The Curse of Gesualdo

The Curse of Gesualdo
Music, Murder and Madness

Joel Epstein

Juwal Publications

Copyright © 2020 by Joel Epstein

All rights reserved. No part of this book may be reproduced or transmitted in any form or by any means, electronic or mechanical, including photocopying, recording, or by any information and retrieval system, without permission in writing from the copyright owner.

This is a work of fiction. Any resemblance to actual persons, living within the last century, is purely coincidental.

Published by Juwal Publications
www.juwalpub.com

To Ziva

Before you begin

My grandfather was a surgeon, and an amateur student of medical history. During World War II he served in the US Army, and after the war he was stationed with the occupation forces in Naples. While rummaging about an old bookstall, he came across a manuscript with an unusual drawing of a trepan. The trepan was a specialized drill for making holes in the skull. Trepanation was a standard treatment in Medieval and Renaissance Europe for a variety of ailments, from migraine to insanity. My grandfather's Italian was very limited, but the salesman said the manuscript contained a detailed description of a trepanation performed by a blind physician, who relied only on touch and smell to perform this complicated procedure. Beyond that, the salesman said the manuscript dealt with the life of an obscure Renaissance composer that no one had ever heard of. My grandfather bought the book.

When my grandfather died in 2017, I took the manuscript to Professor Jacob Messe, a specialist in Renaissance music at Staton University. Prof. Messe said the manuscript was about Carlo Gesualdo. Gesualdo, who had recently risen from oblivion to star status in the pantheon of Renaissance composers, was one of the most innovative and surprising musicians of his age, whose strangely chromatic works have attracted the attention of many modern composers. Gesualdo was also a celebrity for his eccentric and violent life. He was promiscuous and bisexual. Married in his early twenties, he, according to contemporary accounts, suspected his close friend of having an affair with his wife, and murdered them both. He was then so consumed with guilt that he had himself whipped nightly as penance. Moreover, he was reported to have been bewitched – the witch cast a spell that rendered him capable of sex only with her. "I own him from the waist down," she said at her trial. "His wife will receive only kisses."

Professor Messe could not verify the authenticity of the manuscript. For one thing, it contains numerous minor errors of known facts. For example, Gesualdo's father's name was Fabrizio, not Fabio as it appears in the manuscript; Gesualdo's son was born in 1588, not in 1587; and so on. On the other hand, the narrative resolves many of the more puzzling anomalies of the Gesualdo story as scholars have been able to discover.

So I leave it to the reader to decide if this is the real story of Gesualdo or not. In any case, it's a Hell of a good story.

Joel Epstein
November 18, 2018

Napoli, This 20th of May, Year of Our Lord 1622

"She is not dead yet! She is not dead!"

Those words echo in my mind when I remember the white marble halls of the San Severo Palace of Naples – the palace where the Prince who was my Master and my companion murdered his wife and his best friend. Those were the words, according to the official inquest, that he uttered as he stabbed his beautiful bride again and again, in an ecstasy of blood and gore that stained my own love and devotion to my Master with the blood of hatred.

For many years, I was the nearly constant companion of His Excellency the Prince Carlo Gesualdo, ruler of much of southern Italy. As his personal servant and his confidante, I joined him in his wild debauches; I succored him in his depressions; I stayed his hand when he sought to scourge himself; I extracted him from embarrassment when his antic nature offended. Perhaps above all, I followed him on a musical journey to harmonies never imagined in our time. I adored him for his genius, despised him for his callous and repulsive nature, and, in the end, both pitied and abhorred him when, weeks before his death, I understood the vile power of the curse under which he lived.

Though I lived at his side for many years, I was not present at the murder, and so had no first-hand knowledge of what transpired. But I knew that the official inquest was a fabric of lies, woven to cover a more awful truth. And it was only years later that I learned the depth of the depravity, the sorcery, and the evil that cursed my Master's life.

Today I am an old man, but I remember my first meeting with Prince Carlo Gesualdo as clearly as the summer sun on the red roofs of the village that bears his name. I was a boy of 15, the prince was 16. The day was the 14 of June, Year of Our Lord 1582.

My name is Ludovico Forcella, and I come from a long line of musicians. My father Giustiniano, a musician in the service of the His Excellency Don Fabio Gesualdo – Don Carlo's father – gave me a thorough musical education. I learned singing, lute, theorbo, and *Lira da Braccio*. I studied in Naples with the great maestro Giovanni Camillo Maffei, who taught me to support my voice from deep in my chest, and to press my tongue to my teeth to execute complex *trilli* and other difficult ornaments.

On my 15th birthday, my father brought me to His Excellency Don Fabio to seek a position. Fifteen was very young for a musician at court, but I was considered somewhat of a prodigy, thanks to hard work and my father's stern tutelage. Moreover, my father knew that the Prince was interested in keeping a musician the same age as his son, who was greatly enamored of music, and whose well-known eccentricities had rendered him unpopular among others of his age and rank.

His Excellency Don Fabio was one of the most honored and respected men of our country: Count of Conza, Marquis of Laino Rotondo, Duke of Caggiano, Prince of Venosa and feudatory of the king with over one hundred fiefdoms scattered throughout southern Italy including Bisaccia, Villamaina, Santaniello all'Esca, Montefredane. So it was a great honor and not a little intimidating to stand before him as he interviewed my father at length about my education, my skills, and my character. He then asked me to play. I took up my *lira da braccio*, and played a galliard by Pomponio Nenna, one of the bright young composers who served the court, embellishing it nicely with trills and runs of my own invention. I could see my father was pleased with my performance, and the Prince also, for he called me forward when I had finished.

"Ludovico, you are the same age as my son Carlo, who is a great lover of music. My son is afflicted with frequent moods, and music, it seems, is the only thing that can soothe him. He has had many servants, but none have…" He hesitated a moment in his speech. "None have succeeded in satisfying him. I wonder if you might dare to take upon yourself to make an attempt."

I was quite abashed by so direct an address to me, but I gathered my courage and replied, "Your Excellency, I will do all in my power to please my Lord and his son." This answer pleased His Excellency, as he turned to my father, and directly began to discuss the terms of my employment.

That being concluded, I was directed to take up my lira and accompany the party to master Carlo's chamber. It was an odd and uncomfortable procession: His Excellency and his entourage walked silently, my father and myself full of trepidation and put off by so grand a procession. We reached the closed door of the son's chamber. His Excellency stood aside, and, without speaking, motioned me enter.

I opened the door and stepped into the room; the door shut behind me. The scene before me was shocking. The room was a shambles. The curtains had been torn from the windows, the contents of the desk swept away, the inkpot smashed and the ink spattered across the floor. Pages of manuscript paper were strewn about; and, most shocking, the smashed remains of a *viola da gamba* lay before me, its delicate neck broken, its elegantly carved curves broken into a thousand pieces.

And, in the corner of the room, huddled like a fetus in its mother's womb, cowered Don Carlo, rocking, rocking, and uttering muffled sounds that were between humming and sobs.

I stood frozen. My heart was filled with a confusing mix of emotions – terror, pity, wonder. I had a strong desire to turn and rush out the door through which I came. Yet I was also drawn to this strange sight, awed by this boy's overpowering presence. And I knew that, somehow, I was being tested, and that my future hung on my actions of the next few minutes.

For what seemed an endless time, I stood there, transfixed, unable to move and unable to tear my eyes from my new master. If it was a few moments or an hour, I know not. But gradually I realized what I must do. I lifted my instrument. I began to sing *A Morte Re Marítete*, an old villanella, accompanying myself on the lira. Little did I realize how prescient were the words of this song:

> *How I hope to see her husband dead*
> *Yea, my own death do I dread*
> *Death from her radiant beauty.*

My voice, no longer as pure and high as it once was, was still clear and pleasing, and I knew I could rely on it not to split at this crucial time. As I sang, I watched to see how my new master responded. The humming and rocking stopped, and, though he remained curled in a tight ball, I could see he was listening intently. I played through the song, and found my head empty for another tune to play; so I played *A Morte* all over again. Now I could see his body relaxing, and opening slightly. As the second turn of the song approached an end, I began to sweat. My mind was still blank, and I tried, even as I sang, to think of another tune. Panic began to set in. My mouth went dry as cotton. The only tune that came into my head was the children's ditty, *Ambarabai ciccì coccò*. I reached the final chord of my song, and, with no better thought in my head, set into the nonsense song.

> *Ambarabai ciccì coccò,*
> *Three owls perch and hoot, "ho ho"*
> *With the doctor's daughter they did rut.*
> *The doctor, he did split a gut.*
> *Ambarabai ciccì coccò*

As I sang and bowed my lira, my master slowly relaxed his muscles. He turned to me; a thin smile broke on his lips, but his gaze bore into me with an intensity that almost disturbed my concentration. I forced myself to continue, running through all the verses, and between verses improvising on the viol with double and triple stops and turns and trills about the melody.

The song ended. I stood quietly, completely in wonderment at what would happen next. My fear was gone. My master crouched in his corner, the corners of his mouth turned up, staring at me with a gaze that could pierce armor. And then, of a sudden, he leapt up and rushed to me, grasped my head in both his hands, and kissed me full and long on my lips.

From that first encounter, that was the way it was with the Master: sometimes terrifying, sometimes uplifting, often puzzling, always astonishing. Music and carnality were forever mixed in everything he did. Music for Master Carlo was a visceral thing; whether he was listening, or playing, or composing, you could see how the music was physically touching him, grasping him and shaking him with the power of orgasm. And so it was with lust. The Master looked with venery on every living thing, man, woman, animal. Everything moved him with a physical power and rhythmic, harmonic beauty that was music to his soul. Music and fucking – they were inseparably mixed in the master's mind.

Indeed, it took me a bit of reflection to understand that that kiss was not a kiss of mere camaraderie, but of lust. After the kiss, the master summarily dismissed me, and told me to return in an hour. During that hour, I considered long and hard how I must behave with this strange and, yes, dangerous creature. I decided I must conquer my fear, and I knew instinctively that I must never hide the truth from him.

He, for his part, must have worked like a fiend, rehanging the curtains, gathering up the scattered sheets of manuscript, sweeping away the shards of broken viol, and scrubbing vainly at the ink stains on the floor and carpet. For when I returned, the room was restored to order, and the master sat smiling at his desk, strumming a lute, and singing.

"Do you feel it?" he demanded when I entered. "Do you feel this harmony?" I listened to the strangest music I had ever heard. A series of chords, intervals of the fourth, moved down a half step at a time, while the master sang a vocal line that climbed upward along a meandering path that fit no known mode of composition. The words – I imagined they were of his own composition – were about passion, and the melody rose in intensity to match the words. "*Your breasts seize me as I seize them, your body arches to my swelling, your opening pulls me in and in and in and the Glory of God is upon us.*" The harmonies moved faster and faster, the melody spiraling higher even into a shriek, until the master struck a dreaded tritone, the interval of the devil, and then resolved into a heavenly triad.

"What do you think?" he demanded again. "Do you feel it?"

"I… I cannot speak, my Lord."

"You must. You must tell me the truth."

I spoke the truth. "This music, my Lord, defies all the rules of music that I have learned. The melody seems to meander, the harmonies are unlike any I have heard. The tritonus at the end is something that is forbidden, and must never be heard in music. Yet, my Lord, I must say I was swept away by it. It was not mere music. It was physically painful. A beautiful pain."

Master Carlo laid down his lute and again leapt up and hugged me, planting another kiss upon my lips. He was tall and gaunt, with a long face and long fingers, and arms as thin as the bundled twigs of a white birch. Yet his embrace was like an iron clamp. "We must make love," he exclaimed.

I had prepared myself for this moment. I screwed up my courage. "My Lord," I said. "I cannot. I am not that way."

Master Carlo released me, and stared at me for a long moment. I felt the tension in the air – I knew this was either the end, or a beginning. His eyes bored into me, his face a palate of emotions, I knew not which. But then his mouth lifted into a smile.

"I understand. But we must go whoring, you and I. Very soon."

"Very well, my Lord," I replied. I had never had a woman in my life, and, though fantasies danced often in my mind, I had never considered the actual practical possibility of debauchery. So my reply, then, had no real meaning to me.

We talked all that afternoon, and into the night. We found a vital link in our music, for I, too, often felt shivers in my spine and a clenching in my heart and twitching in my muscles when I heard and played music that I loved. His talk flowed with an energy and fluidity that was frightening. Music and fucking: these were the themes that played on my Master's innermost being. And always, his eyes bore the same fire that I had seen that first day. His eyes, and his fingers: they fascinated me. Long fingers with long, oval nails. As he spoke, his hands flashed through the air, his fingers pointing and gesticulating. His lank and height (he was almost a head taller than I) made him look almost sickly. But his speech was animated with a demonic vigor that belied his looks.

My master's passion for music and for love was a source of much tension in the household. It absolutely scandalized his uncle, His Eminence Alfonso Gesualdo, who was a cardinal and Bishop of Albano at the time. His Eminence was the exact opposite of his nephew – cold and calculating, ambitious and cruel. A member of the innermost circle of the church hierarchy, he had his eye set on the Holy See. I recall many screaming arguments tearing through the house about Don Carlo's music, like the one that occurred about a year after I entered My Master's service.

"It is unseemly, and an embarrassment to me," he seethed at Carlo's father over supper. "This total devotion to music is worthy of a servant, not the son of a Prince."

"I am afraid we are powerless to stop him," replied His Excellency. "He has terrible tantrums. Music is the only thing that soothes him."

"I will tell you what will soothe him. Lock him in his room. The birch switch, that is what will soothe him!"

I was in the adjoining room, waiting with Maestro Nenna and the singers to perform a madrigal at the end of the meal. Through the curtain, I could see Master Carlo sitting sullenly, his father the Prince Fabio, his uncle, and Carlo's elder brother Luigi, smirking as he picked at his roast.

His Excellency moved to speak, but the Bishop continued his tirade. "You, Fabio, have a kingdom to rule. And I have a career in the church. How do you think it will reflect on me, and on you, to have this boy shaming us with his lechery and his music and his blasphemy?"

At this, Master Carlo rose in a fury. "Blasphemy? You talk to me of blasphemy? You with your hypocritical posturing and your disgusting fawning over your sissy altar boys? What, you think we all don't know about your sickening perversions? You and your holiness! What do you know about music? You know nothing about music. Music, that is where God is, that is what uplifts and makes things holy! The only place you can see God is in the assholes of your darling altar boys." And he rose and stormed out of the dining hall.

Bishop Alfonso sat in his chair, turning a shade of livid purple. "Thank God it is Luigi, and not that monster, who is inheriting the Principality," he said under his breath.

After this exchange, we gave a cursory performance of our madrigal, and I rushed off to Master Carlo's chambers. There I found him kneeling before the cross, his shirt ripped from his back, weeping and beating himself with his belt.

"My uncle is right," he cried to me. "I am bathed in corruption. I am an abomination in God's eyes. Why can I not live in the light of my uncle Carlo?"

Carlo was Carlo Borromeo, Archbishop of Milan, a man of true saintliness in my Master's eyes.

Master Carlo raised his belt and brought it down with a smack on his back. "I must beat this sin out of me. I must beat this red sea out of me!"

"My Lord, you must stop this," I said. "You must not be so affected by your uncle Alfonso. He is wrong to oppose you so."

"No, he is right, he is right! How can I yell at a cardinal so? Who am I to accuse a prince of the church of blasphemy? He is right. I am the blasphemer!" He gave another swing of the belt.

"You are no blasphemer, my Lord."

"My red dream is a blasphemy. I know it. I am enveloped in the red of sin, in the red of my uncle's robes. I am enveloped now. I can feel the red closing in on me, suffocating me. *Asperges me, Domine, hyssopo, et mundabor: lavabis me, et super nivem dealbabor.* Cleanse me white as snow!" Another blow.

"My Lord, this belt is not hyssop, and it is not cleansing you. Your beating will not purge you of the red dream."

"I am his slave, Ludovico. I hate him so! It is his red robe, I know it, I know it. I hate him, yet I must submit to him. Why, Ludovico, why?" Master Carlo pressed the belt into my hands. "Beat me. Beat me, Ludovico. Beat the red dream out of my soul!"

I took the belt from him, but I did not beat him. Rather, I pressed his shuddering body to my breast. "With love will you purge the red dream, My Lord. With love, not with pain."

Master Carlo told me of his red dream only days after I entered his service. The dream came again and again, sometimes two or three times during a week. He was enveloped in red. Red surrounded him, smothered him. He felt human flesh pressing against him, and a sharp stabbing pain in his side, like a sword. The dream was the same every time, and he awoke from it screaming, bathed in sweat and shaking.

The meaning of this dream was revealed to me only a few weeks before my Master's death. But even now, I felt I had some understanding – that turned out to be wrong – of the meaning of this nightmare. Red, I thought, is the color of pain. Colors are endlessly flashing in My Master's mind – he often describes his music as pink, or deep blue, or pied with many hues. With three colors is he obsessed: red, black and white. Red is the color of pain. Black is the color of death. And white is the color of nothingness, of the void. Red is My Master's color, for he owns the pain – it is his to feel and his to inflict. It can light the blackness, postponing the blessed

11

release of death; and it can fill the white, giving substance to the void. This is in My Master's mind – for me, I must say, these meanings are different. I think, for example, of the main corridor of the Palazzo San Severo in Naples, flagged in the purest white marble. Often, today, when I walk that corridor, I cannot help but imagine it slippery with the carmine of blood, and my ears cannot stop the anguished cries that must have been: *"She is not dead, she is not dead!"*

But, for My Lord, traversing that corridor filled him with an existential dread. Not because he saw the carnage of that fateful day, but because he saw nothing. "There is nothing there!" he cried, grabbing at me. "Lead me! Lead me out of here!"

Indeed, leading Master Carlo – leading him out of tantrum, or out of depression, or out of scandalous entanglement – quickly became my mission. The role of chaperone to his antic disposition was thrust upon me both by his father the Prince and by himself. It was a role of frightening gravity and complexity for a lad of fifteen, and it weighed heavily on my soul. And the love that burgeoned between us – a love nurtured by our mutual servitude to the Muse of music – rendered that role weightier still, yet added to the urgency that I succeed.

For instance, several weeks after I began serving the young prince, His Excellency asked that I attend his son's lessons with Pomponio Nenna. Maestro Nenna instructed Carlo in the art of composition. I knew the Maestro well, as I had also taken lessons from him and frequently performed with him in the court. And it was clear to me that the dispositions of master and pupil would react together like steel and flint. In the first lesson I attended, Master Carlo had submitted two madrigals for the Maestro's review.

"This exercise, My Lord, is perfectly executed," said the Maestro, taking up the first madrigal in five parts. "It proves you have understood the rules of composition I have been teaching, and that you can apply them with art and taste.

"Now, this," he continued, lifting up the second madrigal, "is full of errors. It offends some of the most basic rules of composition. Let me begin with the complete lack of coordination between text and music. I have taught you that each verse of text must be set off from its neighbor by a cadence. Here" – he pointed to the *cantus* voice beginning the verse *Onde te stessa* – "you have introduced the second verse already in the second bar, yet the cadence comes only in the fourth bar – and that on the unstressed third beat of the bar! Now here… "

Master Carlo broke in impatiently. "But, Maestro, do you not listen to the music? Do you not think this is beautiful?"

"I know not what you mean by beautiful," replied Maestro Pomponio testily. "What to me is beautiful – what is inevitable, and what is inviolable – is the structure laid down by the *musica perfecta* that we have inherited from the great masters. You cannot build a house if your timbers are not true, and your joints not fastened securely. And you cannot create beautiful music if you do not adhere to the laws of composition. It is that simple, My Lord: if you are to be an artist, you must learn to temper your invention."

"Invention?" snapped Master Carlo. "This", lifting up the first exercise, "is invention. This is something I made up to please you and to prove I have learned your holy rules. But in this", grasping the second madrigal, "there is no invention. I hear the music in my head, and I write it down. There is no invention here, but discovery!"

I could see the blood rising in my Master's head, his hands shaking with passion, and I sensed that his anger was about to explode into some act of violence. I decided to act. I was already standing, but I drew myself up to my full height (albeit far less than his).

"My Lord," I said. "No one is impugning your skill, nor denying the beauty of your music. Maestro Nenna seeks only your well-being by teaching you the ways of the old masters. And you cannot deny the beauty of those masters! It is, indeed, *musica perfecta*! You can only benefit from his tutelage, no matter how painful it may be for you!"

The color drained from my Master's face. He fell to his seat, and dropped his head in his hands. "You are right, Ludovico, you are right! How can I let these passions rule me? I am so sorry, Maestro, I am so sorry!"

The Maestro was clearly disconcerted by the unseemly sight of my Master's weeping and abject apology. I spoke. "Maestro, perhaps we should continue this lesson at a later time? Perhaps after supper." Maestro Nenna, greatly relieved, rose without a word, and with a slight bow, withdrew.

I retell this incident not to cast aspersions on the character of Maestro Nenna, but only to illustrate the role of chaperone I had come to play. As I said, the role was onerous, and I turned to my father for advice.

"You were absolutely right to terminate the lesson," my father advised me. "Don Pomponio is a fine musician and composer, and a dear friend as well. He is very conservative in his views on the education of musicians, and adamant in his insistence on correct harmony and forms. But I can tell you, that secretly Pomponio greatly admires the Prince. And, while he would never accede to some of the Prince's greater excesses, I have noticed in his recent compositions some of the mannerisms of the Prince's madrigals.

"Your companionship with the Prince has certainly had a tempering effect on the Prince, and you should know that it has not gone unnoticed. For the Prince's father has commented to me, and made a handsome gift of a bolt of silk.

"But, beyond urging you to continue the course you have chosen, I should warn you that not all are pleased with your success. You should know that there are those who would drive a wedge between you and your Master."

"Who are these?" I asked.

"Luigi, and your Master's uncle Alphonso."

"The Cardinal?" I was genuinely surprised by this revelation. "His Eminence has always complained loudly of my Master's excesses. Surely he should be pleased that they are mediated."

"Things are not always as they seem, my son. Luigi sees your Master as a threat to his succession, especially now that he is so sickly. And Luigi is the Bishop's pawn. They are schemers and seek your downfall, for that means the downfall of the Prince Carlo. So beware."

As you can imagine, it was in a somber mood that I left this audience with my father. Far from comforting me, it only added to my concern and to the heaviness in my heart.

I have written of my Master's violent passions and his obsessive love of music, but I have not discussed his licentiousness, beyond mentioning it in passing. This is certainly not by design, but other aspects of my Master's character have occupied my writing until now. But know that every living thing excited in my Master a lubricious flame that he could not, indeed, did not wish to, quench. My Master's sexual escapades were sundry: at least once a week, his friend Don Fabrizio, the Duke of Andria, joined him in a tour of the courtesans and bordellos of Naples. I sometimes joined him in these expeditions. In addition, the courtly, and especially the musical, society of Naples provided numerous opportunities for sexual liaisons. Many women of the court – both married and unmarried – were willing to give themselves to the Prince of one of the leading families of the realm, and, indeed, of all Italy. There were also many women – young girls, actually – in the orphanages of Naples, who were trained as musicians and singers, and who frequently performed in the homes of the leading families. These nubile girls were generally available for services beyond the performance of music, and my Master frequently enjoyed the pleasure of their nonmusical skills. Finally, my Master did not hesitate to enjoy sexual concourse with his subjects – men, women, boys and girls. These escapades continued even after my Master had married, and were frequently followed by the usual bouts of self-loathing, guilt, and self-inflicted injury.

Dalliances with his subjects could be the source of scandal and even tragedy. The following episode – which would later have unforeseen and tragic repercussions – will illustrate.

I came to my Master's study in the afternoon after a rehearsal with the consort. This was about two years after my Master's marriage to Donna Maria d'Avalos. He was much enamored of his bride, yet their relationship would soon be careening toward tragedy. For, enamored though he may have been, yet he was still unable to rein in his passions. My Master was seated in the center of the room, and standing before him was a peasant maid. I immediately recognized her – she was the daughter of the master carpenter Errico d'Angelo, who had spent several months before my Master's wedding, renovating the Gesualdo palace. The girl had often accompanied her father to work, doing odd jobs and playing about the castle. She was only 12 at the time; in the two years that had passed, she had become quite pretty and developed for her young age. Master Carlo was delighted to see me. "Come in Ludovico, come in! See what I have found! A maid with an angelic voice. Sing for us, child."

The girl resumed her singing, and, indeed, had a clear and bell-like voice that was exceptional. She sang the song *Oi Ricciulina:*

> *Oi Ricciulina,*
> *Oi maranchina,*
> *Oi signorina,*
> *Fai la-li-la*

"Let me instruct you," said Master Carlo. "You must sing from the chest, not from the belly." He stepped behind her, and wrapped his arms about her below her bosom. "Now sing. Not from your belly. From here, from here," and he pressed his hands against the bottoms of her breasts, pushing them up until they popped right out of her bodice. The girl was, of course mortified, and her hands flew up to cover herself. Master Carlo sternly ordered, "Put your hands to your sides, child! Now sing! Continue to sing!"

With great reluctance, the child lowered her hands and tried to continue the song. But she had lost her voice, and the notes came out in a pathetic quaver. "Not like that! Sing from the chest! Support your voice, nasty child!" My master grabbed the tender flesh of the bottoms of her breasts and pinched them firmly.

"You are hurting me, Sir," the child cried. "Please stop!"

"Sing. Sing as you are taught, properly, and I shall stop," said my Master, and pinched still harder. The terrified girl winced in pain, but obediently gave her best effort, and, indeed, succeeded in singing with a pure tone again, stronger than before for being supported by her diaphragm. Master Carlo burst into a broad smile. He released his pinches, and moved his hands over her young breasts – breasts that certainly had never been touched by man before. "You see? I knew you could do it!" The girl was clearly shaken, yet she looked oddly pleased by my Master's praise.

"Come tomorrow," said Master Carlo. "I shall give you an exercise to strengthen the muscles of your jaw and tongue. Now tuck yourself in and run along. You look like a hussy."

For the next few days, I was detained in the rehearsals, and arrived at my Master's chambers at suppertime. A week had passed when I arrived from rehearsal in early afternoon. I opened the door and there I saw the girl on her knees before my Master, her bosom bared, and my Master's erect penis in her mouth. "Excuse me, my Lord," I murmured, and made to exit hastily. But Master Carlo called me. "Come in, Ludovico. I am eager to talk to you." So I entered the chamber and closed the door carefully behind me. I was at once transfixed by the sight, yet at the same time unable to look on it. But my Master was completely unself-conscious, and began to chatter.

"Do you know, Ludovico, how many melodies can be created from just three notes? I have done a calculation. With only three notes, and three pitches allowed, one can combine 27 melodies. But that does not include differences in time value. For each note can be a breve, a semibreve, a quaver, or a semiquaver. That is another 64 possibilities. So, together, there can be 27 times 64 possible melodies. How much is 64 multiplied by 27, Ludovico?"

"I know not, My Lord."

"Never mind, I am certain it must be several thousand. But that is only the beginning – for each note can be sung *staccato* or *legato*, *cantabile* or *alla marcia*, *piano* or *fortissimo* – the possibilities are infinite. Ah, ah, more tongue!" and he started gyrating his hips vigorously, until his body stiffened and he forced his member deep into the girl's throat. His body then relaxed. He bent down quickly, and pressed his mouth against hers, probing her mouth with his tongue, licking his own juices off the inside of her cheeks. "I love the taste of my own *sborra*! I am sorry you came so late. You should

17

have heard her sing! I am teaching her *Al Di Dolce Ben Mio.* In another month she shall carry her part in a madrigal!"

The girl, meanwhile, had tucked her bosom back in her bodice, and wiped her lips with the hem of her skirt. Unlike her frightened look of a week ago, her eyes were bright and her lips bore the hint of a smile. "Shall I come tomorrow, my Lord?"

"Of course, of course, my dear." And she hastened out of the room. "What a delightful little *puttana*!" he said, as the door shut.

"She is not a whore, My Lord," I admonished. "She is the daughter of one of your subjects, and I beg you to be wary of such encounters. They can lead to no good."

Master Carlo looked at me with puzzlement. Then his eyes suddenly lit, as though with understanding. "Ah, I understand. You want her. You shall have her, Ludovico. Next time we shall share! It was most inconsiderate of me!"

"That was not my intention, My Lord. What I meant was that, while it may be your right to do with your vassals as you wish, it will not endear you to your subjects to make whores of their children. I merely advise some circumspection." In truth, I saw little harm in this dalliance such as it was, and, indeed, thought how lovely it might be to accede to his proposal. For she was delectable. But, knowing my Master's history, I feared how this liaison might develop. As it did, the very next day.

I was in attendance when the child arrived the following afternoon. She was walking stiffly, in obvious pain. My Master looked at her piercingly. "What is the matter, child?" he asked.

The girl stood stoically and said nothing.

"I have asked you a question," said my Master testily. "Answer."

Still the girl made no reply. But her condition was obvious.

"You have been beaten," said my Master. "Show me."

No response.

My Master rose from his seat. "Lift up your skirts, and show me that you have been beaten!"

With terror in her eyes, the girl lifted her skirts to show the ugly red welts across her bottom.

"Your father did this?"

She nodded.

The sight of the poor girl's tormented flesh set off a turmoil of emotion in my Master, clearly reflected in his face. On the one hand, he was horrified by the sight, on the other, clearly titillated by it. I was about to intervene, but my Master had already pressed the girl face down on the table, and penetrated her swollen buttocks. The girl, apparently no stranger to punishment and abuse, squealed quietly but did not cry out. After a few moments, he came, and released her. He was immediately seized by remorse, and fell to his knees in tears. I quickly escorted the terrified girl out.

It was clear that this episode could only end in tragedy. And so it came to pass that the girl ceased to come to my Master's chambers. After a few days, Master Carlo asked me about her.

"She will not be coming again," I said.

"Why not? We must go and fetch her."

"You cannot fetch her, My Lord."

"Why not? Of course I can fetch her. We will go at once!"

"We cannot fetch her because she is dead."

"Dead? How dead?"

"Her father killed her."

Again, a look of puzzlement clouded my Master's face. This time, the puzzlement gave way to anger. "Why kill her? She had the voice of an angel! I would have had her in a consort! The damned fool. Kill my student? I will kill him!" He went to his closet to gird his sword. But I reached out and placed my hand on his arm to stop him.

"He killed her because you defiled her! He killed her because you sullied his name! You, my Lord, are to blame for her death!"

I could clearly see the warring emotions in my Master's visage. Anger, shame, remorse, and, above all confusion – the thought that sin could have such immediate and dire consequences was always an anomaly to him. But it was the shame and remorse that won out. For the Prince fell to his knees before the cross, his body wracked with sobs. He raked his fingernails across his cheeks, digging in until he drew blood. "Oh Ludovico, what have I done? Perfidy, oh perfidy! Uncle Carlo, I have failed you again!"

I grasped his wrists to prevent him from doing further injury to himself. "My Lord, you will not indulge in this self-destruction. You will go to confession, and you will do the penance that your confessor decrees. You shall recompense the father for the death of his daughter. And, above all, you shall refrain from these abominations from now and forevermore!"

These were noble words. But of course nothing came of them. What is more, I had already found that my own flesh is weak, and I was already joining my Master in some of his escapades. Perhaps I was still a tempering influence on my Lord, but it was by meeting him halfway between the paths of sin and of righteousness.

These things that I have written of heretofore happened long ago. Now I am old, though I am in remarkably good health for a person my age. Most of my friends and colleagues have died, yet I remain. Nonetheless, various infirmities hamper my work. My eyesight is weak, and I find I cannot write for more than a few hours a day – and not at all at night by candlelight. The pain in my hip has made descending stairs a trial, and, since my wife Beatrice died three years ago, my son has kindly agreed to allow me the rear room on the ground floor.

I am blessed with a devoted son who cares for me in my dotage. As long as my wife was alive, I continued to work as a musician, and lived in my own home. But when my beloved Beatrice passed away, my son Carlo urged me to retire and come to live with him. He married Ariana Carlino, the daughter of the Carlino music publishing house in Napoli. Carlo joined his father-in-law's business, and has become quite wealthy. He and his wife bought a large house in Napoli, not far from the Palazzo San Severo, and it is in my son's house that I now reside.

While I am bedeviled somewhat by these minor infirmities of age, my mind is still intact, and the passion I feel for my former master's music and for his tragic story still burns in my breast. And it is this passion that has led me to plunge, as it were, directly into a description of his character, without offering first an orderly biography of the early years of Prince Carlo Gesualdo. This defect I shall now endeavor to correct.

Prince Carlo Gesualdo was born on the eighth day of March, in the Year of Our Lord 1566, in the principality of Venosa. His father Fabio Gesualdo, from a long line tracing back to Roberto Guiscardo of Norman ancestry, was lord over numerous lands, including Venosa, Frigento, Mirabella, Paternapoli, and more. His mother was Girolama Borromeo, sister of the great Carlo Borromeo, Archbishop of Milan, and daughter of Margherita de' Medici. Prince Carlo was their second child, the eldest being Luigi, who was to be heir to the vast holdings of the Gesualdo family.

When he was seven, Prince Carlo's mother died, and he was sent to Rome, into the care of Fabio's brother Alfonso, then Dean of the College of Cardinals, to be trained to take up the cloth. As my Master told it, it was a period of great trial and pain in his life. For the first few weeks, His Eminence Don Alfonso treated the Prince with a deference and solicitude that was (my Master said in retrospect) fawning. The Prince expressed a desire to continue his study of music, and his uncle arranged for the great Annibale Stabile to teach him. The Cardinal was extremely affectionate, hugging and kissing the Prince at every opportunity. At one point, the Cardinal seated the Prince at his side, put his arm around him, lifted the Prince's hand and pressed it against his cassock. The Prince could feel His Eminence's penis hard beneath the robe. "I was quite fascinated by this," my Master told me. "I squeezed it, and fondled it. My uncle took my hand and placed it beneath his cassock, so I could rub his *cazzo*. I played with him until he came. He made a mess all over my hand and on his robe. I thought he would be pleased, but he was very angry. He slapped me hard, and told me to leave.

"The next time we met, he found an excuse to punish me. He accused me falsely of disrespect. He forcibly pulled me over his knees, and pulled down my pantaloons. Then he spanked me on my bare *culo*. When he was done, he took his hand and gently rubbed my sore bum, and then tried to fondle my *cazzo*. But I grabbed his other hand and sank my teeth into it with all my strength. He leaped up with a scream, tumbling me to the floor, and with a curse, dashed out of the room."

This was, my Master told me, the last time his uncle attempted to molest him – indeed, after that, they rarely spoke to each other. But from that time on, His Eminence ensured that the Prince's life was an endless trial. He was beaten with the birch regularly for insubordination. His tutors cursed him, the Priest and his confessor told him he was unworthy, indeed, drove that message into him. And while he rarely spoke to the Prince, the Cardinal often attended his beatings, his face set in a wry and self-satisfied smirk. The Prince had only two comforts: his music, and the visits of his uncle Carlo Borromeo. His music master, Maestro Stabile, a rubicund and jovial man, as stout as he was tall, was a kind and encouraging teacher, and the Prince adored him. It was this treatment that led the Prince to be consumed by his love of music. He would practice and compose at the expense of his other lessons, behavior that led to increased beatings and denigrations.

Of my Master's other uncle, His Eminence Carlo Borromeo, my Master spoke with this highest of reverence. His Eminence was at this time the Archbishop of Milan, and came only rarely to Rome. Curiously, my Master's recollection of these visits was often vague and contradictory: he would tell me a detailed account of a visit, and then later tell me a completely different version. My Master told me once that he met His uncle only four times in his life; but on another occasion told me that the cardinal was a frequent visitor. But whatever the details of the recollections, they were always suffused with a deep sense of the kindness, mercy and holiness of this saintly man.

Thus the Prince grew into a cycle of punishment, rebellion, and remorse, tempered only by his devotion to his art. This continued through puberty, when the Prince's sexual appetites were awakened. With no real spiritual hand to guide him, he quickly fell into a sink of debauchery. At the age of 12, he discovered the pleasures of sexual concourse with one of the altar boys, who had already gained considerable sexual experience at the hands of his uncle the Cardinal. At 13, he was seduced by a servant girl four years his senior. He found his appetite to be voracious, and his station as the son of the ruler of one of the richest principalities in the Kingdom gave him ready access to a variety of men and women. And, while he indulged freely and eagerly his lubricious urges, he was always consumed later with guilt, penance, and a perverted satisfaction from the beatings he received most regularly at the hands of his uncle's servants.

Friends he had but one: Fabrizio Carafa, son of one of the leading families of Napoli, who was, like the Prince, sent to Rome to study for the priesthood. At 14 years of age, Don Fabrizio was already one of the handsomest blades in Rome, and women would swoon at his feet. Quite unlike my Master, who, even at that age, was overtall and lanky, with a sallow face and hooded eyes and a thin, cruel mouth. Don Fabrizio, by contrast, had sharply chiseled features like a marble statue; curly red hair; and, even at that young age, muscles that rippled visibly under his sleeves and hose. Despite their differences in appearance, they would sneak out to go whoring together in the brothels of Rome. They would stroll through the Campo Marzio, where the ladies leaned over their balconies draped with yellow sheets, their bosoms falling out of their bodices, urging the boys up to their apartments with a wink and a quick lick of the lips. Or the boys would head to a basement wine bar in the Via Schiavonia, where the whores would sidle up to them and brazenly grasp at their crotches, cadging drinks and urging them into the back room for a quick *bocchino*.

As boys were wont, they would spend long hours together, talking. Their talk ranged over many topics, but concentrated on two: sex and music. Master Fabrizio was, like every young *cavalliere*, trained and adept in the art of music, and, though his interest could not compare to the single-minded devotion – indeed, obsession – of the Prince, they would talk and play and sing together, often deep into the night. Together they would listen to consorts, and Master Fabrizio marveled at the physical effect music had on the young Prince: his body would respond to the sounds as though to physical contact, his muscles tensing and relaxing, his face ranging through emotions of pain, anger, surprise, love, joy and release in accordance with the mood of the music he was hearing. A great performance could leave the Prince physically drained; a bad performance, with imperfect intonation or a lack of coordination between the parts, could induce actual pain, causing the Prince to clamp his hands over his ears.

It was on the *Carnevale* of the boys' 15th year that Master Fabrizio discovered his true self. The Prince costumed himself as a priest, and Master Fabrizio as a woman. With the aid of one of their courtesan friends, the boy succeeded in so perfectly aping the dress and behavior of a woman that none could identify his true sex. He found this experience so titillating that even before the processional was over, the boys retired to the Prince's chamber, there they took carnal pleasure in each other in a manner as near to male-female intercourse as two men can. From that day forth, Master Fabrizio never missed an opportunity to don the clothing of a woman. To be sure, he lost not his interest in sexual concourse with women, but, like the Prince, developed a broadly catholic sexual appetite.

The Prince's excursions with his friend to the dives of Rome were always followed by pangs of remorse and inadequacy, frantic prayer, and, often, temper tantrums born of guilt. The tantrums usually lead to beatings, which had an exculpatory and purgative effect on the Prince, thus freeing his soul for another plunge into the abyss. It was on one of these excursions that the Prince and Master Fabrizio encountered the Cardinal the Prince's uncle. They were in a dark tavern in the Ortaccio. In a corner sat a man, dressed like a common laborer in blouse and pantaloons, his face turned to the wall, and pawing the hussy who sat beside him. Even though he sat disguised with his back to the boys, the Prince identified him unmistakably. I will confront him, he said to his friend. Don't be a fool, said Don Fabrizio. He is a whoreson and a scoundrel, said the Prince. He will only make your life more miserable, said Don Fabrizio. Despite his friend's remonstrances, the Prince would not be dissuaded. He rose and went to the Cardinal's table. "Hello Uncle," he said. The Cardinal turned and stared at his nephew with a mix of fury and horror. Then, without saying a word, he rose, delivered a tremendous slap to the Prince's face, and stalked out of the bar. Contrary to Don Fabrizio's predictions, the incident had an immediate, salubrious effect on the Prince's life, for, from that moment forward, all corporal punishment of the Prince ceased. However, the Cardinal forevermore entertained a searing hatred for my Master, which would darken the Prince's days to the end of his life.

Shortly before the Prince's 16th birthday, he was called upon to return to Gesualdo. His elder brother Luigi had taken grievously ill, and there was fear for his life. The plans for a life in the church were thus set aside, and my Master began to be groomed as a possible successor to the Principality, should Luigi die. Don Fabrizio also returned to Naples shortly thereafter, the two continued their friendship and their dalliances together.

Is it the concurrence of time, place and circumstance that dictate destiny? Or is it a brand seared into a man's soul, like Orestes, relentlessly searching out the tragic denouement that will make his life complete? Time: time for an uncle's hatred to concoct a scheme for catastrophe, time for a mother's lust for vengeance to brew a potion to poison life and love. Place: the alabaster corridor of the Gesualdo mansion, a white so pure and empty as to strike terror into a sick mind. Circumstance: a tormented soul, riven by lust and anger and piety, joined to a paragon of beauty and innocence, as remote from that torment as the clouds of heaven from the fires of hell. All these converging to rip that tormented cry from his throat: She is not dead yet, she is not dead yet!

White, the void; red, the blood; black, the death: these are the colors that paint every word of this memoir. I was not there on that fateful night – yea, had I been there, perhaps I could have prevented the tragedy – and, until my Master's death, had only a fragmentary and rumor-riddled account of the events. Yet that night lives in my mind as though I was there in the room, sprayed with blood and smeared with gore, ears torn by pathetic cries for mercy and tortured cries for vengeance. It lives on in my memory with every note of my Master's tormented music, music that will live forever as a monument to his twisted soul.

White: the void. I learned of my Master's terror of the alabaster white corridor of the San Severo villa early on in my service. For in the second week of my service, the household moved from the palace in Gesualdo to the winter villa in Naples. And there, on the first occasion that he had to walk that corridor with me, he gripped my hand in panic, as we walked to his room. In retrospect, his reaction could well have been a premonition of the terrible events that would occur there in another six years. But at the time, he spoke to me of the fear of oblivion that seized him. "There is nothing there, nothing!" he cried. That night he was awakened twice by the red dream, and I had to rush into his chamber to calm his screams.

Once I understood the source of his terror, I spoke directly to his father His Excellency. I urged him to paint the corridor a different color, and perhaps to hang some pictures there. His Excellency did not hesitate, and within two days the walls of the corridor were painted a light pink, and there was hung on the wall a hunting scene by Giovanni Antonio di Amato the Younger. This action had the immediate effect of eliminating my Master's anxiety. Indeed, he took an inordinate interest in the painting, sitting for hours and examining every detail of the eight-palm tall canvas – the teeth marks on the hart's neck where the hunting dog had bit, the blood dripping from the arrow stuck deep in the animal's flank, the prey lying with its head twisted back in a pose of death. Standing over the cadaver were the two hunters, armed with bows and spears, gesturing meaningfully, their faces suffused with the light filtering through the trees of the forest. The dogs were prancing or lying at their feet, and their horses were waiting patiently in the background. It was a well-executed picture, I thought, artfully composed and cleverly executed in its detail. My Master would sit on the floor before the painting, enchanted by the drama depicted, and would ask me questions that, of course, I hadn't the vaguest of notion how to answer. "Do you think the hart suffered greatly? I wonder why he didn't use his spear in the kill, but only the single arrow." He would invent a narrative to the picture: "The hart was seized by the dogs, but succeeded in breaking away, and making a dash for it. But the dogs chased the hart into the clearing – here you can see the trampled undergrowth – where the hunters had a clear shot at it with their arrows. Struck by the arrows, the hart leapt high in the air, kicking its legs out. It almost succeeded in kicking this dog in the head, but the dog was too quick, and leapt away at the last moment. Then this dog... " pointing at the greyhound sitting patiently by its master - "leapt forward and bit the hart in the throat. You see the teeth marks here. The hart shook violently, trying to shake the dog off, but could not free itself. Slowly it fell to the ground. It lay breathing heavily for several minutes. Why didn't the hunters spear him to end his suffering? But no, they waited until the hart's struggles ended in death."

After several days of such speculation and examination, my Master suddenly leapt up, and cried, "I must learn to hunt. Ludovico, go and bring me Don Fabrizio." I hastened off, and called on his friend, who lived only a short jog away from my Master's home in San Severo. Don Fabrizio came at once, and was delighted to take upon himself the task of training my Master in the arts of the hunt.

My Master had never had an athletic bent, and, while, like all sons of the aristocracy, had learned the rudiments of fencing and riding, he had never invested any effort into them, especially with a career in the church before him. But now he threw himself into the study with a vigor and single-mindedness that heretofore had characterized only his interest in music. He would practice his archery and spear handling for hours, developing quite a skill. He rode daily with Don Fabrizio, honing his equestrian skills. He even did target practice with the arquebus. Firearms had indeed become quite common as a hunting weapon of late, but Don Fabrizio urged my Master to eschew them for this purpose, for, he said, a misaimed first shot would cause the prey to bolt, and the hunter would be unable to reload and refire before the prey was gone.

Within a few weeks, Don Fabrizio announced that the Prince was ready to sally forth, and he joined a hunting party. To my chagrin, my Master announced that I was to accompany him. I protested that my equestrian skills were rudimentary – aside from being a burden on the advance of the party, I would be risking my neck. But my Master would hear none of this. I was to take up the rear of the party, riding my courser and leading a packhorse, to carry the prey back to the castle at the conclusion of the hunt.

I admit that, despite my lack of technical skills, I found the hunt quite exhilarating. The entire day was enjoyable. The party met early in the morning, meeting with the huntsman, who had set out at dawn to seek the prey and develop a strategy for tracking and killing. The dogs were then deployed along the expected course of the chase. Each breed of hound had its specific function: the lymers were adept at scenting and finding the prey, the running hounds gave the chase, and the greyhounds made the attack, harried the animal and drove it into the arena for the kill. There were special breeds for special animals of prey: the greyhounds for harts, the alaunts and mastiffs for boars or wolves, the foxhounds for foxes, trained ferrets for rabbits.

Once the dogs had been deployed to their locations, the party set out to find the prey. The lymers led the search tugging at their leashes, their noses to the ground, their long ears flopping or pressed to the sides of their heads. The lymers led the party to where the prey was harbored. When the party arrived, the prey unharbored – that is, made a dash to escape – and the chase began. The running hounds sprang at the prey, forcing it along the path of the hunt, until the killing ground was reached. There the party fell upon the prey with spears and arrows, felling it. If the prey was a boar, the bravest (or most foolhardy) of the party would often dismount and dispatch the raging animal with swords and spears. It was not an unknown event for the enraged boar to gore one of the hunters, causing grievous injury before it could be taken down. In the end, the hounds were rewarded for their labors with chunks of meat from the dead animal. The prey was usually carved up on the spot, the sides and parts loaded onto the packhorse. If the animal was destined for stuffing, it would be loaded uncut onto the back of the packhorse, and carried back to the palace.

With time, the Prince gained remarkable skill at the hunt, and within a few years was one of the leaders of the party. By then, he set out not only in the large parties of sportsmen, but would mount for a hunt accompanied only by Don Fabrizio and myself, and a few of the Prince's finest hounds. Don Fabrizio was immensely strong, and was reputed to have once killed a bear with only a spear. We would ride slowly and silently through the forests surrounding the palace of Gesualdo, or the *Astroni* forest outside of Naples, searching out a deer to slaughter. It was on such an excursion, soon after my Master had married, that we had a remarkable encounter of tremendous portent.

It was early evening, and we were about to give up and return to the lodge in the forest south of Gesualdo, when we heard strange music emanating from the forest. My Master immediately headed toward the sound. It was singing in five parts, in harmonies completely strange to the ear: long, sinuating modulations moving chromatically through the range of modes. The counterpoint met in strangely cacophonous chords, suddenly resolving into perfect harmonies. I had never heard anything like it. My Master, as though entranced by the singing, pushed through the pathless forest, oblivious to the danger of becoming lost. The light filtering through the trees was growing dimmer as the sound of the music grew stronger. Don Fabrizio and I struggled to keep up. When we neared the source of the music, the Prince tied his horse to a tree, slowed and crept forward stealthily, reaching a clump of juniper bushes, there we hid and peeked into a clearing. The dogs lay obediently at our feet.

In the clearing was a small pond surrounded by about 20 women, all wearing black dresses and barefoot. Above the pond was a wooden platform, with an elaborately carved panel in the back – an inverted cross, and, above it, a pentagram. On the platform a billy goat was tethered, clearly agitated, scratching his foot against the platform like a bull before a charge. Also on the platform was what appeared to be a small, low table.

Two women were standing thigh-deep in the pond, their skirts floating in the muddy water. One woman – apparently the leader or priestess – was supporting the second at the small of her back, her other hand gripping the woman's nose. The priestess bent the woman over backwards, submerging her entirely in the water, chanting a strange Latin chant that rose seductively above the chanting of the other women:

> *Concupitio mala, tu nequamquam dilige Christum;*
> *Daemona secteris, nec pete salvifcum;*
> *Despicias, rogo te, Christum: nec tempore toto*
> *Conspice praesentem te fore judicio.*

> *Lust after evil, and do not at all love Christ;*
> *you follow the devil, do not seek Him who gives salvation;*
> *despise Christ, I beg you, and realize*
> *that never will you stand before a judgment.*

Each woman, in turn, stepped into the pond, to be baptized in this catechism of blasphemy. The ritual proceeded slowly, and by the time all the women had been so blessed – or cursed – darkness had fallen. Yet the clearing was lit by a full moon that bathed the scene in a ghostly white light.

With this part of the ritual completed, the priestess took the hand of a girl, who must have been about 14 years of age, and led her up to the platform. With a swift gesture, the priestess grasped the hem of the child's garment, and lifted it over her head, leaving her completely naked on the platform. The chanting of the women grew higher and more frenzied, and the women started gyrating lewdly about the platform. The priestess bent the girl over the table, lifting her buttocks high in the air. She then untethered the goat, who approached the recumbent girl, and pressed his nose into her private areas. He then mounted the table with his front paws, straddling the girl, his priapic member jutting from his loins. The singing reached a climax of dissonance as the goat humped his loins vigorously, entering the prostrate girl. Within seconds the goat spilled its seed into the girl. The priestess took up a long knife, and grabbed the goat by the collar. She raised the knife. We gave a gasp as we imagined we were about to witness a human sacrifice. But the priestess brought the knife down with a swift thrust, severing the goat's throat. The head hung loosely on the spine and skin of the back of the neck. The goat's hooves kicked out spasmodically, as the murdered animal fell to the floor. Blood spewed from the body, painting the girl and the priestess in dark carmine. As the dissonance of the singing resolved into a remarkable cadence, the priestess raised the knife over her head, with the blade pointing down, and chanted a continuation of the dark incantation:

> *Veridicos preme, nec laudes, sed carpere gesta*
> *Quaerito cujusvis, non tua respicias.*
> *Dispereas male, ne quaeras tu coelica, verum*
> *Crimine frangaris, ne fuge delicias.*

> *Suppress those who speak the truth,*
> *and do not praise the deeds of anyone, but seek to slander them;*
> *do not consider your own; let your end be an evil one,*
> *do not seek the things of heaven;*
> *let yourself be broken by crime,*
> *do not shun pleasures of the flesh.*

The girl took the priestess's hand and pressed it to her lips, then donned her dress and descended from the platform. The chanting fell silent. The three of us cowered behind the juniper, I quivering with fright. There was a moment of silence. Then the priestess spoke.

"Bring the musician."

It was like a physical blow. We thought we were lurking undetected, yet this witch knew all along that we were there. Moreover, she knew who we were. My Master, the excitement glowing in his eyes, rose and started forward. Filled with trepidation, Don Fabrizio and I followed. But the witch raised her hand.

"Not the boy and the *ricchione,*" she said. "Just the musician."

Strong hands grabbed us. We could have shaken free, but three women stood before us. They raised their skirts, and wiped their hands across their vaginas. Then they raised their hands to stop us. Their hands were smeared with blood. The sight of menstrual blood, a powerful poison, stopped us in our tracks. My Master was oblivious to all this, He walked up to the platform as in a trance. The platform was slippery from the blood of the slaughtered goat. He stood and faced the priestess. His eyes were shining in the moonlight, his lips in a slight, beatific smile. She grabbed him by the hair, and forced him to his knees. Goat's blood smeared over his hair and face and knees.

"You have had a wretched life, musician." The Prince looked down at the floor like a chastised child.

"Forgive me, mother," he said in a near whisper.

"You have offended my brothers," said the witch. "You will suffer for that."

"Yes, mother."

"You will offend my sister. You will suffer greatly for that."

"Yes, mother."

The priestess lifted her skirt, and shoved my Master's lips forcibly against her crotch. "Eat, *stronzo.*" The women below began again their gyrations, obscene gestures and cries of delight. My Master eagerly lapped at the priestess, until she shook violently, and threw him to the floor. Then, silently, the women filed out of the clearing, leaving us alone.

When they were gone, I rushed up to my Master, who was lying motionless on the platform. "Master, rise," I cried, shaking him. He awoke from his trance, sat bolt upright, and cried, "Follow them! Do not let them get away!"

"I shall not leave you, Master," I said.

"Don't be a fool. Find them, Find them now. Fabrizio, go after them."

Fabrizio roused the dogs, and tried to set them on the scent of the witches. But the dogs could not, or would not, rise to the hunt, and stubbornly sat down, facing Don Fabrizio. "Cur, follow," cried Fabrizio. But the dogs would not budge. The women had disappeared without a trace.

My Master broke out in tears. "They are gone! I have failed again! *Pater noster, qui es in caelis, sanctificetur nomen tuum.*" He dug his fingernails into his face, scratching to draw blood. I grabbed his wrists and held him firmly to my breast. "My Lord, you must forget these witches. These are evil, they will destroy you."

"Destroy me? Am I not already destroyed? Did you not hear what she said? I have offended her, I have offended her brothers and sisters. Wretchedness is my fate, and it is my due. *Lasciate ogne speranza, voi ch'intrate!*" He tried to wrench his hands free to do himself more damage, but I held him fast.

"My Lord, there is hope, but only if you abandon this evil way. These are witches, and they consort with the devil. Do not seek them."

"Did you hear the music, Ludovico? Was that music not divine? I have never heard sounds so hypnotic. I must hear that music again, Ludovico. I must make that music mine!" He ceased his crying, and filled with resolve. "Unhand me. We will sleep here tonight. Tomorrow we will mark this spot, I must return here and hear them again."

We were, in fact, unequipped to spend the night in the forest. We had planned to return to the castle by nightfall. But we were completely lost and had no hope of finding our way out in the dark of night, even with the aid of the moonlight. So we stretched out on the ground and slept as best we could. We awoke before the moon had set. We rose, stiff and groggy and hungry, mounted, and set off to the north. After riding for several hours, we encountered a stream, and followed it out of the forest, to the road leading to Gesualdo.

The following four days were spent scouring the forest, searching for the coven's secret altar. We retraced our steps from the original march, at least a dozen times. But no trace of the pond or the altar could we find. My Master woke every night in screams, harrowed by the red dream. By the end of the week, I urged the Prince to abandon his search. "You must abjure this obsession, My Lord. Your duties call you." With reluctance, My Master agreed, and we returned to the palace in Gesualdo.

My Master, however, did not return immediately to his duties. Instead, he shut himself in his chamber for four days. He allowed no one to enter. He directed me to bring him bread and water only, once a day, which I was instructed to leave by his closed door. No one other than myself had any concourse with him.

At the end of the four days, he allowed me into his chamber. He was sitting, cross-legged, on the floor in the middle of the room. His shirt back was stained with blood where he had apparently beaten himself; the blood was clotted and the fabric adhered to his body. Yellow pus oozed out of the wounds and through the shirt. Greatly moved by the sight, I moved to comfort him, to free him of the bloody shirt and to begin dressing his wounds. But he raised his hand in a motion so definitive that I halted in my steps. Without a word, he handed me a sheaf of manuscript paper, and motioned me to sit. I took the pages, sat down and read through the music. It took me well over an hour. It was a transcription of the singing of the witches. My Master remembered it far more accurately and completely than I. Hearing it was remarkable, but, seeing it written on the page, this music was no less than miraculous. The main contrapuntal subject wandered through all the known pitches of the octave. The voices entered one after another, each at a different interval, reproducing the subject precisely. The intersection of these voices created a fabric of dissonances and resolutions which defy description. Sometimes a resolution would last only a moment, falling on a weak beat so as to pass almost unnoticed, only to return again for a true cadence. It appeared to obey all the complex rules of counterpoint, yet defy them at the same time. The music followed the rules, not in the letter, but in the spirit, transforming the rules themselves into a higher order.

Reading this manuscript, I broke out in a cold sweat. It induced in me at once awe and terror. Never had I seen such powerful music. This was not mere *musica secreta*, music to be heard only by a select aristocratic few and never to be published. This was *musica prohibita* – music, I knew intuitively, that would never be performed, and that would be read only by me. And when Prince Carlo Gesualdo's soul departed from this world, destined to reside eternally wherever God decreed, he left for me an envelope with the manuscript.

m'involate hor mi redete il core

I wrote earlier that I had urged my Master to leave the forest in order to return to his duties. For by the time this episode occurred, my Master's brother had died, his father was infirm, and the responsibilities for ruling the principality of Venosa fell upon him. In the three years since his return home from Rome – and the period of my service with him – Don Carlo Gesualdo had grown from a quixotic and unstable boy to a man of remarkable maturity. He had, it turned out, a remarkable talent for governance, and was a competent and fair ruler of his realm. To be sure, his extreme mood shifts continued, his frequent forays into libidinous and often perverse escapades continued untempered, and his obsession with his music consumed large quantities of time. Yet, despite this, he took his responsibilities for the well-being of his subjects and the prosperity of his fiefs seriously and discharged those responsibilities with honor and skill.

From the moment of his return home, it was clear to Prince Carlo that Luigi would not survive. His elder brother was pale, his breathing shallow, his chest fallen, and he was often too weak to rise from his bed. Indeed, within a few weeks he regained some of his strength, thanks to the ministrations of numerous excellent doctors sent for his care by Don Carlo's uncle Alfonso, the cardinal. But even in his recovered state, he was weak and lacking in vitality. Moreover, it was clear to their father His Excellency Don Fabio that Luigi had neither talent nor interest in ruling the realm, and that his younger brother Carlo was much better suited to be heir. His Excellency ordered his sons Don Carlo and Don Luigi to sit with him in court, and to observe as he managed the accounts and directed affairs of the estates. In these sessions, Don Carlo paid rapt attention, and often asked questions. Don Luigi, on the other hand, displayed no interest, and, indeed, after a few weeks, ceased to attend. In spite of this apathy toward the arts of governance, Don Luigi was greatly angered by what he saw as the usurpation of his seniority by his younger brother. Not only Don Luigi, but also his uncle, His Eminence Alfonso Gesualdo, who bore toward my Master a biding antipathy ever since, as a seven-year-old boy, my Master sank his teeth into the Cardinal's hand. The Cardinal sent Luigi, accompanied by Giulio Gesualdo, his nephew and protégé, to speak with the Prince. My Master was present when the interview took place.

"My Lord," said Don Luigi, "It is most unseemly that my younger brother accompanies you in your princely duties. Am I not the heir?"

"My son," replied His Excellency, "it is most unseemly that *you* do not attend. Did I not invite you to join us? How else are you to learn the arts of governance?"

"My Lord, I cannot attend when you treat my younger brother as though he is the elder. I cannot abide this. I will not abide this!"

The father now grew angry. "You shall not tell me what you will abide and what you will not abide! I instructed you to attend. You failed to do so. And now you come to me with complaints that I do not favor you. You are yourself to blame."

Don Giulio now intervened, seeing there was no profit in this confrontation. "My Lord, your anger is justified. The Prince Luigi is my dear friend, and it pains me to see him slighted so by Your Excellency. Allow me, my Lord, to urge you to forgive him and to allow him to continue to profit by your tutelage. I will personally encourage him to attend your sessions, and may he profit greatly from your boundless wisdom."

"I do not need your intervention, and he does not need my forgiveness," responded His Excellency Don Fabio. "All he need do is attend when I sit in court, pay attention when I review the accounts, and learn how I manage the estates. Without his presence, there is no way he will learn to rule, and I will rue the day when he ascends to the Principate in my stead." And, with a wave of the hand, he dismissed his son and his advocate.

Indeed, for the next few days, Don Luigi tagged along sullenly as Prince Fabio performed his duties. But after a week, the elder son fell again ill, and sent word to his father that he was unable to rise from his bed. And so, again, my Master was the only attentive pupil to receive his father's instruction.

Don Giulio, and the Cardinal himself, nevertheless persisted in their efforts to drive a wedge between father and son. The Cardinal's protests about Don Carlo's music, which I referred to earlier, is an example of these efforts. Don Giulio missed no opportunity to report to the father on my Master's dalliances, often in the most lurid terms. He likewise reported on my Master's bouts with depression and self-deprecation, which, he insinuated, rendered him unstable and unfit to rule. He even went so far as to suggest, at one point, that my Master's mental vicissitudes eroded his allegiance to his father, and that my Master was contemplating subterfuges to undermine His Excellency's suzerainty. This suggestion so infuriated Don Fabio that he dismissed Don Giulio from his presence, and refused to see him again. This was, however, not the end of Don Giulio's influence in the court. For he had succeeded in insinuating himself into the confidence of my Master himself.

Personally, I found Don Giulio an obsequious sycophant, and his efforts to ingratiate himself with my Master disgusting. Don Giulio was nondescript in every way. He was not tall, neither was he short. He was heavy, but neither strong nor fat. His features drooped like the face of a basset hound – limp, hanging jowls, drooping eyelids, nose bulbous without being large, lips thick without the set of authority. His visage was mildly repulsive yet eminently forgettable. His lips were turned down in a permanent glower, but one that expressed neither discontent nor boredom. Indeed, the only time he showed any expression at all was when my Mistress, Donna Maria, entered the room. His eyes then lit up in a lecherous leer, but immediately faded back into his inscrutable but uninteresting mug.

When he walked, he oozed with an unpunctuated gait, yet he was anything but graceful. Don Giulio had studied for the priesthood, and was, in fact, ordained. His vows, of course, were as chaff to the wind, and the main way he set about ingratiating himself in my Master's eyes was by accompanying us on our frequent excursions into the dens of Neapolitan iniquity. He always drank the least, yet acted the drunkest, urging my Master and his friend Don Fabrizio to acts of greater and greater debauchery, and always carefully observing the proceedings, I presumed to use as blackmail at a later date.

These dens of Neapolitan iniquity – I feel I must explain, for those who have not probed this underworld of vice will have no inkling of its nature or organization. I certainly didn't, for when I began in my Master's service, I was innocent as the driven snow. For sure, the church had set its canon against fornication and sodomy, and the civil authorities, likewise, made feeble efforts to limit the scope of this underworld. But in reality, neither the church nor the state made any effort to curtail the extensive world of sin. At one point, the viceroy attempted to herd all the prostitutes into a single section of the city, but his efforts were bootless. It is said that Naples was a city of 300,000 people and 30,000 whores.

The elite of this underworld is the *cortigiana onesta,* the honest courtesan. These are women of great culture and beauty, and their skill in lovemaking is matched by their skills in music, poetry, and the arts of conversation. Such was, for example, Francesca d'Aragona, said to be the granddaughter of the great poet and lover Tullia d'Aragona. It was with Donna Francesca that I lost my innocence. I escorted my Master to her home on the Via Stella, there she entertained us with beautiful singing, accompanying herself artfully on the lute. Her servant, too, sang beautifully, and the two of them performed a rendition of the villanella *Ch'all'acqua vai,* which took my breath away. Not only because of the quality of the singing, but because of the raw erotic energy that these ladies effused. I fully expected my Master to retire with Donna Francesca, perhaps leaving me to cavort ineptly with the servant girl. Of this possibility I was, in my total inexperience, in terror. So it was to my great surprise that he turned to the courtesan, and said, "My darling

Francesca, I must ask a great favor of you. My servant here – indeed, he is more than a servant, he is a friend – is still a stranger in the field of love. Pray, take him for the night, and return him to me a man." That night was my introduction to the world of the flesh, an introduction that would lead to a life where service to my Master and physical pleasure became inextricably entwined.

I often wonder what my father, may his spirit enjoy the peace of Heaven, would have said were he to have known of my promiscuous forays into the world of the night. His Excellency, my Master's father, provided my father with a house of his own, where he resided with my sister. When I entered the employ of Prince Carlo, I moved into the manse, and so saw less of my father, and he was unable to follow my comings and goings, as he did when I used to live with him before my service. In any case, he died of *mala aria* just a year after my employment. My sister, two years my junior, was given into my charge, and the Prince my Master graciously agreed to employ her as a maid. Subsequently I married her to the son of a cheesemaker in Naples, and she bore him four children.

As I recall him, my father was a straightforward, honest and devout man. He was dedicated to his wife, who died when I was still a child, and thereafter lived, I believe, a life of celibacy. Never did a prurient thought cross his mind – he was as remote from venery as day from night. He was fastidious and meticulous, very exacting in his music-making as in his life. At least, that is how I remember him.

Yet, devout though he may have been, he was a tolerant man who did not impose his own values and behavior on others. He religiously attended mass, and confessed once a week, though I cannot imagine what he had to confess. But he never forced religion on me, and when I skipped mass occasionally, he never censured. What's more, his work as a musician brought him into contact with people of diverse habits and beliefs, and he never reproved nor hesitated to befriend them. For example, many of his friends and fellow musicians were Jews, of the Amani and other families. He never viewed these as infidels, and, quite the contrary, continued to perform with them even after the Guild banned Jews from all performance. So I believe he would not have been excessively censorious of my behavior. And, in any case, when I married at the age of 22, during a sojourn in Cremona of which I shall soon tell, I renounced all such behavior.

But I digress. I was describing the underworld of sexual depravity that spread throughout the fabric of Naples as a cloth soaks blood throughout its fibers though just a corner be dipped in carmine. Beneath the respected *cortigiana onesta* was the *cortigiana di lume,* the common prostitute. These ladies emerged at night, wandering the streets or leaning over their balconies beckoning passing gentlemen, or loitering in the wine bars and taverns. When the dusk darkened to night, these whores swarmed the city, and every woman you encountered you could be sure was selling her body, for no honest woman would venture into the streets of Naples unescorted after the sun went down.

These, the *cortigiane* of different flavors, constituted most of underground Naples. But there were, beyond these, places where one could seek sexual pleasures of a rarer and more sinister kind. There were taverns where there gathered men who preferred the company of other men; there were places where men like Don Fabrizio could indulge in their strange penchant for dressing as a woman; there were dark, subterranean taverns where one could buy the services of prepubescent boys or girls, and where one could, for a high price, attend the degradation, rape, and even torture of enslaved victims.

It was to one of these places that my Master, Don Fabrizio and Don Giulio had, apparently, visited on one occasion. We had attended a musical soiree at the home of a wealthy patron of the arts, who owned an excellent Flemish *clavecin*, and who hosted a talented consort of young female singers from a Naples orphanage. The girls sang delightfully. After the performance, I flirted gaily with the *canto* singer, who had charms beyond her charming voice. One thing led to another, and I soon asked my Master to excuse me, and accompanied the young lady to my chambers in the palace of San Severo. There we did what we did, and I sent the young girl on her way. Though it was by then late at night, I felt it my duty to attend to my Master, and I quietly opened the door to his chamber. There, I saw a young boy of no more than 11 years, stretched over a table. My Master was pumping vigorously into the lad's posterior, while Don Fabrizio, attired as a woman, had his dress lifted over his hips and had his member plunged in the boy's throat. In a chair watching was Don Giulio, his hose and breeches clumped about his knees, his hand gripping his *coglioni* and a lascivious grin on his lubberly lips. I turned to leave immediately, but my Master spoke. "Ah, Ludovico, so you ploughed the ditch of the little *soprano puttana*, eh?"

"Yes, my Lord."

"And how was she?"

I pride myself in being a tolerant man, as was my father. But this scene was far too extreme even for my liberal tastes, and I chose not to answer. Instead, I excused myself, I admit, in a most disrespectful manner. "I shall take my leave of you now, my Lord. We can discuss this in the morning." Another master would no doubt have taken umbrage at so direct a rebuttal, but my Master merely chuckled and continued debauching the unfortunate child on the table.

I repeat this episode not as mere gossip, but to illustrate two points: first, the extreme variety of depravity that was available in Naples at this time; and second, to show how Don Giulio succeeded in insinuating himself into my Master's society, becoming as frequent – if not intimate – a companion as his friend Don Fabrizio.

LIB

m'involate hor mi redete il core

Red, the color of blood. Red, the color of pain. Red, the color of sin.

Red is the color of the robes of the cardinal.

Two cardinals cast their scarlet shadows over this narrative. One – Alfonso Gesualdo – is already familiar to you, and appears as a living player in the drama of my Master's life. The second – my Master's namesake, His Eminence Carlo Borromeo – makes only a cameo appearance; yet his shadow is as long and as scarlet as the first.

Both cardinals were my Master's uncles: Alfonso Gesualdo was his father's brother, and Carlo Borromeo was his mother's brother. As I have mentioned, my Master's accounts of his rare meetings with his uncle were often clouded by contradiction and vagueness. The Archbishop, my Master told me, was never censorious, and was kindly and attentive. He had an aura about him which instilled confidence and encouraged confession. He remembered the Archbishop's kindly brown eyes, eyes that seemed huge, protruding, bright, intelligent and unblinking; a sharp, aquiline nose above firmly set lips; a face that radiated authority and charity at the same time. His charity, his modesty, his honesty, and his faith: these were the source of his authority and his rise in the Church.

My Master recalled a soothing balm that the Archbishop would rub on the angry welts that often covered his back and bottom from his tutors' beatings; His Eminence's touch, said the Master, was like velvet. My Master found comfort in burying himself in his uncle's scarlet robes; not the terrifying feeling of drowning in red as in his red dream, but comforting, soothing, and nurturing a yearning for devotion and penance.

Penance, for the Archbishop was unwavering in his faith. He believed passionately that suffering was the wages of sin, and that he who suffered on earth would find his reward in Heaven. This was his message to Don Carlo in later visits. Here is how my Master recalled his the Cardinal's message: "My son, pain and suffering are God's signposts. If you suffer, you should not look to others. You should look inward, and seek to correct your ways. Prayer without thought will never Heavenward reach. And you must always remember, that your suffering is as naught – look to the suffering of our Lord. Accept your pain, and your reward will be in Heaven. *Si fuerint peccata vestra ut coccinum quasi nix dealbabuntur*"

It was a lesson that seared its mark in my Master's soul. Don Carlo believed that, though his sins be scarlet, they shall be washed white as snow; that pain was the path to Heaven; and that suffering was his just deserts for his own faults. The Archbishop was to the Prince – as he was, indeed, to the whole world – a paragon of virtue and charity. So, while the Prince basked in his aura during their visits, he returned to his quarters with a feeling of inadequacy that he could not live up to his uncle's high standards. And he began to view his repeated punishments and humiliations at the hands of his other uncle's minions as a proof of his own failing.

For his other uncle, His Eminence Alfonso Gesualdo, was, in the eyes of my Master, the opposite of the Archbishop. Where Carlo Borromeo was charitable, the cardinal was avaricious; where the first was chaste, the Cardinal was lecherous; where the first was modest, the Cardinal was ambitious and ruthless.

Consider this: when Carlo Borromeo was only 12 years of age, he was granted the income from two wealthy abbeys in the family perquisite. The child priest (for he had already been ordained and received the tonsure) took only the income he needed for his minimal existence and turned the rest over to the poor. His Eminence Alfonso, as Archbishop of Conza, impoverished the diocese, seizing the tithes for his own aggrandizement.

Consider this: it was said that Carlo Borromeo never once took pleasure in woman, man, child or beast. His Eminence Alfonso, had a reputation for venery. It was said of him that he wavered between the pleasures of the peach – the smooth, round buttocks of young boys – or of the fig. *Le pesche eran giàcibo da prelati*, wrote Berni. And, indeed, the peach was the preferred fruit of this prelate, if not to the exclusion of the fig.

Consider this: Carlo Borromeo accepted his appointments with submission, and fulfilled his duties with diligence. His Eminence Alfonso had set his sights on the Holy See. Twice did he conspire to create cabals in the College of Cardinals, playing ambitions against enmities, cabals that were foiled only by the intervention of His Eminence Carlo Borromeo, acting on the instruction of the sitting Pope. And, while His Eminence Alfonso never achieved his Papal ambitions, he succeeded in twice having elected Popes who were weak and sickly, and who brought weakness and dissent and shame upon the Church.

One characteristic of His Eminence Alfonso: he never forgot and he never forgave. That one act of self-defense, when my Master as a young child sank his teeth into his uncle's hand, marked my Master forever. As the years passed, his uncle's hatred would destroy my Master's life.

m'inuolate hor mi redete il core
L I B

Maria d'Avalos – just the name conjures in me a cacophony of feelings that claw at my heart like the talons of a hawk: tenderness, love, terror.

Maria d'Avalos: beautiful, honest, pure, devoted, faithful, innocent, true.

Maria d'Avalos: gifted, clever, wise, intuitive.

Maria d'Avalos: dead. Murdered.

Maria d'Avalos was my Master's wife, my Mistress, for four years. In all the time I knew her, I could not imagine her doing an impure act. In all the time I knew her, there was never a moment when her devotion to her husband, to her child, and to the houses of d'Avalos and Gesualdo swerved. And that is why the events that led to her death seem to me so incredible.

Maria d'Avalos: I often try to expunge that name from my memory. For whenever my thoughts turn to her, my mind tries to reconstruct the horror of that night, when blood painted the alabaster steps of the Gesualdo mansion red and brown and black. I had read the inquest. I had read the reports. I had seen the evidence, seemingly incontrovertible, of her faithlessness and the justice of her bloody demise. Yet so many questions remained in my mind.

Three men, said the witnesses. Three men joined the Prince in the incursion to her chamber that night. My friend Pietro Bardotti, servant of the Prince, identified them as men in my Master's service. But at least one of those he identified, Ascanio Lama, I knew was not in Naples at the time – for he was in jail in Cremona. Could Pietro have erred? Or was he lying? Why would he do that? Why would he refuse to say who were those faceless men who, with steel bared, burst into my mistress's chamber?

And there they slew them. Don Fabrizio, the man who killed a bear with only a spear. Donna Maria, who had never killed or harmed a being in her short life. Why? Why?

Questions. The name Maria d'Avalos awakens in my mind this flood of questions. But, in the end, these questions are washed away in a carmine flood that leaves me limp and shuddering and bereft of all capacity for rational thought.

Yet there is no avoiding it. For I have come to that point in my narrative where, perforce, I must speak of my Mistress. For, on the fifth day of June, in the year of our Lord 1586, my Master married Donna Maria d'Avalos, an event that set their lives on a blind course to tragedy.

Indeed, the events leading up to the marriage were auspicious. A half a year before, Prince Carlo's brother Luigi died, despite the best efforts of the doctors provided by his uncle, the Cardinal Alfonso. The cardinal made no secret of his displeasure with this turn of events, but there was nothing to be done: my Master was now the heir to the principality. The Prince his father called Don Carlo to arrange the match.

"Do you know of the widow Maria D'Avalos?" he asked.

"Who does not know of Maria D'Avalos?" replied his son. "She is the greatest beauty of the realm."

"I have arranged for you to marry her."

My Master was disinclined to wed. He was much enamored of his crapulous life, and the constraints of marriage had no appeal for him. On the other hand, he certainly understood the new responsibilities that rested upon him with his brother's death, one of which was certainly to provide a male heir. And for this, Maria D'Avalos seemed eminently qualified. Though only 21, she had already wed twice before, and was mother to two boys from her first marriage. Both her husbands had died, her second within the last two months.

So my Master, resigned to his fate, consented to the match. "It shall be as you desire, my Lord," he said with a bow. "But she is only recently widowed, and still in the compulsory period of mourning."

"I shall ask your uncle to arrange a papal dispensation to allow you to marry her as soon as possible," replied his father. "I have already concluded the terms. Go and begin your courtship."

So the very next day, I set out with my Master to Montesarchio, a half-day's ride from Gesualdo, with two horses laden with gifts for the bride to be. Donna Maria's father, Carlo D'Avalos, received us handsomely, and honored my Master with a feast that included an entire wild boar slaughtered that very morning. After supper, my Master sat with Donna Maria, and presented her with a friendship ring wrought of solid gold.

In the morning, we set out for home. My Master was uncharacteristically silent for the entire journey, and I was quite concerned that the match did not meet with his approval. My fears were, however, completely unfounded; quite the opposite, Prince Carlo was completely smitten by love for the beautiful Donna Maria. This I soon learned, for on our arrival in Gesualdo, he bade me accompany him to his rooms, there he spilled his heart out for over an hour. "Such grace, such beauty! I am unworthy of so great a gift! Oh, Ludovico, did you see how she cast her eyes down. Such modesty! How can I live up to such a standard? I today renounce all debauchery! I shall be her slave forever!" And so on, in a litany that, I dare say, soon became monotonous and slightly embarrassing to attend. However, the flood came to an abrupt halt, when he declared, "Ludovico, leave me! I must write! I must write music for my wife!"

Thus began a period of two days, during which my Master did not leave his chambers. I brought his meals to him, and reported to his father the Prince that my Master was well and more than enthusiastic about the match. Sore tempted was I to enter his chamber unbidden, to assure myself of his well-being, yet I knew him well enough to refrain. Wisely did I act, for at the end of two days, he called me to his chamber. He was disheveled, but had done no harm to himself; on the contrary, he was filled with a manic energy. He handed me a sheaf of paper on which he had composed two madrigals, and instructed me to copy out the part books from the score. This I did, in my finest hand, and delivered the pages to the bookbinder, who illuminated the manuscript and bound it in fine leather. Here is the text of the first of the madrigals, a poem by Donna Maria's great uncle Alfonso D'Avalos:

> *Sento che nel partire*
> *il cor giunge al morire.*
> *Ond'io, misero ognor, ogni momento*
> *grido "morir mi sento"*
> *non sperando di far a voi ritorno.*
> *E così, dico mille volte il giorno*
> *"partir io non vorrei"*
> *se col partir accresco i dolor miei.*

> *I feel that in the parting*
> *the heart touches Death,*
> *and so, forever sad, I cry, at every moment:*
> *'To die I feel',*
> *for now I cannot hope for you to come back,*
> *And, thus, I tell myself a thousand times each day: '*
> *I have no wish to leave, if my going increases my sorrow.'*

Here I must pause to make a surprising observation: the madrigals that my Master wrote in the throes of love, inspired by the extraordinary beauty of his bride to be, were to me a singular disappointment. They had none of the daring, the originality, the genius of his prior work. They adhered strictly to the rules of composition as professed by his teacher Pomponio Nenna and by the other court composer, Scipione Stella; they never challenged those rules, and they displayed none of the chromatic daring or complexity of his other madrigals. Indeed, they did not rise above the most pedestrian compositions of Scipione Stella himself.

Please do not take this to suggest denigration of Don Scipione. Don Scipione was a fine musician, and a dear friend. Even today, though he has taken vows and changed his name to Pietro Paulo, we meet frequently and reminisce about old times. For in those days, we played or sang together almost daily. His Excellency owned a fine harpsichord built by Giovanni Antonio Baffo, and we would often play songs, me on the lira da braccio and he on the harpsichord, often entertaining the Prince and his guests late into the night. He was a fine performer and composer for the keyboard, as well as a composer of madrigals. Indeed, I regret that I earlier called his compositions pedestrian – they were original and showed a high mastery of his craft.

This has often caused me to wonder: what is it that sets great music apart from merely good music? I am, of course, not the first to speculate on this weighty question. Many of our writers have noted that composers of the greatest music have a melancholy disposition, and are often seized by bouts of despair and conflict. This was certainly the case with my Master, whose tormented soul produced some of the most astonishing and original music I have ever been privileged to hear. Yet there are compositions by others, great masters, who were unflaggingly cheerful, gentle souls who, I daresay, never suffered a day of depression in their lives. I think of Luzzasco Luzzaschi, whom I had the pleasure and honor of meeting, and who was something of a role model for my Master during his time in Ferrara, or Lodovico Agostini, whose ingenious musical riddles I sometimes spent hours trying to crack. Indeed, even the great Monteverdi, whose newfangled musical forms I despise, but who, I cannot deny, is as great an innovator as was my own Master, is not known as a melancholy person.

My friend Padre Pietro (whom I often still call Don Scipione, much to his chagrin) and I often sit in the garden of my son's house, and lament the decline of the great art of music. This newfangled style of opera – of which Monteverdi is the master – seems to us so superficial and foolish. Where has gone all the great art of polyphony? One hardly ever hears madrigals these days, everyone is infatuated by *L'Orfeo* and *L'Arriana,* Monteverdi's operas. Such noise! Such bombast! An orchestra with 37 instruments, all blasting away with a racket to awaken the sleeping Vesuvius! And no viols! All these new instruments, violins, violas, cellos. No, says my friend Padre Pietro, we are simply old fashioned. This music, it is not bad, it is simply different. We are simply stuck in the old ways. But I say – no! This new style of monody, this style of solo singing with no polyphony, none of the glorious richness of voices weaving in and out, this is simply dross. And I miss the velvet tones of the *viola da gamba* and resonance of the *viola d'amore*. Not that violins are bad – I myself was one of the first people in Naples to play on a violin. But can they replace that royalty of the instrument family, the viols?

I must tell you of the first time my Master heard a violin. It was a few months after I had entered his service – already he had taken me to the courtesan, and we had developed an intimacy that went beyond that of master and servant. We had spent the day in musical pursuits. In the morning we enlisted Don Pomponio, my father, and another musician of the court, Dominico Avrabanel, to open the chest of viols and read through some madrigals. We played some of Don Pomponio's and of Don Scipione's, which we could read off in a single effort. We played some of my Master's, which required several attempts before we got them right. Each madrigal inspired a lively discussion of its merits. My Master was in a good and generous mood, and was quite complimentary of the madrigals by the court composers. Some of the more surprising modulations disturbed the older masters, and they had interesting criticisms of what worked and what did not. It was most instructive as well as a joy to play with such talented and accomplished musicians. We then dined, and after a rest, I set out with him to the home of his friend Don Fabrizio, where we heard a lovely new singer, who sang villanelas and frottole, accompanying herself on the lute. She had an exquisite voice, and was equally beautiful to look upon. Sadly, she was an indifferent lute player, but her voice and delightful figure more than compensated. I was sure that my Master would tarry a bit and seduce her after the performance, but he was eager to move on.

As we were in the northern quarter of the city, I suggested that we visit my friend and mentor, the doctor Moise Amani. I had mentioned this remarkable man to my Master before, and he was curious to make the acquaintance. So we made our way to the *Porta San Gennaro*, and turned left along the outer side of the wall. The wall was lined with tents and makeshift tenements built by the poor, who could not afford to live in the security of the walled city, or who had been expelled for various civil or criminal offenses. We had not gone 100 steps when we heard the sound of my mentor playing. It was a remarkable sound, a sound that my Master had never heard – an instrument, sounding similar to a *Lira da braccio*, but far stronger and clearer, almost bell-like. Each note was clearly distinguished from its neighbor, even in the quick and virtuosic passages, like a string of perfectly round pearls, perfectly matched, each pearl with its own shine and depth. My Master was so taken with the sound, that he stopped in his tracks, listening intently, and, I could see, moved to the depth of his soul. He stood thus, transfixed, until the end of the tune, and then strode apace to the source of the sound.

There, in the garden of a prim wooden house, sat my teacher and mentor. He was a tall, lanky man, dressed in ordinary clothing. On the lapel of his cloak was a round yellow circle the size of a hand. But the most riveting aspect of his appearance was his face: long and narrow, with thin lips, a wispy beard, and a large, ugly scar slashed across his head nearly from ear to ear; and, where the eyes should have been, dark holes.

He was seated on a wooden bench. The garden was a tidily kept rectangle, with a wicket fence, in sharp contrast to the surrounding slum. The bench was in the shade of a spreading lemon tree; to the right was a large herb garden, neat rows of carefully pruned shrubs of tarragon, wormwood, and other plants, many of which I could not identify. Beside my teacher sat his servant and assistant, a small, stocky man with an oversized head, and, like his master, a yellow circle sewn on the lapel of his cloak. My teacher held in his long, slim fingers an instrument, familiar to me but unknown to my Master. It was somewhat similar to a lira da braccio, but smaller and far more graceful in shape. It had only four strings, rather than the usual seven, with no drones; it had an elegantly carved peg box, with fluted pegs of ivory; it had no frets; and the back, rather than flat, was carved like the top in a graceful arch.

My teacher, though he had no eyes, immediately sensed my presence. "Ludovico!" he cried. "What a joy to have you here! And who is your friend?" It was always a source of wonder to me how, without benefit of sight, he could identify me perfectly and know if I was accompanied. There were occasions when he could even tell what I was wearing, or if I was carrying my instrument. The sharpness of his other senses compensated for his loss of eyesight.

"My honored teacher, this is my Master, His Highness Prince Carlo Gesualdo. I am taken into his service. My Lord, this is my teacher, il Dottore Moise Amani. And this is his assistant, Don Salamone."

The Dottore bowed from the waist, but without rising from his bench. "Your Highness, what a great honor to make your acquaintance. Your name goes before you. Your father is a great Lord and a man of the highest esteem."

My Master was slightly taken aback by this greeting. It was unbecoming of his station to have others greet him without even rising from their seats. But if he was offended, his intense curiosity about the instrument that the doctor held in his hands overcame any other emotion he may have had.

"I was listening to your playing," said my Master. "I was enchanted. You must play more on this... "

"Violin, your Highness. It is a violin, imported from Cremona."

"I long to hear it."

Without another word, the doctor lifted the instrument to his chest, and, holding it snugly against his breast, drew the bow across the strings. The music again worked its magic. My Master stood entranced, drinking in the sound with his eyes shut and a beatific cast to his lips. The doctor played a long *cantabile,* and then followed with a *tarantella Napolitana,* his long fingers dancing on the fingerboard with the speed of the leaping spider. The music rolled on for perhaps twenty minutes, with my Master standing immobile the entire time. As the last chord died away, my Master opened his eyes and looked with amazement at the doctor. He stared mutely at the doctor and his instrument, as though the music had stolen from him the capacity of speech. The doctor, sensing his plight, spoke for him.

"It is a violin," he said. "A new development, growing not from the viol family, but from the line of *vielle* and *rebec*. Your servant Ludovico also plays the violin very beautifully."

My Master turned to me. "Play," he commanded. I took the violin in my hands, tucked it securely under my chin, and proceeded to play an *arioso*. I embellished the tune with chords and double stops, and the long notes I enhanced with the close shake, a trembling of the hand which lent a pleasant warbling sound to the note. I had not the facility of my teacher the doctor, so I did not attempt a fast tune like a *giga* or *tarantella*. But I believe I acquitted myself admirably, showing off the deep tone of the instrument to best effect. My Master was as enchanted by my playing as he was by the doctor's.

"You hold the instrument differently," my Master noted.

"There is really no generally accepted method for playing the instrument; indeed, many of the best players keep their technique a deep secret, lest some upstart should best them," replied the doctor. "I have even seen players in the North hold the instrument on their knees like a *viola da gamba*."

"I want one," said my Master.

The doctor smiled dryly and shook his head. "There are only two or three makers who know the secret of the violin's construction – Gasparo da Salo, of Brescia, and the Amatis of Cremona, father and son, Andrea and Antonio. I received mine as payment for a medical service, and thus avoided a long wait. Now the violin is the rage in all of the North, and I fear you will wait for years to acquire one."

"I do not want to wait years. What was the service you performed?"

"It was for Antonio Amati. I treated him for bad dreams."

My Master and I looked at each other quizzically. My Master turned to the doctor to speak, but no words came. I spoke in his stead.

"My Master also suffers from bad dreams."

The doctor turned to face my Master. Eyeless, he could see nothing – yet his visage had an intensity as though he were staring, examining every contour of my Master's countenance and body. After a long moment, he spoke.

"May I invite you in for a bit of *grappa* and a *tissana*? Don Salamone, would you be kind enough to prepare an infusion of verbena and peppermint for our guests?" He rose and led the way into his house.

I must say, it was a day of astonishment for my Master. First the music, then the remarkable instrument, and now the interior of my teacher's home. For this was no ordinary dwelling – it was also the doctor's clinic and laboratory. Two walls of the main room were lined with shelves bearing the instruments and materials of his profession. On one bank of shelves, a myriad assortment of vessels – crucibles, retorts, alembics; vessels of glass, of copper, of iron; squat vessels with wide mouths, tall jars with narrow necks and glass stoppers, flat dishes with conical ceramic lids. A second bank of shelves contained rows of jars, tightly sealed. Each jar was labeled with its contents in an elegant, flowing script. Laudanum, bismuth, oil of tartar, verdigris. A third bank held medical instruments – oddly shaped knives, drills, and pincers of all sizes and shapes. A fourth shelf held the doctor's books – rows and rows of tomes in Latin, Greek, Hebrew and Italian. Along a third wall, a high plank bed stood, with a strange framework built above it, for holding a patient suspended in a permanent position while the doctor performed operations. The main room opened out into a second room, where were the stove and sleeping quarters. In the center of the main room were a simple table and three chairs. The doctor bade us sit.

We sat about the table. My Master looked about the tidy room with a look of fascination. His gaze settled on a small parchment tacked to the wall, and he stared fixedly at it. It was a rectangle about a hand span wide and two long, on which were inscribed ten circles, interconnected by what appeared to be interwoven tubes or tunnels. Together they formed a most intricate pattern. The entire design, as well as the interstices between the forms, was filled with writing in a tiny and very exacting script, in an alphabet I knew (from my previous acquaintance with my teacher) to be Hebrew. This parchment – a talisman of some sort – seized the imagination of my Master, who could not lower his eyes from it.

The doctor, though blind, had an uncanny sense of all that was taking place. "What is it you are looking at, My Lord?" he asked. "I imagine it is the *kamea*."

"It must be powerful magic," said my Master.

"There is no such thing as magic," replied the doctor. "Magic is simply a name for things we do not understand. When we understand them, they cease to be magic. At one time the seemingly erratic motion of the stars across the firmament were thought to be magic. We know now that the motion of the earth through space is what inscribes that movement. One day, we shall understand the power of that image, and it shall not longer be magic."

"What is it?" asked my Master.

"It is an ancient Jewish amulet, showing the ten aspects of God."

"I have seen it before," said my Master. "I have seen it on the wall in my uncle's room in Rome."

"Your uncle?"

"His Eminence the Cardinal Carlo Borromeo. My namesake."

I have noted how much one's expression is conveyed by the eyes. It was therefore remarkable to me how expressive was my teacher's face, even though he had no eyes. For his face turned to stone. The color of his cheeks was replaced by a ghostly pallor, and his lips set in a sphinxlike expression. The coldness in his mien was arresting, and even my Master, as fascinated as he was by the other trappings of his surroundings, was paralyzed by the pall that fell over the room. We sat in silence for what seemed an eternity. The pall was broken only when Don Salamone brought small cups of grappa and ceramic mugs filled with the fragrant verbana and mint infusions. The arrival of the tea shook my teacher from his reverie. As quickly as the pall had been cast, it was lifted, and the doctor resumed the conversation.

"Now, tell me about your dream."

My Master described the red dream – the drowning in red, the stabbing pain in his side, the terror, the screaming, the cold sweat. Just retelling the dream had a frightening effect on him; he shuddered as he spoke, and finally buried his head in his hands, unable to continue.

"Don Salamone, prepare a pipe for our guest," said the doctor to his assistant. He then continued to address my Master. "This dream, I believe, is rooted in some terrible hurt," said the doctor. "It is a hurt that you have driven from your conscious mind, but it resides deep in your soul. Perhaps one day the memory of this hurt will rise out of the abyss, but until that time you shall continue to suffer from this nightmare.

"There is only one known cure for this condition. Love. If you will love another, a total, unwavering love from the depths of your heart, then the dream will be banished. For there is not room enough in the human heart for a great love and a great terror. Of course, if the love should die, there will again be room in the heart and the dream will return.

"Until such time as you shall love, I can offer only a palliative." Don Salamone had returned to the table, carrying a small, curiously shaped brass bowl with a small tube protruding from the lower rim. The doctor dropped a lump of gray resin into the bowl, and with an ember that Don Salamone had brought from the stove, ignited the resin, inhaling vigorously through the tube. He then passed the device to my Master, and instructed him, too, to inhale the vapors from the burning resin. My Master took a deep breath through the tube, and immediately broke out coughing. The doctor smiled.

"It takes some getting used to, but you will soon be able to inhale the smoke without irritation. This is hashish, made from the oil of the hemp plant. I import the hashish and pipe from Morocco. Inhale some more."

My Master took another breath from the pipe, and this time was able to hold the vapor in his lungs without coughing. After several puffs, the effect on him was clear – his features relaxed, and the tension in his face was replaced with a benevolent smile.

"As long as you take a daily dose of hashish, your dream will not return," said the doctor. "Alas, I cannot supply you with a daily dose. I myself have not discovered the secret of extracting the oil of hemp and condensing it into a cake like this; what is more, the varieties of hemp we have here in Italy have very little potency. So I am reliant on my relatives in Morocco, who send this to me periodically. And I can provide you with no more than one or two doses per week. So I fear you will have to suffer your dream periodically until such time as you shall love."

The doctor wrapped three lumps of hashish in a small piece of paper, and handed the wad to my Master.

"How shall I pay you?" asked my Master.

"There is no need for payment," said the doctor. "I do this as a gift to the master of my pupil. And I could not take money from the nephew of so illustrious a cardinal as Carlo Borromeo." This last sentence was spoken with ice in my teacher's voice.

As we left the house and headed back to the city gate, my Master turned to me. "Why does your teacher hate my uncle so?"

"I know the reason," I replied.

"Then tell me."

"You may not know, my Lord, that a few years before we were born, the Inquisition ordered the expulsion of all Jews from Naples. My teacher told me the stories of those terrible times. There were many Jews then, and they were forced to abandon their homes and property. Of those who refused, many were burnt at the stake as heretics. My teacher was at that time a young doctor, but already very successful, with several patients of stature and power. These patients petitioned the Viceroy to allow the doctor to stay, but the Inquisition was adamant. As my teacher told it, there was a crisis between the church and the Viceroy, which reached all the way to the Pope. The Holy Father sent his emissary to Naples to resolve the conflict. The emissary decreed a compromise – the dottore would be expelled from the walled city, and not be burned at the stake – only that his eyes be burned out with a red-hot poker.

"That emissary was your uncle, His Eminence the cardinal Carlo Borromeo."

---

m'inuolate hor mi redete il core

My teacher's prognosis proved to be remarkably accurate. My Master suffered from the red dream regularly, except on those nights when he inhaled the hashish vapor. I made monthly visits to my teacher's home outside the city gate, to collect as much hashish as he had. My Master often accompanied me on these excursions. On the one hand, he was eager to hear the violin as frequently as he could; on the other hand, he was profoundly disturbed by my teacher's execration of my Master's uncle. My Master held up Carlo Borromeo as a paragon of perfection and virtue, and the thought that the cardinal had acted with such callous violence toward someone whom my Master had come to respect was a painful dissonance to him. With time, it was a dissonance that my Master learned to live with, for over the years he accompanied me more and more; for my teacher's wisdom and extensive knowledge of music, science and philosophy made conversation with him a delight – not to mention the beauty of the music that he played.

But it was the second part of my teacher's prognosis that proved the most compelling in its accuracy. For, the moment my Master fell in love, the red dream ceased to trouble him. Quite the contrary, from the moment of his first meeting with Donna Maria, he embarked upon the two happiest years of his life. As I have written before, from that first moment he was smitten with a love, for which he was totally unprepared, and, indeed, completely unsuitable. That is, if it is possible to be unsuitable for love, this was the case. His impetuous nature, his frequent descents into dark moods of self-recrimination and guilt, and his unbridled submission to his libidinal urges, made it nigh impossible to maintain a stable, loving relationship. There was, however, one cardinal factor which made such love possible: the total devotion, the forgiving nature and the support of Donna Maria. For, as much as he was smitten with love for her, so was she smitten with love for him. This became clear upon my second meeting with her, when I brought her the bound manuscripts of the madrigals my Master had written in her honor.

As I said, these madrigals were not the best productions of my Master's art; on the contrary, they were, in my opinion, bland and pedestrian. Donna Maria, however, did not feel that way at all. She received the volume with unbridled delight, and, though she had not the skill of reading the notes and hearing the music in her head, she enthused effusively over the illustrations, the beauty of the handwriting and binding, and the texts (with which she was familiar). And when the *capella* sang the madrigals for her, she experienced the same visceral joy in the music that my Master felt. No critical examination for her: she was swept away by this expression of my Master's devotion to her.

When I was just a child, my mother took me to a holy man whose blessings, it was believed, could change the course of a man's life. The man, a hermit, lived in a cave on the slopes of Vesuvius. There, in the hermit's cave, the wizened old man placed his hands on my head and chanted Latin verses that I could not understand. He then turned to my mother and said, "The boy will find favor in the eyes of men."

And that, indeed, has been the case. People meet me and often have immediate confidence in me. Total strangers will sometimes confide in me their most intimate secrets. It is this trait of mine, I believe, that has made it possible to serve my Master where others have failed. And it was, I believe, this trait that made me an instant confidante of my Master's fiancée. For from that second meeting, she took me into her most intimate confidences.

After the *capella* sang, my Master and Donna Maria sat together and conversed for long hours, while the servants and family milled about the great hall. My Master had brought along more gifts on this visit, and the bride's family had reciprocated with gifts of their own: a bolt of fine silk, a silver repoussé chalice with a fine, intricate design, a set of silver dishes embossed with the D'Avalos seal, and more. I busied myself with organizing and packaging the gifts for the journey home, while the lovers caressed each other – with their eyes only, of course, for chaperones were everywhere. It was, indeed, quite remarkable for two partners thrust together by the convenience of political alliances to be thus enamored of each other, but this was the unusual case of His Highness Carlo Gesualdo and Donna Maria D'Avalos. For those of us who were mere spectators, it was, I suppose, a bit tedious; in any case, by the time the morning star glimmered above the castle, my Master had run out of blandishments, and readied to go. I was to remain behind to pack the gifts on the pack horse, and return later to Gesualdo.

But when the hall had emptied of family and servants, and there remained only the Lady and her personal attendant, Donna Maria called me over. She was still wide awake, and began to pour her heart out to me.

"Such a gallant man, and so handsome. Oh, Ludovico, I am so blessed to have him as a husband. So sensitive, so gifted. And his music – it simply carries me away. I fear I am a boor in matters of music. I so fear that I will be unable to speak to him on this subject so dear to his heart. Do you think I can live up to the level that such a brilliant man deserves?"

I have no idea how I could have answered this question, but, fortunately, she expected no answer, but continued her panegyric. "His hands are so gentle. Did you see how he took my own hand in his? So strong, yet so soft! I could hardly breathe, I was so moved by love. Love, Ludovico, I am crippled by love. Twice have I been married, but no husband did I have for whom I felt this feeling. Indeed, my first husband was a gentle man, and treated me fairly and with respect. And I bore him two children. But no love did I feel for him, though we were cordial and kind to each other. I suppose my children – I loved my children very much. My son died an infant, but my daughter lives with her father's family. How painful was the parting! I still love her, it is a constant source of sadness that she is not with me now. Alas, when I remarried, my children stayed behind in my first husband's home. It was such a painful parting. I see her only once a month or less, it is the most painful part of my life. And my second husband – he was a lout. I despised him. He had no manners, he was rude and violent. He even tried to beat me one time, but he was drunk and I evaded him. His death, God forgive me for saying so, was a blessing. But now, this – this paragon of beauty, of aristocracy, I feel so blessed! Is it not so, Ludovico? Is it not so?"

Again, I found myself at a loss for a response, and, this time, it seemed, she really did expect me to interject some comment. So, rather than attempt an answer to her question, I posed one myself. "How did your husbands die, my Mistress?"

"Don Federigo, my first husband, died of the *mala aria*. He survived three sweats, on the fourth he died. It was an awful death – I was at his side the whole time. The fever rose like fire, he was consumed, delirious, screaming. Then of a sudden it passed, and he lay drenched in sweat. But then two days later it returned, and then again and again. By the fourth time he was destroyed – he chose to die rather than live this nightmare.

"My second husband – I do not know from what he died. He was drunk and sick the whole time I was his wife. At the end he had black warts all over his body – perhaps it was plague. But I don't care. I hated him.

"But now I shall have my true love. I swear to you, Ludovico, I swear by the Blessed Virgin, my love for my prince will fill my heart to the day of my death."

I must say, as I listened to my Mistress speak this litany, I felt no little unease. For the Hyperion she thought she was marrying was no Hyperion at all, but rather more of a satyr. Should I speak? Should I disavow her of her misconception, before she should be rudely disappointed? I, I thought, alone, could perhaps divert a tragic mismeeting of the couple, before it was too late.

"My Mistress," said I, "You should know that your betrothed is not the paragon you seem to believe."

"Paragon?" she replied. "Oh, not at all! My father was careful in researching the character of your master. I know about the moods, I know about the peccadilloes. My father has told me all. He has told me about you, too – I know that you are close to Don Carlo, much closer than a servant to his master, and that you join him often in his debauches. I do not love him for his faults, but for his beauty, and his genius, and his soul. Give me that soul, Ludovico, and I shall forgive whatever faults he may have!"

"Madam, may I speak freely?"

"Of course, Ludovico. I trust you to guide me in this."

"My master is a man of strong appetites, and – how shall I say this – a love of variety. You cannot expect him to rein in his passions, for, I believe, he cannot. And he may well make demands of you that are – not in the ordinary way."

"Ludovico, I have given him my heart. After that, he can take any part of me that he desires. Oh, I only wish that he indeed desires."

This was the first of many confidences that my Mistress placed in me. At the time, I did not suppose that she intended for me to record her words in a memoir for all to read. Yet, today, she and he are both dead, deaths that rake across the heart like a maul, deaths that wrench at my innards with waves of pity and revulsion and love and hate, like the torment of Prometheus. Considering the circumstances of their deaths, I do not believe that Donna Maria would object to my divulging the sentiments that she expressed that day; quite the contrary, I believe she would want the truth to be told – the truth of her love, of her fidelity, of her submission to a terrible fate that pursued her and him like the Furies.

I hope it is clear from my recounting of this encounter that the current story of my Mistress's murder is rife with lies and slanders. For example, Asconia Corona writes in his chronicle *Successi tragici et amorosi* – the most popular and accepted version of the events – that "human nature... implanted in the bosom of Donna Maria unchaste and libidinous desires..."; and the author goes on to describe intimate conversations, completely spun from the imagination, wherein my Mistress encourages her lover in the most brazen and vulgar fashion to acts of venery. Now the identity of the architect of these fabrications, and the reason for their promulgation, I was to learn in due course. But I must make clear that, even on the very first reading, I knew this account was a transparent and wicked attempt to destroy my Mistress's undisputed (until then) reputation for chastity and modesty.

m'inuolate hor mi tedette il core

The next three months – and indeed, the next three years, up to the date of the hex on my master by the witch Aurelia d'Errico – were the happiest of my Master's life. He was seized by an exquisite joy of life, a frenetic flurry of activity and creativity, and a relative freedom from the dark torments of his life. The red dream fled from his sleep entirely, just as my teacher the Doctor had predicted. The bouts of self-destructive depression that had punctuated his days, albeit never ceased, but were much mitigated. These occasional depressions – which were far fewer as well as less intense than previously – focused primarily on his fears that he would be inadequate as a husband and a lover. These fears were, in my mind, completely baseless, given his extensive experience in the field of Amor; yet they nonetheless occupied his thoughts and sullied the otherwise halcyon period of his life. I once encountered him in his chambers, gazing at his naked body in the mirror. "Tell me Ludovico, is it too small?"

"It is neither too small nor too large, My Lord," I replied. "*Non è quanto grande, è come lo si utilizza.* It is not how large, but how you use it. Surely, you, who have had hundreds, perhaps thousands of partners, should be assured in this matter."

My Master sighed, clearly dissatisfied with my reply. "I just wish I could be sure. I so do not want her to be disappointed with me." He stroked himself gently, causing the member to stand straight into the mirror.

"My Lord, I have spoken with the Lady, and I promise you, your unconditional love is all that she seeks in you. Whatever physical prowess you may bring to the marital bed will delight her perfectly."

But, as I say, these manifestations of depression had none of the intensity or frequency of his former self. That said, I must note that his pursuit of fleshly pleasure continued unabated throughout the period up to the wedding, and, indeed, beyond. And my Master was often seized by guilt and self-recrimination after his evenings of debauchery. He would beg me to beat him – which, of course, I refused to do – and wept by the cross. These bouts of remorse, however, passed quickly, and he soon rationalized away all moral or philosophical doubt; on the contrary, any attempts on my part to dissuade him from further shows of unfaithfulness to his bride to be were met with dismissal: I must stay in shape for my wife, he would reply.

Musically, this was a period of intense work. For my Master was exceedingly prolific, writing madrigal after madrigal, inspired by his love. And, while I considered these works to be inferior to his previous efforts, he expected the capella and the camerata to sing or play these to perfection, and rehearsed us mercilessly for hours every day. I both sang in the capella and played in the camerata, so I was myself occupied completely during the course of the day.

My Master's father, His Excellency Don Fabio, was a *cavalliere* of taste and refinement, and he had gathered to his court the finest musicians of all of southern Italy. We had eight singers in the *capella*, of whom four (including myself) were full-time musicians – the others were servants in different capacities, but with fine voices and good musical training. The *maestro di capella* was Bartolomeo Roi, a crusty old musician with a long white beard and sparkling blue eyes. Maestro Bartolomeo was very old school, and disapproved of the harmonic liberties of my Master, as well as his prodigal life style, but was wise enough to keep his opinions to himself. In any case, he was much more satisfied with my Master's current efforts, firmly rooted as they were in the old tradition, than with his earlier experiments with chromaticism. The organist for the *capella* was my friend Scipione Stella, whom I have already mentioned. Don Scipione was a barrel-chested man with a *basso profundo* laugh that resounded through the halls of the palace like a huge bass drum. His wife was fat as a goose and just as tyrannical, gabbling away at him incessantly. When she died, he left the service of the Prince and took up the cloth.

We had seven instrumentalists in the *camerata*. I mention only a few: myself on lira de braccio, Don Pomponio – my Master's counterpoint teacher – on theorbo and violone, my father on viola da gamba, Giovanni de Macque on cembalo and organ. Don Giovanni was the only member of the academy who was of the *oltramontani* – the "musicians from across the mountains", composers and performers imported from the north of Europe. It was fashionable – indeed still is today – to believe Italian musicians inferior to those of the low countries. The Prince, my Master's father, did not think so, and therefore eschewed the many Flemish musicians recruited to serve in the Italian courts. To be sure, the Flemish had developed a very high form of the contrapuntal art, but, His Excellency averred, they were no better than our own artists in technique, and lacked the passion of our home-grown musicians.

Don Giovanni in fact, despite being foreign born, came to Italy as a youngster, and did not speak with the barbarous accent that characterized other *oltramontani*. Nonetheless, he had a distinctly non-Italian face, with the short, upturned nose, round eyes and pallid complexion typical of these Northerners. He was the only one of the members of the *camerata* who composed instrumental music – everyone else composed vocal music only – and was thus, in my eyes, a blessed addition to the *camerata*. And, though his features were Northern, his temperament was distinctly southern; for he loved to joke and he shined as a leader of our musical fraternity.

We were a closely knit society within the Gesualdo court. Working together as we did daily, we developed close friendships, and shared confidences. My Master shared our dedication to music, but, if only by nature of his position, was decidedly an outsider to our little community. This greatly annoyed him and he longed to be accepted as one of the community. However, quite aside from the barrier on any fraternization posed by his high station, he was socially quite inept. He really had no circle of close friends; indeed, apart from Don Fabrizio and myself, he had no friends at all (I don't count Don Giulio as a friend). He was, in the society of a group, a poor conversationalist and, worse, given to inept and inappropriate interjections which could be quite embarrassing. Here is an example: Don Giovanni (who, with my father, was one of the eldest of the musicians of the court) had married a lovely Italian woman. The admixture of the musician's cold Northern blood with the fiery temperament of a Neapolitan belle had produced an offspring of striking beauty and character. Their daughter, then 13 years old, was perfectly constructed and had a delightful personality. We were sitting after rehearsal, drinking wine, and Don Giovanni was telling us what a talent she was on the lute. Don Pomponio remarked, "She will make some lucky man a fine husband in three or four years!" to which my Master commented,

"I wonder what it would be like to fuck her?"

Needless to say, this question fell like an earthquake on the group. All conversation immediately stopped, and the gathered musicians looked upon my Master aghast. And then, naturally, their eyes turned to me; for, as Don Carlo's personal servant and faux chaperone, I was expected to deal with situations like these. I must say, from my intimate acquaintance with my Master, I knew this not to be an actual proposal to seduce his servant's daughter, but simply an incompetent attempt to be witty and to join in the conversation. My Master had no inkling that this remark was in any way offensive.

In an attempt to defuse the situation, I said, "I think my Lord only means that he believes your daughter will one day be an excellent wife in every respect, and will bring you many grandchildren."

"Well, I can say Amen to that," replied Don Giovanni.

"Yes, of course," said my Master, realizing that something was amiss with his previous comment, but uncertain exactly what it was. This exchange indeed served to relieve some of the tension. But the very next day, Don Giovanni sent his daughter to live with his cousins in Mantua, and she did not return to Naples until she married three years later.

I can say in all modesty that my closeness to my Master, and my ability to rein in his more outrageous behavior had won me the respect of both my musical peers and the Prince himself. As the youngest member of the *camerata*, I was paid the minimum that His Excellency offered to musicians, 12 ducats per month. However, I had no expenses whatsoever – my Master provided me with all my needs, including clothing, transportation, lodging (in the Palace), and, of course, entertainment. Moreover, His Excellency raised my father's salary to 24 ducats per month, and provided him a house, a servant and a horse. This was the highest salary paid to musicians in the court, and, indeed, in all of Naples, excepting of course the salary of Battista di Pavola. Don Battista was a *castrata* that His Excellency hired away from the court of the d'Estes of Ferrara. *Castrati* were – and still are – paid absurdly high sums, and were in desperately short supply. Indeed, Don Battista gave our *capella* an absolutely shimmering tone, making our *capella* by far the finest in Naples. So we were willing to live with Don Battista's obnoxious behavior; for he was foul-mouthed and salacious. He had an uncanny attraction to women, and he lured dozens to his bed every month. And after every sordid episode, he would regale us with the most anatomical details of how he gave these women the most extreme pleasure. All this despite the fact that he himself was incapable of full intercourse, and had never had an orgasm.

I suppose that Don Battista's narratives were one of the reasons that my Master thought his off-color interjections would be acceptable or even of interest to the gathered musicians. In fact, my fellows were a staunchly conservative lot. My friend Don Scipione, I have mentioned, took up the cloth later in life. Don Giovanni, like all *oltramontani*, came from the land of Martin Luther, where anything but the strictest decorum of speech or action resulted in public punishment and humiliation; we had heard of the stocks and the brandings. And, while Don Giovanni was born Catholic, he brought with him from his childhood much of that Northern strictness. And my father, as I have told, was devout and modest. So there was certainly no audience here for comments of a sexual ilk.

I should mention that, when my father died, His Excellency, in his great bounty, granted me my father's salary, even though I was still one of the youngest members of the *camerata*, as well as usufruct in the house, the horse and the servant. I sold the horse – my Master had provided me with a horse already – and I rented out the house, which provided me an additional four ducats a month, making me a man of considerable means.

m'involate hor mi redete il core

Dreams, writes Santa Synosius, are a window to the soul. While the intellect holds objects that are, the soul holds objects that are becoming. And the dream, he writes, is a mirror unto itself that reflects those incorporeal objects that are not yet but which will be.

I have written of the red dream – the dream that happily had fled from my Master's nights during this period of love and courtship. But there was another dream, equally disturbing, that cast its dubious shadow across those halcyon days.

My Mistress Lady Maria confided in me. She dreamed she was sleeping in her bed. She awoke and saw the floor around her bed crawling with vermin. Roaches, rats and mice, snakes, large spiders, covered the floor entirely, a black, rippling sea of vermin. In her dream, my Mistress stood up on her bed and began screaming. The vermin crawled onto her bed, and started climbing up her body. The creatures did not bite her, on the contrary, their slimy bodies slithered over her like oozing oil. She screamed louder and louder, as the vermin crawled into her mouth and eyes and ears, and into the private spaces between her loins.

At this point in the dream, my Mistress's maid entered and awakened her; for she was screaming not only in her dream, but in reality. After a few minutes wherein she was disoriented and unable to express herself or think, she understood that this terrifying experience had been an invention of her sleeping mind. And she angrily reproached her maid for awakening her; for, she said, wakening her had prevented her from dreaming the dream to its conclusion.

"I know there is more to this dream," she told me. "Now I will never know how it ends. I must understand this dream."

She knew of my Master's red dream, and of the treatment I had assisted in obtaining by introducing him to my teacher. But Donna Maria, rather than forthwith put her faith in a Jewish doctor, preferred first to consult her priest. She therefore went to confession, and the confessor proscribed a penance of fasting and prayer.

"He said the vermin were my lecherous thoughts," she told me. "He said it is the nature of woman to be lustful and promiscuous, and that I must rein in these impulses that are ingrained in me. Oh Ludovico, do you think it is so?"

I assured her on this account. "My Lady, I have known you only a few short months. But in that time I believe I have come to know you well, and I can attest that you do not have a lecherous thought in your head. I have never met a woman more modest, more chaste, and more faithful than you are."

This prejudice, that women are creatures driven by lust, and, consequently, must be ruled by men and that men must constantly be on their guard, is widely believed, and, indeed, seems to be a tenet of our clergy. I am, of course, a product of my times; but in this particular matter I find this prejudice to be untrue. It is my experience that there are lustful men just as there are virtuous women; God did not give women an extra measure of lustful thoughts, just as he did not slight men in this respect, either. I have known many men who were far more driven by lust than the average woman: my Master and his friend Don Fabrizio are certainly examples. Moreover, a person's lecherous leanings are not constant throughout his life – I myself am testimony to this. Until my 15th year, when I was engaged as my Master's servant, I had not a lecherous thought in my head; and, were I to have one, I would not even have recognized it as such. Immediately upon my engagement to my Master, I was swept up in my Master's life of venery, and, indeed, every nubile female awoke in me a burning desire to have carnal knowledge of her. I was, it is true, not as consumed with lust as my Master, but the pursuit of sexual pleasure became a motive force in my life, and there was not a moment when it was not in the back of my mind.

When I was sent to Cremona, where I met my wife, this all-encompassing sea of lust in which I bathed subsided. My thoughts turned to her, and to family, and, while I can say that we had an excellent relationship in every respect, the carnal urges ceased to be a primary motive force in my life.

Now there are, of course, women who are driven by lust. Aurelia d'Errico is one such person. This is the witch who put the tragic curse on my Master, destroying his love and his life. The d'Errico woman longed to possess not only the body of her victim, but his entire soul – it was an all-consuming lust to conquer and destroy. It was purely evil.

But I digress. I believe that I succeeded in reassuring my Mistress that the priest was wrong in his interpretation of her dream, and his assessment that she was a creature of depravity. I convinced her to accompany me to the home of Doctor Moise my teacher, and allow him to recommend a solution. Encouraged by my recital of his success in ameliorating the effects of the red dream in my Master, she agreed. So, on a visit to Naples some weeks later, she came with her chaperone and maid and myself to the home of the Dottore.

The Dottore listened patiently as Donna Maria retold the dream. He sat a while in silent thought. Then he said, "There is more to this dream than you are telling."

Donna Maria looked at him quizzically. She thought back on the night of the dream, the awakening, the confusion, the sense of the dream being unfinished. "Yes, that is so," she said.

"Tell me."

"I believe there were people in the room. I do not know how many or who they were. They rose up out of the sea of vermin, and were themselves covered with vermin. There were two or three or four. And they were looking at me."

"And then?"

"My maid awakened me. But I know now how the dream ends."

"You do not have to tell me if you do not wish."

"No, I wish to tell you. The vermin disappear. The people disappear. Everything becomes white. I, too, become white, an empty space. There is nothing left – everything becomes a void. And there is no more terror, no pain, no body – there is nothing!"

Again, the Dottore sat in silence, deep in thought. Then he spoke.

"This is, for you, a very disturbing dream. But I can assure you, it has no deep meaning. It is certainly not a dream of prophecy, you have nothing to fear on that count. It contains frightening images, but these images are merely unformed objects of the imagination, and do not signify dark forces within you. I think it is likely that there is some somatic source to this dream, perhaps an illness that was attempting to attack your body, but which, through these images, your mind succeeded in repulsing.

"I believe you should put your concerns behind you. But, as I know this is advice difficult to take, I am prescribing a dose of the same medicine I gave your fiancé to repel the ill effects of his own dream."

And so, the doctor's assistant Don Salamone prepared the brass device with the gray lump of hashish resin, and my Mistress inhaled the vapors, inducing, as it did for my Master, a new calm.

That was the end of the episode of the dream, as far as my Mistress was concerned. She never gave it another thought. For me, however, there was an epilogue. On my next visit to my teacher, with my Master, the doctor took me aside.

"I lied to your Mistress about her dream," he told me. "I said it was of no consequence, and thus calmed her. But the truth is different: it was, I believe, not a mere *insomnium*, nightmare. It was an *oraculum*, a prophetic dream. I believe this dream foretold some terrible event, indeed, a course of events leading to a tragedy, in which she shall be swept up and which she shall be powerless to deflect. I did not tell her this, for there would be no point in burdening her needlessly. But I tell you, for, perhaps, you will have the power to intervene and prevent a catastrophe."

Oh, how wrong he was! For, when the curse drove to its tragic conclusion, and the corridors of San Severo filled with blood, I was far away, sent packing by a Master already too far in the sway of the witch and her confederates to resist.

m'inuolate hor mi rédete il core

Enough! I have written that this was a happy period, the happiest in my Master's and Mistress's lives. Yet I keep returning to the horrors of that tragedy: the curse, the murder, the bloody aftermath. I must cease to perseverate on these dark events, for there is so much of joy and rejoicing at this time.

There was the music. Not only did my Master write prolifically, the other composers of the court offered their productions to the happy couple. Don Pomponio wrote a case of wedding madrigals, dedicated to the couple. As a gesture to my Master – and, perhaps, as a sign of his own developing tastes – he wrote these using many of the chromatic gestures that characterized the earlier works of my Master. There is, to my mind, a certain irony in this: the compositions of my Master were becoming more conservative in style just as those of Don Pomponio were becoming more daring! My friend Don Scipio, and Maestro Giovanni de Macque also contributed their works. Maestro Giovanni gave us a number of instrumental works, which the *camerata* performed with delight.

Not only in the field of music, but in all the arts was there a flowering. My Master commissioned two large canvasses from the painters Bellisario Corenzia and the Florentine Giovanni Balducci. Balducci was commended to my Master by Maestro de Macque, who had met him when he sojourned in Florence. He came to Gesualdo to execute his work, a large seascape depicting the launching of Odysseus's fleet. He was a man of fiery disposition, constantly getting involved in fistfights with other artists – painters in general were a very disorderly bunch, constantly arguing and dueling. That notwithstanding, he and my Master had an instant rapport, and Balducci resettled in Naples and never returned to Florence. My Master later commissioned him to do the altarpiece in the church Santa Maria delle Grazie. This work depicts my Master kneeling before our Savious, apparently pleading for the souls of his murdered wife and his friend. At his side is the saintly Cardinal Carlo Borromeo. How ironic!

The poet Cesare Cortese wrote several *epithalamia*. Usually, these wedding poems extol the virtues of married life and the importance of family values and fidelity. Don Cesare was, however, very much an iconoclast: his poems are full of the slang of Naples, and written with a sailor's bawdy wit. Here is one of them:

> *As smooth as peach your pouty cheek,*
> *Like milky fig your lips so sweet,*
> *If I should breach your garden wall,*
> *I'll steal your cherries, steal them all,*
> *God Strike me dead if one should fall.*
>
> *For o'er that wall I'll snoop and peer,*
> *Until you say, "Come enter, dear!"*
> *Then I will climb your garden wall,*
> *I'll steal your cherries, steal them all,*
> *God strike me dead if one should fall.*
>
> *And once I pierce that garden wall,*
> *You'll laugh, you'll cry, you'll gasp, you'll call,*
> *"Come steal my cherries, steal them all!"*
> *For once it's breached, there is no wall,*
> *Your fruits are mine, I'll take them all.*
> *God strike me dead if one should fall.*

In preparation for the wedding, and for the receipt of the new bride in the Gesualdo castle, my Master had engaged workmen of the village to make an extensive renovation. The castle was built 700 years before, and the last renovation was 100 years ago. It was old and drafty, the roof leaked, many of the windows were unglazed. His Excellency my Master's father had delegated the management of the Gesualdo fief to my Master, who undertook a major improvement of the castle and its environs. To this end, he engaged the master carpenter Errico d'Angelo, whose daughter, you may recall, later met her death at his hand after my Master had trysted with her. Don Errico performed a remarkable transformation of the old castle: the walls were paneled with oak, beautifully carved with wreaths and vases and faux pillars, the old window casings were replaced, new doors with finely wrought hardware were hung. The granite floors were reflagged with marble, the walls hung with tapestries and paintings, sculptures were commissioned to grace the halls. In the great hall, My Master ordered that dark oak panels be hung from the ceiling, and the floor laid with a plush carpet imported from Stamboul, a deep wine red with an intricate design in green and blue and ivory woven into the thick nap. The result was that the strong echo in the hall was deadened, yet the hall still had a lively resonation, so it was an ideal room for our nightly performances.

In preparation for the wedding procession through the main thoroughfare of Gesualdo, workmen were preparing huge decorative floats. I was in a bit of a quandary about these floats. There were two dealing specifically with the subject of music: a float for Orfeo – an upper level depicting a meadow with the heavens above, and an opening leading to the lower level, where were shown different chambers of purgatory and hell through which Orfeo would pass as the float rolled down the street; and a float for the forest nymphs, decorated with woods and clearings, and Gods and Goddesses suspended from the superstructure of the float. On the Orfeo float the camarata was to play, accompanying Orfeo. As I was one of the few musicians who could both sing and play, I was to be cast in the role of Orfeo. Don Pomponio had composed a new setting of the arias of the story, especially *Ecco pur ch'a voi ritorno,* that I was to sing, accompanying myself on the lute, with the *camarata* in the background. Don Pomponio's arrangement was achingly beautiful and I was eager to perform it. On the other hand, on the forest nymph float the *capella* was to sing new love madrigals composed by my Master; I certainly would not want to miss singing in this. Alas, there was no way I could do both. Before we started the rehearsal of Orfeo, we talked about this dilemma. "You could sing the aria," suggested Don Scipione, "then, with lightning speed, leap behind the float, strip off your Orfeo costume, slide into your nymph costume, and dash back to the nymph float."

"The cheers and applause for your Orfeo performance will still be ringing as the nymph float rolls up, with you lolling against a pillar in the nymph float, ready for the first madrigal," said Don Pomponio.

But I knew these suggestions, well-intentioned as they might be, were completely impractical. For one thing, once I began the role of Orfeo, I could not leave the float until Charon had ferried me back from the underworld, with fair Eurydice at my heels! It was Maestro Roi who settled the matter. "You shall play Orfeo to the last. The *capella* shall manage without you!"

The floats were truly magnificent. Each guild made a float to honor the newlyweds. The carpenters, despite the fact that they were busy ten hours a day with remodeling the castle, nevertheless found the time to build an intricate reconstruction of the *Via Dolorosa*, with each Station of the Cross built in the most meticulous detail. The weavers and dyers guild's float presented leading figures in the history of their craft: Penelope, weaving her shawl endlessly while waiting for Odysseus; Santa Lydia, who brought the Tyrian purple dye to Christendom; San Mauritius, patron saint of the weavers. All this behind a giant spider web stretched across the frame of the float; and in the middle of the web, Arachne, with the eight legs of a spider and the face and body of a woman. Arachne plucked at the strings of the web with her eight legs, while, behind the scene, a lute player plucked out a tune, giving the appearance that the spider was playing the music on her web.

These things I saw a day before the processional, for I knew that on the day of the march I would be too engaged to see anything. And, indeed, my performance on the day of the event was one of the most taxing – and rewarding – of my life. There was, of course, much noise and commotion, and initially I had to sing at the top of my lungs to make myself heard. But once my voice broke through, I sensed a hush fall over the crowd, and our performance held the people spellbound. At the end of our *favola*, the people broke into thunderous applause. The float then moved on, and, five hundred steps beyond, we repeated the performance. Thus we made our way gradually up the *Via Roma*, from the fountain, and up to the *Chiesa Madre di San Nicola*, where the mass and nuptials took place. The entire route was lined with well-wishers and spectators, from the castle to the church, and our float must have stopped and our show repeated at least a dozen times. We parked our floats in a circle in the plaza, and this was the only moment I regretted my choice; for the *capella* abandoned their float and rushed into the church, to sing in the ceremony. We of the *camarata*, on the other hand, were not needed, and we sat biding our time on the float. Thus, I missed seeing the *tradere filiam suam* and the *uxorem ducere*, and hearing my comrades sing the mass. At the end of the ceremony, My Master and Mistress mounted two matched, pure white *Lipizzano* stallions and led the way up to the castle.

One hundred and fifty people attended the wedding feast. This was a banquet the likes of which had never been seen in all of the province of Avellino, perhaps in all of southern Italy. There must have been 70 or 100 antipasti, laid out on a sideboard that stretched the entire length of the great hall: artichokes stuffed with prosciutto, figs filled with chopped nuts, peaches in the French style, dozens of spiced fish dishes. The broiled octopus tentacles *alla Catalena* was simply superb. After the buffet, the guests sat down at long tables, and servants came around with the *pasta* and *mines*: at least ten different kinds of soup, and as many of pasta. This much of the meal took the better part of two hours, for the guests needed time to digest and to consume tuns of Fiano wine. All the while, the *camarata* was playing – *villanelle, mascherate, moresce greghesce, villota, giustiniane*. Popular songs, and, as the evening wore on and the wine flowed, people joined in and sang along. In the short breaks in the music, servants brought us trays full of the delicacies.

There followed the *lesso* courses – veal stew, *pasticcio di seccaticcia alla Francese*, a dozen types of salami. Then the roast – an entire boar, pheasants stuffed with rice and chestnuts, venison, *lonza di vitello, pulcinelli con aceto*. By the time the *fruttarie* arrived, it was well past midnight.

But the party was still just warming up. For after the feasting, the dancing started. We started with the more traditional and staid court dances - *bassadance, pavane, almain* – and became gradually faster and wilder. The *Galliard*, the *Volta*, and the wild *Tarantella*. As the music became faster and more compelling, many of the more conservative guests – including the parents and siblings of the bride – retired, leaving the younger and more libertine to revel. With tumbler after tumbler of wine, brandy and grappa acting as lubricants, gradually the conventions of chastity, fidelity and discretion fell by the wayside, and the party became wilder and wilder. The ladies pulled at the hems of their blouses, until the tops of their pink aureolae showed; the men did not hide their lascivious intent when, during the *Volta*, they grasped their partners by the crotch and hurled them skyward. Couples, unmarried or married, to each other or to others, no matter, disappeared from the dance floor, only to return later, the woman's cheeks flushed with pleasure. My Master disappeared early in the evening with his bride, returning an hour later. He then disappeared a second time with Don Fabrizio. Again returning to the dance floor, he grabbed a young servant girl, and dragged her behind an arras near the stage where we were performing. I could hear her weak protests and subsequent sighs as he took his pleasure. Nor did the orgiastic spirit of the evening pass me by. For, during a brief break in our playing, a guest, the daughter of a local squire, grabbed my hand and led me to a chamber upstairs, there, quite oblivious to the differences in our stations, we had fleshly pleasure in each other – all quick enough for me to take my place on the stage before the *camarata* resumed its playing.

The party finally broke up as the first light of dawn was turning the great hall a delicate pink. Who would have believed that the festivities would continue unabated? Yet by midmorning, the tournaments began. It was a day of jousting, archery and racing, fencing and *guerre di pugni*. The star of the day was unquestionably my Master's friend Don Fabrizio. At the first event, the *garosello*, mounted contestants used their lances to spear wooden rings hanging on threads. Points were given both for the number of rings and the speed of the horses. Don Fabrizio succeeded in spearing all five rings, one after another, without reining his horse for a single halt. It was a performance unapproached by any of the other contestants. He was eager to do a real joust, but His Excellency Don Fabio, my Master's father, had forbidden it since the last time, when one of the contestants was permanently crippled. However, there was a tilt, and Don Fabrizio knocked the target aspin with astounding accuracy.

Not only at jousting did Don Fabrizio shine; he took second place in the sabre contest, and first place in the grappling. In the *guerre di pugni,* he succeeded in casting opponent after opponent to the ground. In strength and skill, there was none his equal.

My mistress excelled in the archery contest. Using the long bow, she skewered ten gold ducats on her arrows in the coin shot. I was secretly pleased that one of the big losers was Don Giulio, who had posted most of the coins she hit. He was himself a very indifferent shot, and did not hit a single coin. He looked quite set back by his defeat, especially at the hands of a woman. But at the end of the match, he acknowledged his defeat, oozing up to my Mistress in his clumsy, greasy manner, and bowed obsequiously. There was also a mounted crossbow competition – horsemen fired an arrow at a wreath hung on a board, with their horses at full gallop. Only three succeeded in hitting the target. Finally, in the afternoon was the horse race. Each village in Avellino sent its fastest horse and rider for 40 laps around the *campo.* The winner was a squire from Montesarchio, who rode a Calabrese stallion – a surprising win for a horse standing only 15 hands high.

Between events there was entertainment: *Arlecchino, Dottore* and *Pantalone* performed their antics in a riotous *Commedia dell'Arte.* A lovely lady actress joined the farce, entering the stage in cartwheels, her dress flapping down exposing her bare bottom, and her breasts fell out of her breastbags. It was a lewd site that drew excited cheers from the audience. Jugglers with five balls in the air walked a tightrope suspended high above the fairground. And we musicians broke into small groups, and strolled through the crowds singing bawdy folksongs, with the revellers roaring along with us. Then, when evening fell, another banquet, as extravagant – and, later, as lascivious – as the first.

m'inuolate hor mi tédette il core

There! I have done it! I have written an entire *ottavo* without once mentioning the murder, the witchcraft, the suffering. I have done this because this was truly a joyous time, and because this is how I personally experienced it. Do not think, though, that the festivities were without portents of an encroaching doom. I feel justified in omitting this because I did not personally witness it. The episode occurred in the church, while I was outside. My friend Pietro Bardotti, my Master's valet, related it to me.

My Master's father the Prince had wanted his brother, His Eminence the Cardinal, to conduct the mass and the nuptials. To this, my Master adamantly refused – understandably, to me, considering the misery he had suffered at the cardinal's hands during his childhood in Rome. The Prince then suggested that his other uncle, His Eminence Carlo Borromeo, conduct the mass. To this my Master agreed, but, unfortunately, His Eminence Don Carlo was suffering from a condition of the throat and had lost his voice. So the ceremonies were conducted by the parish priest, with the two cardinals standing by.

The mass went without incident. After the mass there was to be a ceremony of exchanging of rings. The priest asked the cardinal to bless the rings prior to the couple taking the vows. The chief usher, so Don Pietro told me, handed the ring case – an elegantly carved box of olive wood, lined with velvet, and which contained a ring that His Eminence had given as a gift. The Cardinal Don Carlo took the ring and lifted it to his lips, then handed the emerald ring and the box to his brother-in-law, His Eminence Don Alfonso. Don Alfonso took the ring in his left hand. With his right hand he covered his face, and muttered a verse in Latin, that Pietro could not make out. It was certainly not the Latin that Pietro knew. The cardinal gripped the ring with a fist so tight that his whole hand and arm began to shake. His face, mostly hidden by his hand, was contorted into a look of intense concentration: his eyes were shut tight, his lips twisted in a grimace as though he was in great pain. He then opened his eyes and instructed my Master to hold out his hand, and dropped the ring into his upturned palm. "The Master let out a sharp cry, and dropped the ring to the ground," Pietro said. "Donna Maria looked startled, but then smiled gently and bent to pick up the fallen ring. Our Master grabbed her and pulled her away, his eyes fixed on the ring on the floor. We all turned to look. The emerald ring, the gift of his uncle, was glowing a bright red, as though it had been taken this moment from the furnace.

"It was a terrifying moment. The people in the congregation, of course, could not see what was transpiring. But the entire wedding party looked aghast, their eyes shifting from the glowing red-hot ring, to the cardinals, to the horrified bridal couple. Thus they stood for several minutes, while the ring, apparently, cooled as it lay on its spot. Then the priest, who was greatly perturbed, bent down and lifted the ring, and handed it to the groom, and the ceremony continued."

But that was not the end of the incident. "The priest completed the prayers," Don Pietro said, "Our Master slid the ring onto the finger of his betrothed, and they exchanged their vows. Then the priest turned again to the cardinals and asked that they bless the newlyweds. His Eminence Don Carlo lifted his hands, but was unable to speak. My Master's other uncle turned to his nephew, a scowl on his face, and said, 'Bring an heir. Bring an heir and then you shall have my blessing.'

"The Master muttered under his breath, 'Or your curse.' His Eminence heard the remark, and replied, "Blessing, curse, it is all the same. For Satan, too, is one of God's creatures.'"

This story was so remarkable that it was hard for me to believe that Pietro had seen and understood things correctly. But there were two corroborations of the episode. First, in my first meeting with my Master, after the wedding festivities, I noted that his right hand was bound in a cloth. I asked him what had happened, and he responded, somewhat cryptically, that he had burned his hand. He refused to tell me the circumstances of the accident, and refused to remove the bandage to let me examine the wound. The searing ring left a deep scar in the center of his right palm, the symbolism of which was not lost on either him or me. He referred to the scar as his stigma, and would remark, I need to burn my other hand to make myself complete. The second corroboration of Pietro's story came when I went to visit the church and examined the floor. There I found, on the tiles where the couple would have stood, a small indentation, charred black.

Not that I doubted Pietro. He was an honest and trusted friend, reliable in every respect. It is true that, as I have mentioned before, in the inquest into the murder, he lied to the inquisitors as to who were the three persons who attended my Master when he entered my Mistress's chamber and committed the dastardly crime. I knew this to be a lie, because one of the persons he named was at the time with me in Cremona. I was later to learn the reason for this lie; it was completely understandable, and did not in any way degrade my trust in him.

But it was not only I who trusted Pietro – my Master, too, had complete faith in him. Aside from myself, Pietro was the closest servant to my Master in the entire household. Pietro had no ear for music, and, being of a markedly conservative bent, looked askance at my Master's prurience, and, therefore, did not enjoy the personal closeness that obtained between myself and my Master. However, of all matters of management of my Master's affairs, both personal and governmental, Pietro was charged with complete oversight.

Among his duties was the preparation of My Master's abodes prior to his arrival. My Master traveled a good deal between his fiefdoms, and every such move was a complex operation. In general, the court spent the winter in the San Severo mansion in Naples, and, in the summer, moved to the palace in Gesualdo. However, during the course of each sojourn, my Master would visit his other principalities to attend to affairs – primarily to Venosa, where he also had a handsome villa. Each of these moves was a complex and difficult operation. Each residence had its own skeleton staff of five to ten servants, whose job it was to ensure that the house was ready at all times to receive the Prince and his entourage. This meant not only keeping the residence clean and the stables in order, but also to have the kitchen prepared to create meals for upwards of fifty people at a moment's notice. Of course, the chief of the kitchen did not keep provenance for fifty people on hand at all times. But he made arrangements with the residents of the town, so that, at any time, he could visit them and draw on their reserves of meat and vegetables and grain and dairy products to assemble the ingredients of a banquet within a few hours.

A few days prior to departure of the court, Pietro organized all the provisions and baggage required for the journey, and then set out with an advance team of three servants to the destination, On the way, he made arrangements with innkeepers on the road for the entourage to sojourn during the journey. At the destination, he worked with the resident staff to make sure that everything was in order for the court's arrival. A few days later, the court set out. For the two annual moves between Naples and Gesualdo, this was a major operation: a caravan of fifty people, courtiers, servants, musicians, artists, carts of baggage, provisions for the way. My Master rode on a horse, his wife and father in a closed carriage. His father was at this time infirm; he could not walk without assistance, and was mostly wheeled about in a special chair. His mind was intact, and he was as cogent as a man of 20, but he tired very easily and could not keep up a conversation for more than a few minutes. The journey was for him very tiring, and it was necessary to stop the carriage – and consequently the entire brigade – for a short time every couple of hours. In truth, His Excellency the Prince would have preferred to forego these journeys. He was, however, still the Prince, his son acting as regent, and his presence was therefore required.

The trip from Naples to Gesualdo took two or three days. On the way, the entire court stayed at the inns specified by Pietro. Arrival at the inn was an operation in itself, The horses had to be unharnessed and set to pasture, the pack horses unloaded and the baggage secured, accommodations assigned, meals prepared. After dinner there was usually music, so we musicians had to unpack our instruments and prepare a stage for the performance. In the morning, it generally took two hours or so to reassemble the caravan and set out for the continuation of the journey. To complicate matters, our caravan was normally accompanied by a small host of hangers-on, who joined us for the journey for reasons of security. The roads in our region were relatively safe, thanks to the frequent policing by my Master's guards, but there was still a risk of brigands attacking unprotected travelers. So many people who had to make the journey along the Avellino highway chose to make the trip along with our band. These travelers usually did not take up accommodations in the inn, but set up tents in the court of the inn, and prepared their own meals.

When making shorter visits to his principalities, my Master took a much smaller group of eight or ten servants. These always included myself and at least one other musician, the court chancellor, Pietro, a few personal servants, and three soldiers at arms. On these occasions, as well, Pietro would set out in advance to make sure the residence was prepared. So, while in principle, every residence was kept in a state of perpetual readiness for a surprise visit, in fact such visits never occurred – my Master was always careful to apprise the staff of his impending arrival, giving them a few days to make final preparations.

That is, except on one occasion – the night of the murder. Immediately after the murder, as reported by the inquest and confirmed personally to me by Pietro, my Master took two courtiers and set off in the middle of the night for the palace of Gesualdo. Pietro was eager to accompany him, but my Master commanded him to remain behind, and to offer his testimony to the inquest which, my Master was certain, would immediately follow. Thus, my Master arrived in Gesualdo the following evening – they rode straight for 18 hours – with no advance warning and no entourage. This in itself was extraordinary, and put the staff into a quandary. But my Master was at that point in such a state of distraction that his unannounced arrival was the least of the difficulties. Pietro, meanwhile, organized the rest of the court as quickly as he could, and, within a day, the entire court had evacuated the palace in San Severo and moved precipitously to Gesualdo.

But I get ahead of myself. I was telling of the episode of the ring, and the cardinal's statement that he would withhold his blessing – or curse – of the couple until they had produced an heir. And in this he was true to his word. For the married couple enjoyed a year and a half of peace. The principalities prospered. The region produced the finest olive oil in all of Italy. The wines of the region – *Greco di Tufo, Fiano* and *Taurasi* – graced the finest tables of the highest aristocracy. Through the graces of my Master, and the fine taste of the Viceroy of Naples, Naples and Avellino became centers of culture, Neapolitan painters and sculptors were commissioned frequently, as were masters of the highest reputations from Rome, Florence, Ferrara, Venice. As for the musicians – well, my natural modesty prevents me from oversinging their praises. Suffice it to say that I felt honored to be performing with the finest musicians of the realm.

My Master's bounty contributed to the overall prosperity. He improved the Avellino highway from Naples to Gesualdo, and his soldiers succeeded in virtually eradicating the highway robbers that had plagued travelers. He also graded the roads to Montesarchio and to Venosa. These improvements were a great lubricant to trade, and the produce of Avellino flowed to the capital and from there to ports throughout the civilized world – the oil of Avellino was not unknown to tables as far as London and Paris. He erected fountains all around Gesualdo and Venosa. And he was bounteous to supplicants throughout the principality who came to beg his assistance.

During this time, the red dream retreated entirely from his sleep. He still suffered from bouts of depression. They were rarer than before, and less intense. These often occurred as a reaction following one of his more egregious sybaritic episodes. He would be seized with remorse, particularly for failing to live up to the vows of fidelity he had made to his wife. He would close himself in his chamber, and forbid any from entering. After a day of this, I would demand entrance, and he would allow me to bring him food and drink. He would receive me kneeling, facing me so I could not see his back, which he had beaten raw with his belt. Only by the third or fourth day would he allow me to enter and speak with him. I would embrace him, comfort him, reassure him that his wife forgave him his peccadilloes. Sometimes we would kneel together before the cross in his chamber, and pray for the redemption of his soul. After that, I would bring my lute or my *viola di braccia*, and play him music until he was restored. Only then would he allow me to dress the wounds on his back, and help him bathe and dress. During this time he would never allow his wife to approach, only myself. This was a great trial to Donna Maria, who cared not at all about his philandering, but was concerned only and entirely about his welfare. "Please tell him that I love him, that all I wish for is for him to return to me," she would tell me. This message I faithfully conveyed to my Master, but it rarely helped in assuaging his depression.

Upon his emergence from the depression, there followed a period of intense activity. He composed, administered, and attended his wife with a manic energy that could be as frightening as the depression that preceded it. He would often sit me down for a lengthy harangue on the topic of music. Once, for example, he subjected me to two hours of analysis of a madrigal he had received in manuscript from Luzzasco Luzzaschi, the Ferrarese composer who was to become his friend and rival in a few years. "See this modulation," he said, speaking with the rapidity of a wildfire. "It is very effective. It is masterful, but he fails for follow up with a proper progression. See here," he continued, pointing to a point in the manuscript. "Here, he should have repeated the modulation – but he goes off in another direction. The piece loses its consistency, its energy." and on and on.

This mania lasted, like the preceding depression, for a few days. He then returned to his normal self – engaged in the hunt with his friend Don Fabrizio, attended the rehearsals of the *capella*, attended to affairs of the principality. A week or two would pass, and then the pressures of his libidinous soul would overcome his prudence, and he would return to a life of dissipation. In Naples, this meant a return to the apartments of the *cortigiane* and the dives of the back alleys of the port, in the company of Don Fabrizio and myself. In Gesualdo, the options were more limited. There was only one prostitute in all of Gesualdo, and my Master found no pleasure in her. There were, to be sure, no shortage of courtiers, both male and female, who were pleased to attend to my Master's needs. More complicated were his dalliances with his subjects, especially his subjects' children. I have told of the tragic episode of the carpenter's daughter. That was an extreme case. But there were many of his subjects who lived in fear that the Prince's capricious eye should fall upon their sons or daughters or wives. I did my best to prevent my Master from seizing on some unwilling subject or subject's child, not always with success. Of course, there were those who were quite willing to offer up their daughters' virginity on the altar of the Master's bed, in hopes of his siring a bastard child, thus ensuring the family's welfare for this and future generations. Such siring never occurred.

When in Naples, Don Fabrizio was my Master's constant companion. Don Fabrizio preferred Naples to Gesualdo, and complained constantly about how provincial and backward was the town whenever the court was there. In Naples, it was much easier for Don Fabrizio to indulge in his particular perversion. The two of them would not infrequently attend parties or concerts in Naples, Don Fabrizio dressed consummately as a woman and acting the part of my Master's consort. The masquerade was successful more often than not, for Don Fabrizio was so masterful at acting the part of a woman that, even though his reputation was well known among the Neapolitan party set, none succeeded in penetrating his disguise. After the party, they would retire to my Master's residence, there they would continue the masquerade to its mutually satisfying conclusion.

In Gesualdo, this masquerade was much more problematic. In Naples, Don Fabrizio had an entire closet of women's attire from which to choose; in Gesualdo, he had somehow to cadge his garb from the local residents. The one who solved this dilemma was none other than Donna Maria herself. An astute observer of my Master's predilections, she quickly understood the predicament, and offered her husband her own boudoir for Don Fabrizio's use. So, whenever visiting, Don Fabrizio would steal into her bedroom of night, go to her closet and choose an outfit, then continue to my Master's bedroom, there the two would engage in their illicit affair. This, too, however, was problematic, since Donna Maria's wardrobe could barely stretch over Don Fabrizio's broad shoulders and massive arms. Here, again, my Mistress's ingenuity served. She sent her handmaiden, who was the same height as Don Fabrizio and broad and solid as a horse, to the tailor, to create an appropriate wardrobe for her husband's lover. Thus, Donna Maria became a willing and active confederate in her husband's philandering. I once asked her how she felt about this. "I do this because I love him," she replied to me. "This is what he wishes so it is what I wish."

"You do not find it distasteful, even repugnant?" I asked.

"Nothing my husband does could I find repugnant. Should he find pleasure in murdering me, I would go to my demise a happy woman."

Of course, my Master found no pleasure in murdering her; on the contrary, it was an act that he regretted even in its execution, and he reviled and tormented himself for it ever after. Just as she loved him, he loved her, an unconditional and blinding love, and it was only through trickery and bewitchment that he could be brought to commit a deed that he considered so vile. Not that I am making excuses for him. It was his hand, his willful hand, that put an end to my Mistress's life, and for that I will never forgive him, indeed, I will hate him as much as I love him.

For, during these years, my own feelings toward my Master had changed. What started as a sense of duty and grew to a staunch feeling of comradery grew gradually into a genuine love. Not a physical love, for, however acceptable in our time is a physical love between man and man, I could never entertain the idea for myself. But it was love nonetheless, My devotion to him engendered a physical feeling in my breast, a tightening of the breath. I felt that, in serving my Master, I was serving a higher calling, a calling that engaged me totally, heart and mind and soul. And that feeling extended almost immediately to his beloved. Their love, I felt, was in a sense a love not of two but of three; that I was a silent partner in a relationship that transcended the human, and tied us to the divine.

All that would change – and, yet, not change – with the impending events.

But again I digress. I fear that I am a very disorganized diarist, and when I finish this memoir, I will have to go back and reorganize it completely so it follows some logical or chronological sequence.

I was describing the manner in which Don Fabrizio indulged his deviance in the difficult environment of Gesualdo. And what I wanted to add was that, both in order to protect my Master from scandal, and to heighten the romantic nature of the affair, Don Fabrizio would not enter through the door, but would, under cover of darkness, climb the trellis to my Mistress's window, and enter in presumed secrecy. Of course, this little subterfuge was ridiculous. The entire household knew every detail of the arrangement, and it was the subject of no little merriment among the staff. (The musicians, I should note, never gossiped and the subject was never brought up, though I am sure that they, just as the others, knew all.) Don Fabrizio, for his part, drew so much pleasure from this bit of play acting, that he insisted on copying it in Naples as well. Needless to say, no one divulged the truth of this arrangement to the inquisitors after the murder; aside from needlessly sullying the names of their master and mistress and friend, they would have put the Prince in mortal danger. For the murder of an adulterous wife and her lover would be acceptable, and even expected behavior for a prince of honor; but without that motive, the D'Avalos and Carafa relatives would certainly seek revenge for the killings. Which left the question: if not adultery, what was the motive for this murder? This mystery puzzled me until the final days of my Master's life. And the truth was more chilling than the explanation of adultery, which was believed by all.

In any case, this little bit of theater of climbing the trellis was enjoyable to my Master and Don Fabrizio, and Donna Maria was pleased that in this, also, she could be of service to her lord. So Don Fabrizio, despite his preference for Naples, was a not infrequent visitor to Gesualdo. He would often come with the household when it moved in spring, and stay for several weeks or months, before returning to Naples. This was also fortunate because Don Fabrizio was my Master's hunting partner, and the hunting was much better in Gesualdo than in Naples. The hunting parks outside of Naples were over-hunted, the harts easily spooked, and the wild boars reclusive. Gesualdo, on the other hand, was surrounded by stadia of virgin forest, where many beasts had never had the scent of man. So, with the weather clement, the landscape lush and verdant, and the company compatible, hunting in Gesualdo was a delightful pastime.

I had an opportunity to speak with Don Fabrizio after the wedding. I congratulated him on his success in the games, and he responded with a frown. "I got no pleasure from those games," he said.

I was quite surprised by his response. "Why might that be, my friend?" I asked.

"Ludovico, I will tell the truth. I have lost all interest in the manly arts. Nor do I have any more interest in intercourse with women. Indeed, I am no longer a man. I think as a woman, I act as a woman. I am a woman trapped in a man's body. All these manly pursuits, I do them because my body remembers them. But I have no pleasure in them; quite the opposite, I hate them. I do them because it is what is expected. And, like other women, I am not attracted to women – I am attracted only to men, My dream, Ludovico – my dream is to lose this horrible appendage between my legs. My dream is to marry and settle down, not as I am now, but as a woman, with a man. Nor do I desire to consort with many men, as I once did. I desire only one person – my friend and liege, Carlo Gesualdo. Ludovico, I am in love with the Prince."

I mulled this over a bit. "This is exceedingly awkward," I said. "My Master has just married, and you are well nigh a year married."

"In truth, I despise my wife. She is devout, and insists that I lie with her once a month. I find this chore abhorrent. As for your Master being married, I have only one wish – that the conjugal bed shall not overshadow his lust for me. For I know that I can give him pleasure in ways that his wife cannot."

This wish of Don Fabrizio's was, I suppose, fulfilled, for, as I have said, he continued his trysts with my Master, with the assistance and abettance of my Mistress.

In the autumn of the Year of Our Lord 1588, the court did not move from Gesualdo to Naples as usual, for my Mistress was in her sixth month and the journey was ill-advised. So the court remained for the summer in San Severo, enduring the heat, humidity and fetid air of the city. This sacrifice was compensated for on the first day of February in the Year of Our Lord 1589, when Donna Maria gave birth to a delightful boy. My Mistress proved herself as strong and productive a mother as she had been for her two previous children. She came out of the delivery full of strength, and her child was strong and healthy. He was perfect in every respect except one: he had a strange deformity of the hands, whereby the fingers were joined by what appeared to be a dermatic membrane. At my urging, and with my Master's full consent, we took the child to my teacher, the doctor Don Moise, who examined the child, and declared the condition easily corrected.

"I have seen this only once in my life," said the doctor. "In that case, I surgically separated the fingers. The child developed perfectly, and I see no reason that should not occur in this case as well. The procedure, however, is very painful to the child, and I therefore recommend that neither the mother nor father be present during the operation."

Thus it was that I was assigned to hold the tiny Emmanuelle, for so he was christened, who wailed most woefully while the doctor carefully sliced through the membranes that rendered the hands like the webbed feet of a duck. After the procedure, the doctor gave Emmanuelle a cloth soaked in wine. The infant suckled eagerly at the cloth, and quickly fell asleep.

"The last time I did this," the doctor confided in me, "the child's hands recovered completely. But, interestingly, the child grew up, albeit with normal hands, but with pronounced duck-like behavior. As he grew, he waddled as he walked. And he spoke with a whining, almost quacking voice. He was constantly complaining, and his look was wall-eyed and unblinking."

As it turned out, Don Emmanuelle Gesualdo grew to be nothing like that. From an early age, he was nasty and vindictive, conniving and deceitful. His parents he despised. This was another thorn in my Master's crown, for he loved his son and doted on him endlessly.

As an infant, Emmanuelle bawled incessantly. His nurse was haggard from sleepless nights, and his mother distraught. Nothing seemed to calm him; if his father would approach, the infant would treble his efforts, and issue forth a piercing whine that made proximity to him literally painful. It was on one such occasion that my Master visited his son with me. On sensing his father's presence, the infant Emmanuelle let forth an ear-splitting howl. "Calm him," commanded my Master. With no little trepidation, I approached the screaming child, and took him up in my arms. At first, the infant arched his back and flung out his arms, in what appeared to be a violent protest against my approach. But then, quite surprisingly, he stopped his crying and looked at me with a quizzical stare. It was the first time I had ever held an infant in my arms, and I was at a loss as to what to do. I looked to his nurse, but she was as astonished as I at the child's sudden calm. With no other idea in my head, I started to sing a song – *Vidi hor cogliendo rose* - perhaps not the best choice for a lullaby, but, again to my surprise, with a markedly soothing effect on the petulant creature. With the infant calmed, I approached my Master with the intent of giving him the opportunity to hold and caress his son. But the moment I approached, the child gave out a new piercing scream. The moment I retreated, the screaming abated. It was clear, even then, that Emmanuelle wanted no truck with his own flesh and blood. It seemed that the only one with the capacity for calming the child was myself, and I forthwith had this role thrust upon me. Frequently was I called upon to take Emmanuelle in my arms and lull him to sleep – or at least to silence – by singing him bawdy songs. It was the beginning of a special relationship that obtained between us until his untimely death 12 years later.

At the age of two and a half, Emmanuelle still did not speak. His parents and advisors began to think he was feeble minded, or perhaps deaf. My Master even took the child to visit Don Moise, who, after a thorough examination, declared the child to be physically normal in every respect. A few months after that, Emmanuelle began to talk, and his vocabulary consisted primarily of one word - "No!" His abhorrence of his father continued, and, if my Master dared to approach, he would throw himself on the floor in a tantrum. Still, the only person who had any semblance of communication with the child was myself. He would offer me toys in a semblance of play, and would sit calmly while I sang my bawdy songs.

Shortly prior to his third birthday, Emmanuelle developed into an imaginative caprophile. He would climb up on a chair, and smear his bodily wastes over the hunting canvas that hung in San Severo. The child's work obscured the face of slaughtered hart. The vandalism of this painting, so loved by my Master, was a sophisticated expression of hatred in one so young; I marveled at how the child knew how painful this act was to his father. A servant had the unpleasant task of gently scraping the fecal matter from the work; but the following day, the child had reapplied his fulsome revision to the work. After several days of this, my Master ordered the painting hung higher. The top of the frame was now flush with the ceiling, and the bottom at eye level – presumably out of reach of the child. But the next morning we were alarmed by an awful cry. Emmanuelle had piled chair upon chair and attempted to climb up to reach the painting, his hand smeared with excrement. However, on reaching the seat of the upper chair, the precarious structure toppled, and Emmanuelle suffered a nasty smack on the head. The doctor (not Don Moise) ordered him confined to his bed for three days, but the recalcitrant child refused, and, head smarting, continued to roam about the mansion and wreak havoc.

And so his life continued. When he reached school age, he refused adamantly to study. My Master had by then moved the court to Ferrara. He implored me, as the only one with a relationship with the child, to speak to him. I therefore rapped on the door of his room. He was eight years old at the time.

"Who is there?" he demanded.

"It is I, Don Ludovico."

"What does my father want now?"

"He wishes for me to speak with you."

Emmanuelle flung the door open, and then returned to lie on his bed.

"My Lord, you must know you are heir to your family's estates, and the heir apparent to the title of Prince."

"So?"

"My Lord, if you are to rule, you must learn the arts of a gentleman."

"Fuck gentlemen. And Fuck Prince. And Fuck my father."

"My Lord, we do not always choose our destinies. I fear you shall become the Prince of Venosa, whether you wish it or not."

"Well, Ludovico, I do not choose to be Prince of Venosa, and I do not choose to be heir to my father's estates. My father can shove his estates in his arse."

"What, then, are you planning to do?"

Here Emmanuelle's face broke into a sly, conspiratorial smile. "You will tell no one?"

"You have my word, My Lord."

"I am going to the New World."

Now of course we had all heard of the New World. In Naples, sailors would sometimes claim to have traveled to lands where savages roamed about naked and of strange races of people whose heads grew beneath their shoulders. The existence of a new world was dim in our consciousness. So it was a mystery to me where little Emmanuelle had learned of this.

"Very well," I replied. "When do you plan on departing?"

This stymied the child. He frowned and said nothing.

"May I suggest, my Lord, that it would be impractical for you to undertake such a journey before the age of 15 or 16. Until such time, might I suggest that you develop some of the skills that the journey will require? Mathematics, literature, music..."

"Get out," the child interrupted me.

"As you wish, my Lord."

Of all the subjects that Emmanuelle did not learn, music was the one that most rankled my Master. Unfortunate, since the child had a true aptitude, and, I believed, a suppressed enjoyment in music. Already as an infant, he could clearly identify a piece of music that he had heard only once; by the age of three he could carry a tune. Yet, knowing his father's love of music, he staunchly refused ever to be caught by him attending to it. Occasionally I would play for him, and he would listen eagerly, showing the same visceral joy that was shared by his father and myself. Yet, if his father would enter the room while I was playing, he would immediately shout, "Stop that racket!"

Indeed, the only pastime he seemed to take any interest in was riding. Already at the age of 9, he would mount and set off in the morning, and return only after dark. And, while he spent many hours in the saddle, he was an indifferent and reckless equestrian. At age 10 he failed a jump with a prize Calabrian gelding; the horse broke a leg and had to be put down. He was thrown again and again. At age 11 he broke his arm, and lay bandaged for a month.

My Master's associates and staff all urged discipline. Corporal punishment, they advised, will straighten the child out. But my Master would not hear of it. "I must follow my uncle Carlo," he said. "Forgive, forbear, accept."

"Your uncle knew to be firm when required," I replied. I was thinking of my teacher, Doctor Moise.

My Master did not reply, but I could see tears forming in the corners of his eyes. It was strange that one who had suffered beatings so regularly at the hands of his other uncle, and for whom flagellation was, as it were, beaten into his psyche, should be so opposed to corporal punishment where it indeed appeared to be called for. But there was clearly more to it than that. For my Master's lip trembled as he spoke of it, clearly hiding some deeply suppressed emotion.

"Perhaps this is the punishment I deserve. Who more than I has earned this child's hatred?"

What he said was true. And, where before the murder, I would have rushed to his side, embraced him and held his hands to prevent him from injuring himself, I now stood aside, torn by feelings of love and hate. For the torment of his soul did not excuse in my eyes the egregious deed, and until the day of his death, I would no longer protect him from his own self-destruction; indeed, I would take an active hand in it.

m'involate hor mi tedete il core

In the nine months between my Master's marriage and the birth of his son Emmanuelle, his uncle the cardinal did not once visit the Gesualdo family; not to visit his aging brother, not to greet the young couple. Not even when the Gesualdo court was in Naples, and His Eminence was also in Naples, did he betake himself to visit. This was a remarkable breach of accepted practice – the maintenance of close familial alliances was crucial to the protection of one's status – but not surprising given the animosity between my Master and his uncle. However, at the christening of baby Emmanuelle, he reappeared. There had been a contentious confrontation between my Master and his father the Prince: His Excellency wanted his brother the cardinal to be Godfather, my Master adamantly refused. My Mistress was present at the confrontation, and, asked by His Excellency for her opinion, she said, "As my husband wishes. But I think it would be a great honor for His Eminence to hold the child." It was the first – and only –

time that I heard my Master reply to her sharply. "This is none of your business. If my uncle holds the child, I shall not be there!" This was the end of the argument, and my Master prevailed. So His Eminence attended the christening, in no ritual capacity. Nonetheless, the priest who performed the ceremony – the same priest who performed the wedding – turned to His Eminence and asked, as he had at the nuptials, for the cardinal's blessing on the child and the couple.

His Eminence ignored the child, but turned to my Master. He quoted the passage from Jeremiah: "*Ego Dominus scrutans cor et probans renes qui do unicuique iuxta viam et iuxta fructum adinventionum suarum.*" He made the sign of the cross with an insulting haste and nonchalance, as if to say, you do not deserve this blessing. And, indeed, a strange blessing it was: that the Lord reward him according to his conduct and according to what his deeds deserve. What sort of blessing was this? Was His Eminence suggesting that my Master's reward shall be not in Heaven, but in Hell? His blessing (or curse) left the entire congregation in an awkward silence as we digested the words, a silence that continued until the priest regained his presence of mind and continued to the singing of the final hymn.

Be that as it may, from then on, His Eminence visited the Naples abode albeit infrequently. On those occasions that he did visit, he paid his respects to the Prince, and then usually huddled for a lengthy talk with his protégé Don Giulio. He assiduously avoided meeting my Master, though he would occasionally take a stroll with Don Giulio through the house, touring in particular the infamous hallway which had so terrified my Master until it was painted and the hunting canvass hung. I personally never had concourse with His Eminence.

About two months after Emmanuelle's birth, I had an extremely disturbing conversation with my Master. I was visiting my Master in his chambers in San Severo, and we were chatting on this and that. And then, in a sort of off-hand manner, my Master said, "You know what Don Giulio told me?"

"I am consumed by curiosity, my Lord."

"He told me that Donna Maria's previous husbands... well, they died of, as he said it, an excess of marital bliss."

"An excess of marital bliss, my Lord? What does that mean?"

"Exactly. I asked myself the same question. Curious, is it not?"

"My Lord, the suggestion is simply absurd."

"Absurd, you say? Quite so, quite so."

"My Lord, I have it on first-hand knowledge that that is not the case. My Mistress's first husband died of the *mala aria*, and her second husband died of drunkenness and obesity. Certainly neither died of 'an excess of marital bliss'!"

"I am sure you are right. Silly of me to entertain such a thought."

I could see that this vicious innuendo had nonetheless implanted itself in my Master's mind. "My Lord, no one knows your wife better than yourself. Has it ever been your impression that she is of such an intense sexual hunger that she could drive you to your death with her own demands?"

"Certainly not! I mean, she is passionate enough, but, er, certainly not demanding in that way."

"Then you should consider the matter settled."

There was a pause while my Master digested this. Then he replied.

"That is precisely what disturbs me. Why, why is she not so demanding with me? When she, well, when she fucked her first two husbands to death? And with me, she is, er, merely normal? Why is that? Does she not love me?"

I allowed the ire to be heard in my voice. "My Lord, she did not fuck her first two husbands to death. This is a lie, a vile canard, invented to defame the most loyal, the most faithful, the most loving wife you could possibly wish for. I do not know who is the author of this slander, though I imagine it is Don Giulio himself. And why he should make up tales like this I also do not know. But you must expunge this matter from your mind. It is a lie, a lie, I tell you. Do you understand me?"

As was typical when I chastised him in this way, my Master fell silent for a while, and then responded with a maelstrom of self-recrimination.

"Oh, you are right, Ludovico. How could I be so vile? *Abominatio Domini cogitationes malae.*"

I completed the verse: "But the Lord loves gracious thoughts. So purify yourself of these wicked thoughts, my Lord."

"Pray with me," he demanded, and grabbed my blouse, pulling me down to my knees before the cross.

"My Lord in Heaven, Jesus Christ our Savior," I said, "Hallowed be Thy Name. Cleanse this man of the evil thoughts that have been implanted in his mind. Make him whole again, and make his love for his wife pure and everlasting. Amen." I rose, but my Master remained kneeling, his head in his hands, his eyes streaming tears. And in that pose, I left him.

I suppose it was because I was so angry with him that I did not stay, as was my wont and my duty, to comfort him. Whenever he was bedeviled by these bouts of depression, I would stay with him, hold him, rock him, and sing and play for him until his mood was stable enough for him to be left alone. But in this case, as I say, I was so angered that he should entertain such a transparent and vile slander against my Mistress, that I was in no mind to perform what was, most certainly, my duty.

This exchange did not take place in isolation; there were other conversations that I found unsettling, conversations that suggested his mind was being infected with traitorous thoughts. On one occasion, after we had been playing a duet, me on the *lira di braccio* and he on the lute, he looked at me piercingly.

"Do you think my wife loves me?" he asked.

"It is a silly question, my Lord, a simple question. You know quite well she is completely devoted to you."

"And Don Fabrizio?"

I was somewhat stymied how to respond to this. For Don Fabrizio was as in love with and as devoted to my Master as his own wife. I did not wish to denigrate the love between the two men, yet it felt odd putting this on a par with the love of his own wife in Christ. In the end I answered, "My Lord, he, too, loves you very much."

My Master thought about this a while. Then he said, "Odd, isn't it?"

"What is odd, my Lord?"

"Being loved. I mean, it's… odd."

"It seems to me the most natural thing on earth, my Lord. They love you. You love them. What is odd about that?"

There was another pause, while my Master framed his response. I could see that, while his tone was quiet, his lower lip was trembling, as though suppressing some violent emotion. "Ludovico, I find it… uncomfortable. Being loved. I find it… "

"Yes, my Lord?"

"Depressing."

"I know not what to say, my Lord."

"Sometimes, I wish to be free of this Love. Devotion. It is… it is repugnant to me."

I felt it was time for chastisement. "My Lord, you must put these feelings out of your mind. Love and devotion are not repugnant. They are the most noble of human emotions. You should revel in their love and devotion, not repulse it."

Now my Master suddenly buried his face in his hands. "O, Ludovico, I have these terrible thoughts. Thoughts that my wife and my friend will die. They will die and free me of their love." He shuddered in his whole body, tears flowed freely.

"My Lord, I cannot say whence these thoughts come. But, believe me, they are foreign to you. I know how much you love your wife and your friend. You do not wish them dead."

But my exhortations were too late, for my Master was already in the throes of another deep depression. "These are wicked thoughts, the Devil's thoughts!" he cried. "I must beat them out of me." And, as he did so often, he kneeled before the cross, took a rope and began lashing himself, until I stayed his hand and pressed him to me to calm him.

It was only later, following a far more ominous episode, that I realized that there was more to these encounters than only suggestion.

m'inuolate hor mi redete il core

The ominous episode of which I speak occurred in the spring. We had spent one summer in Naples, due to Donna Maria's confinement and birth, and the following year affairs of the estate required the court to remain almost the entire year in Naples. So, after a two and a half year absence, my Master was eager to make the move back to Gesualdo, and we did so in the early spring. We arrived in time for carnival, and my Master, as well as His Excellency my Master's father, marched in the processional. My Mistress, tired from her journey and from caring for her colicky child, chose to remain in the castle. The procession was winding its way along the Piazza Neviera on its way to the church, my Master and the Bishop walking at the head and His Excellency in his wheeled chair was pushed alongside. The crowd cheered the Princely family as it walked along, reaching out to touch or grasp the hand of His Excellency or my Master. And my Master was reaching out, grasping the outstretched hands, and muttering words of greeting and blessing to the people. He was clearly having a wonderful time, basking in this well-deserved adulation from those whose lives his works had helped make prosperous.

Of a sudden, a woman burst through the crowd, rushed up to my Master, and pressed her lips against his in a passionate kiss. When she drew away, I could see that her lips and those of my Master were smeared with red. She then backed into the crowd, and disappeared as quickly as she had appeared. My Master stopped in his tracks. He looked at first surprised and confused. Then his countenance changed, and he took on a hollow and distant look. He ceased greeting his subjects, and appeared to have lost all interest in the processional. Indeed, I had to take him by the arm and urge him forward, otherwise he would have halted completely.

My Master went through the rest of the day as in a trance. He spoke not a word, did not participate in the Mass nor the festivities and revelry. When we returned to the castle, he turned to me, and grasped me by the shoulders. "Ludovico, find that woman!" he commanded me.

"My Lord, listen to my advice. Forget this woman. No good can come of pursuing her. I saw her for a moment only, but I saw enough. I can assure you, this is an evil woman."

My Master's eyes were glazed as though his spirit was not in his body. His hands gripped my shoulders with an intensity, indeed a violence that frightened me. "Ludovico," he repeated, "find the woman."

I saw there would be no purpose in arguing. So I replied, "Very well, my Lord. I shall set out first thing in the morning."

"Not in the morning. Now. Now! You must bring me this woman." His fingers dug deep into my flesh.

"Very well, my Lord. I shall go now. Now go in and greet your wife. She is waiting for you."

My Master released my shoulders, and stood, motionless, making no move to go to his wife. So I grasped his hand, and led him up the stairs to my Mistress's chambers. There I left him facing the door. Whether he entered I know not, for I turned and began my search for the kissing woman.

I thought my task would be simple. Dozens of people had seen the incident, which was so singular that it was undoubtedly engraved in their memories. Yet when I asked townspeople, they all said they had no idea of what I spoke. No one, they all claimed, had seen or remembered seeing such an incident. I returned to the castle when night had fallen, and rose early the next day to continue my search. I knew numerous townspeople, including several who would certainly have heard about the kiss. Such a thing, they all averred, had never transpired.

So I returned at noon to my Master, and reported that my efforts had failed. I was, personally, quite satisfied with this result, as I was certain that this woman could bring no good to my Master. But to my Master this failure was completely unacceptable. "Leave and do not return until the woman is in your hands!" he commanded. He was completely implacable, and completely unreasonable.

So did my search continue for three days. That is, my presumed search. For, in reality, there was no more search at all. Townspeople hastened to close their doors when I approached, and refused to respond to my knocks, or to my questions when I succeeded in stopping someone in the street. This was not ignorance of the event, I was sure; this was active refusal to divulge some dark secret that the entire town shared.

But on the evening of the third day, my efforts came to an end. For the woman came herself to the door of the castle. She rang the bell, and demanded audience with the Prince. The guards, who had no inkling who she might be, were about to turn her away, when my Master himself came barreling into the antechamber and rushed to her. "You have come at last," he cried, and tried to embrace and kiss her. But she raised her hand and pushed his face away ignominiously.

"So ye missed me, eh?" she said. "Never mind, I gottcha now." She turned to the guards, "Yer Master's goin' on a li'l vacation," she said. She took his hand, and led him away. He followed obediently, like a six-year-old child being led by his mother.

I witnessed this entire exchange, and had the opportunity to examine the woman closely. She was a peasant woman, about 35 years old, plain, not ugly but certainly not attractive. Her face was lined, her hair mousey, her gray dress soiled. She was thin, but with stout legs. Her breasts were small and fallen, and hung loosely under her dress. Her only remarkable feature was her eyes – in sockets sunken deep in her skull, they were an intense green with small black pupils that seemed to burn with an inner fire. She walked with a firm and decisive step, leading my Master down the road to the cluster of houses by the Fontana Danusci. I followed a few steps behind, without attempting to hide my presence. The woman was clearly aware that I was accompanying them, and made no sign of displeasure. We reached the house, a sturdy stone structure of two stories. Downstairs was the stable, wherein resided three sheep and a family of chickens; and a workshop, apparently a carpentry shop, that seemed to be in considerable disarray. The woman led my Master up the steps to the residency. When I attempted to follow, the woman turned to me and made a gesture with her hand that I was not to follow. The gesture was so decisive that I hesitated for a moment; and in that moment, she led my Master through the open door, slammed it shut, and I could hear the latch falling in place.

Destined to await them outside the house until they did whatever they were going to do, I decided to investigate who this woman was. By good fortune, a peasant was leading a horse and cart to a neighboring house. I hailed the man.

"Tell me, whose house it this," I asked, pointing to the woman's house.

"That were the home of Errico d'Angelo," he replied tersely.

"Was?"

"He dead," was the reply.

"How did he die?"

The peasant made no response, but stared at me malevolently. He then turned to continue his passage to his home.

"I say, man, tell me how he died."

The man paused in his steps. He turned to me slowly. "Ye best ask the Missus 'bout that." He then turned back to enter his home, and refused to utter another word.

It was enough, though. I now had some idea of with whom I was dealing. This was the widow of Errico d'Angelo, the master carpenter who had been responsible for the remodel of the castle, whose daughter my Master had debauched, and who had murdered the poor girl when he discovered her shame. And now he, too was dead. This was, I realized, a situation pregnant with danger. Determined to protect my Master, I marched up the steps of the house, and pounded on the door. I shouted, "My Lord, open the door!" Inside I could hear grunts and cries of passion. I redoubled my efforts, but to no avail. No one opened the door, and the couple inside made no sign of even hearing my cries. I considered the possibility of returning to the castle, calling the guard, and breaking down the door. That would be, I thought, the precise opposite of what my Master would have wanted me to do. He would, I felt, wish for me to wait patiently until he had tired of his tryst and left to return home. So, despite my profound trepidation, I sat on the landing, wrapped my cloak around me, and resolved to wait until my Master should emerge.

It was a long wait. Night fell. I dozed uncomfortably on the landing. Inside, I could hear occasional sounds of activity: shuffling of feet, the clank of what sounded like a heavy iron pot on a stove, later another round of lovemaking. In my state of excessive anxiety, every sound seemed amplified and clarified, like the sound of footsteps in a forest on a moonless night. There was quiet in the house, and I napped. Then I heard gentle snoring. My Master did not snore, it must be the woman. Then I heard a sudden cry. A rustling, perhaps of bedding, footsteps, pounding. More movement. Heavy breathing – was it sobbing? More quiet. More grunting and cries of passion. Silence.

With first light, I rose, and resumed my hammering on the door. "Open, My Lord!" I cried. No response. I heard movement inside – moving about, more sounds of cooking, eating. An hour passed. The door opened. My Master emerged. I tried to read his mood from his look, but he was detached, his eyes not meeting mine, but peering into the distance. He spoke no words, but descended the steps and turned to the castle. The woman did not follow, but shut the door again and threw the latch. My Master walked briskly, yet there was no sense of determination in his gait. He walked as though his mind was elsewhere. I followed on his heels. When we arrived at the castle, he turned to me. "Return to her," he said. "Tell her that I wish for her to come to live here."

"Yes, my Lord," I replied, and turned to return to the woman's house. I of course had no intent of proffering such an invitation, but I welcomed the opportunity to visit the woman and make clear in certain terms that her continued involvement with my Master would not be welcome. I considered momentarily the possibility of taking with me a captain of the guard, but decided that, on this first interview, I would try to deal with her alone.

I made my way quickly back to the Fontana Danusci. As I approached the steps, the door to the house opened, and the woman stood there with a wry smile on her angular face. "Come in, Ludovico, I have been expecting you." How did she know to open the door without any sign of my approach? Had she been looking out the window? But there was no window opening on the street. Another eerie and frightening fragment in this increasingly ominous puzzle.

I climbed the stairs and entered the house. It was a dingy room, with only one small window opening in the back. In the dimness, I could make out the bed, in disorder, the kitchen with an unwashed soup pot on the floor, a small table and two chairs, a small pallet on the floor where the woman's daughter must have slept. It was not a well-kept house – there was dust on the floor, grime on the window, a pile of rags on the floor in a corner.

I opened my mouth to speak, but she raised her hand in the same definitive gesture that had given me pause the previous afternoon. "Ye needn't speak," she said. "I know what ye want ta know, an' I know what yer wantin' ta tell me. An' I kin promise ye, I ain't gonna leave yer Master alone. He belongs ta me now, ta me from the waist down."

"I do not know what you mean, Madam," I said, with as much coldness in my voice as I could muster.

"I'll tell ye what I mean," she said. "Sit ye down and have some soup."

"No thank you, Madam," I said, and remained standing.

"Yer a smart fella," she said. "If yer Master were as smart as ye, he'd be a free man now."

"My Master is a free man," I replied with disdain.

The woman's face darkened, and she glared at me with a malevolent gaze. Her green eyes seemed to glow. "Yer master shamed me daughter. Me husband killed me daughter. I killed me husband. And now I aim ta shame yer master."

"Madam, I advise you... " I started.

"Shut up!" she shouted, and gave me a shove, so I stumbled backwards and fell into a chair that was behind me. "Ye lissen ta me, and jist keep yer trap shut." Then she, too, sat, and, inexplicably, broke into tears. She buried her face in her hands, and her body was wracked with sobs. I was oddly moved to go to her, touch her, comfort her; yet, on the other hand, furious with her presumption, her insulting remarks, and her despicable seduction of my Master. Torn between these conflicting emotions, I sat, unable to make a move one way or another.

She lifted her head. "Do ye think I want this?" she said between sobs. "Ye think I chose this? I here be a pawn, a toy in the hands o' evil! I don't want any o' this! I don't want yer Master! I want me husband back! I want me daughter back!" And her head dropped back onto the table, onto her folded arms.

Thus we sat across from each other, me in silence, she sobbing and breathing heavily. Then, as suddenly as she had broken down, she rose up. The tears fell away, and the malevolent stare returned. "I'll tell ye all," she said, poison in her tone. "I'll tell ye why yer Master's a slave ta me now.

"I weren't no witch. I tell ye, I were a decent, lovin' mother and wife. I tell ye, e'en now I love Jesus Christ. I ain't no devil-worshipper. But ye can't be both ways, can ye? So, yea, I'm sinkin', I'm sinkin' inta the dark side.

"What could I do? When me husband killed me daughter, what could I do? He killed it all, he did. He killed me love, he killed the joy in me life. I said, right then, he ain't gonna live after what he done. So I went. I went to Polisandra. She give me the poison. But she ain't givin' nuthin' for free. No, I had ta swear, make a pact. I din't want ta, ye know I din't want ta. I love Jesus Christ, I be a good

Christian I am. But I hadda kill him, don't ye see? He killed me love, he killed everythin'.

"So I gave him the poison. It looked like black death, but it wasn't. I tell ye, he suffered for what he done. He suffered what he deserved. He was four days a-dyin'. An' I enjoyed every minute of it. Well, I paid for it, din't I? I made the pact.

"So then I went back ta Polisandra, she tol' me what ta do ta the Lord. So I done it. I took me blood, the blood from me time, I collected it in a bladder. An', like Polisandra tol' me, I put that little bladder in me mouth, an' I went to meet the Lord. An' I went up, right up ta him, an' I kissed him on the mouth. An' I took me teeth an' I burst that little bladder, an' I filled his mouth with me blood. An' just like Polisandra tol' me, he become me slave. But she says, it ain't enough. The blood, it works for a few days, but then ye gotta give him somethin' more, somethin' stronger. So I wait a coupla days, an' I bring him to the house. An' I take some bread, an' I stuff it in my *fica*. An' we fuck an' fuck, an' in the mornin' I take that bread, an' it all soaked with his seed and me seed, an' I make a soup, and I feed him the soup. An' now he mine, he mine forever. Now I own him from the belt down. His wife, all she gonna get from him is kisses."

I listened to this tirade in a mixture of horror and disgust. Words failed me. But then, as suddenly as before, she again collapsed in tears. This time, I was unmoved by her distress. "What have you to weep for, woman? You have what you wished for."

"Ye think this comes fer free? Ye think I don' gotta pay fer this? I gotta go ta the wood. I gotta take the waters. I gotta fuck the goat. I be damned fer ever! Oh God, help me! Help yer poor li'l creature gone astray!" And, again, she buried her face in her arms, and her whole body was wracked with sobs.

What an odd and disturbing admixture of emotions was I witnessing: the purest evil, mingled with her strange vulnerability, her guilt, her yearning for penance, her unwavering resolve to do ill. But I steeled myself against any pity, and did what I had come to do. I drew out a purse.

"Madam, this purse contains 70 gold ducats. You will take this purse, and you will leave Gesualdo. You will leave forever, Gesualdo, Naples, Avellino, Venosa. If I meet you or hear of you in these environs again, I shall most certainly see to your death."

I placed the purse on the table between us. She reached out, took the purse, opened it and peered inside. Her tears subsided. Then she drew the strings of the purse shut, and hurled it with all her might at me. It struck me hard on the temple. She rose to her full height. "What ye think, yer me pimp? Get out, get out! An' tell yer Master, I'll do his biddin'. I'll be there tonight. Now Get out!"

m'inuolate hor mi redete il core

This music, dark, demonic, cursed, fell,
　Imparts no pleasure, only inflicts pain.
　Like searing coal impressed on naked skin,
Its harmonies do ope the gates of Hell.

Is music not a salve to wounded soul?
　A solace to bereaved, light in despair,
　A fan to lovers' passion, strength in fear?
A balm to join the rent, to make it whole?

But in these strains no solace can be heard,
　No pleasure, only lust without desire,
　Just passion without pleasure: Deathly pyre
where border between life and death obscured.

This deathly song is sung by voices four,
　But did they choose to meld this harmony?
　Or was it destiny that did decree
That they shall call the strokes to Charon's oar?

Tenore sings the Prince, of ancient blood,
 whom ere the witch's curse did demons hound,
 And even in his art no freedom found,
But slaved in Calliope's servitude.

In love alone the Prince did find succor,
 From Cupid's arrows all his demons fled.
 But witchcraft banished Eros from his bed,
No joy now in coition, only chore.

The canto sings Maria, perfect, blessed,
 devoted, faithful, model of beauty
 She, too, victim of sorcery,
Her lover wrenched by Satan from her breast.

Between these, alto, sings the cursed witch,
 Assassin, whore, her heart with hatred filled,
 Her child debauched and murdered, husband killed,
With Satan she contracted, now his bitch.

And who is bass, to ground the harmony?
 His voice is heard, his shadow hides the light.
 Yet nameless, faceless creature of the night,
This cantus firmus hides in mystery.

These are the voices of this ghastly choir,
 Their song foreboding death and misery,
 Their fundament shrouded in mystery,
Their final cadence in eternal fire.

I have included this poem in this memoir against my better judgment. Don Scipione, who read the manuscript, remembered the poem and urged me to include it. It is customary for authors of this type of chronicle to include their own poems here and there. But the truth be told, I am not a good poet, and this is not a particularly good poem. At the time I wrote it, a few weeks after the witch had moved into the Gesualdo castle and turned our lives inside out, I showed it to Torquato Tasso, who was, in addition to being a dear friend of my Master and myself, the leading poet of the Italian peninsula. He pointed out numerous errors of scansion and rhyme, but, by that time, I had found the task of writing verse so onerous that I never bothered to correct them.

In any case, I have included the poem for two reasons: first (if you actually read the poem) you will clearly detect what a dark and miserable mood I was in after the witch's intrusion into our lives; and second, because it expresses my concern that another evil force, beyond that of the witch, was at work destroying my Master's life. It was not clear to me until a few weeks before my Master's death who or what that force was. My Master's uncle, His Eminence Alfonso Gesualdo was a possible candidate, but he visited us only rarely, and did not seem to have enough of a presence to cast the oppressive shadow that darkened our days at that time. This mystery was to grow more compelling as the dire events of the next year unfolded.

As the witch had promised, she appeared at the door of the castle the very evening of my unfortunate interview with her. The Master himself greeted her meekly, and led her to a chamber adjoining his own. That night, the Master was awakened twice by the red dream – the first time since his betrothal. I rushed to his chamber upon hearing his screams, but when I arrived, I found that the witch had suppressed his cries by pressing his lips to her *fica*, and forcing him to stimulate her with his tongue until orgasm. In addition to this, I learned, she forced him to have intercourse with her twice a night. This the Master told me about a week after her arrival.

"I hate it," he told me, his head in his hands, his eyes moist. "There is a vile odor from her mouth, and an even worse one from her *fica*. I try to will my erection to collapse, but it refuses."

"You must simply refuse her, and send her away, my Lord," I said.

"Do you understand nothing?" he said in exasperation. "I can do nothing. Nothing, I tell you! She commands, I obey. I am her slave. This," he said, looking at his loins, "is her slave. It is erect as the penis of Priapus, all through the night. Painfully erect. Even after I dump my seed, it stays hard. Yet when I visit my wife, or when Don Fabrizio visits, it is as limp as a dead worm."

My Master was completely exhausted from these nights of incessant intercourse, and lay about in bed most of the day. He ceased to attend to affairs of state, ignored his friends, and ceased writing music altogether. I tried to think of ways to mitigate what appeared to be the witch's voracious sexual appetite; but I soon learned that what I thought was voraciousness was something else entirely. For the witch herself came to me to complain. I was in my chamber. It was late at night, and I was working on my poem. She knocked at my door. I opened a crack and peered out.

"What do you want?" I asked coldly.

"I wish ta speak to ye," she said.

"I do not wish to speak to you," I said, and shut the door, and threw the bolt. I returned to my desk, but to my astonishment and horror, the bolt slid back of its own volition, and she entered the room.

"I must speak ta ye," she said.

"Very well, I see I have no choice." I laid down my quill and turned to face her. She stood before me for a few moments, and then, suddenly, collapsed to the floor in an ecstasy of sobbing.

"I be afeared. I be so afeared!"

I was, naturally, taken aback by this display of emotion. I found my natural compassion weakening my disdain for her, I made an effort to put steel in my voice.

"What, Madam, do you have to be afraid of?"

"Tomorrow be full moon," she said between sobs.

I was aware that the night of the full moon had special significance for the Satanic sisterhood, but only a vague understanding of what that significance might be. So I waited for further explanation.

"I be baptized," she said, still crumpled on the floor.

"Ah, the goat," I said.

With that, she rose and rushed to me, and clung to me like a drowning woman. "Oh, Ludovico, I don't wanna go. Please don't let me go."

I was at a complete loss as to what to do. This woman, who had enslaved my Master, and was destroying our lives, indeed the lives of the entire principality, was appealing to my pity. And I could not deny that I did feel pity for this wretched creature.

"Madam, it is not I who is sending you to this meeting. Why do you appeal to me?"

"Because ye be me only friend."

"Madam, if you wish for me to be your friend, you must do one thing. You must leave this house immediately and forever."

With that, she released me, and pushed me away violently. "Ye fool. I kinna do that. Don't ye understand? I kinna. Ye understand nothin'."

"Then perhaps you would be wise to speak to someone who does understand. Perhaps a priest."

"I spoken to a priest," she replied, matter-of-factly.

"And what did he say?"

"He tole me say 25 *Ave Marias.*"

I was incredulous. "Twenty-five *Ave Marias* penance for murdering your husband, making a pact with the devil, and enslaving my Master? Who is this priest?"

"Padre Giulio."

"Giulio?" I replied furiously. "Giulio is no priest! He is a fraud! He is a slimy, degraded and disgusting excuse for a human being! Twenty-five *Ave Marias*! It is ridiculous!"

"Ye understand nothin'!" shouted the witch, again enraged. "I kinna say even one *Ave Maria*! I kinna pray! I be a prisoner of the devil!" And she broke down again in tears.

"Perhaps I understand nothing," I replied coldly. "But I understand that you are slaking your depraved needs on my Master."

"My needs?" she replied, with venom in her voice. "I hate it. I hate the sex. Orgasm is painful to me. The feeling of him inside me makes me wanna vomit."

"Then, Madam, why do you not surcease?"

She turned her green eyes on me with a look of disdain that could freeze water. "Acause," she said, "I mean ta fuck him ta death."

"You should beware, Madam, that you do not fuck yourself to death first."

This remark gave her pause. She stood silent for a long moment, her eyes boring into me. Then a strange smile stole across her face. "Oh, how I wish that that would happen," she said. "Pray for me, Ludovico. Pray that I should die. Even the fires o' Hell would be better'n this Hell I be livin'."

And she turned and left my chamber.

Early the next evening, the witch left our castle. I immediately went up to my Master's room, and took my lute along. This was wise, for, for the first time since the witch's arrival, my Master wished to hear music. Already in the room were Don Fabrizio, who was visiting us, and Don Pietro Bardotti. Don Fabrizio was wearing a plain gray dress, which I recognized as the witch's. On the witch it was oversized and shapeless; on Don Fabrizio it was stretched tight like a doublet, the seams about to split over his broad shoulders and brawny arms. I played for hours, singing *villanelle, frotole,* many love songs. He asked me to sing *O Rosa Bella,* and to repeat it again and again. I must have sung it six or eight times. The singing continued late into the night. My Master insisted that we light no candles, but the room was bathed in the ethereal white light of the moon. As midnight approached, my Master began behaving strangely. He rose from his bed, and waved to me to cease my singing. He strode as though to walk about the room, but, after the first step, halted and grabbed his neck, as though restrained by a leash. He stamped one foot and then the other. He shook his head, nodded restlessly, scraped one foot against the floor, snorted. "Are you well, my Lord?" I asked, but he made no reply. He turned and twisted more and more restlessly, tugging all the while on the collar of his nightshirt. "My Lord, perhaps you should lie," said Don Fabrizio. But instead, speaking only in grunts and snorts, my Master reached out to Don Fabrizio and pushed him with surprising force onto the bed, face down, so his buttocks was in the air, With a sudden swift gesture, he lifted the hem of Don Fabrizio's dress, and lifted his own nightshirt, exposing his now erect member. With great force, he thrust his penis into Don Fabrizio's posterior, pumping violently for a few short seconds, until overcome with orgasm. His whole body then stiffened, and he fell with a crash to the floor, his body wracked by an overpowering convulsion. He coughed and choked, his teeth chattered, gnawing at his tongue, his arms twitched crazily at his sides. Blood started to pour from his nose and mouth, and from the scar in the palm of his hand. All the while, he cried out in unintelligible grunts.

The three of us lifted the Prince onto the bed, and held him down, attempting to prevent him from further harming himself. Don Pietro and myself held down his arms, while Don Fabrizio grasped his head, and pressed the corner of the pillow into his mouth, to stop him from chewing his tongue. The Master's body continued to stiffen and spasm wildly. The sheets – and ourselves – were covered with his blood. I thought, surely my Master is going to die, just as the goat was slaughtered by the leader of the coven. However, after a few minutes of this, the shaking subsided, the flow of blood slowed, and my Master laid back on the bed, exhausted and drenched in his own sweat and blood.

The crisis past, I resolved to set out immediately for Naples, and to bring my teacher, Il Dottore Moise Amani, to examine my Master. I asked Don Fabrizio to accompany me, but he preferred to remain at his friend's side. I therefore called the captain of the guard, Ascanio Lama, who directly readied the two fastest horses of the stable, and we set off before dawn. We rode through the day, and by the time we arrived at the doctor's house the sun was setting. I was greatly agitated, but the doctor calmed me. "Before you tell your story, you must sit and have a cup of *Verbana* infusion," he insisted.

Thus calmed, I described the events of the last few weeks – the bloody kiss at the ceremony, my encounters with the witch, and the nature of my Master's distemper. I told him what the witch had said: that her goal was to kill him with excessive sexual stimulation, even though she herself hated to engage in sex with him.

"Your Master is seriously bewitched," said the doctor. "I am a doctor of the body, not of the spirit. I fear I am not qualified to attempt to exorcise the demon that has seized him, nor to counter the spell the witch has cast upon him. For that you will need to call a priest who specializes in these matters. The best I can do is treat him, and perhaps her, for the bodily symptoms that this spell has entailed."

"That is all I ask, my friend," I said.

"Then let us be away," he replied. "Salamone, load the cart."

I was eager to set off that same evening, but the doctor adamantly refused. "You will rest here, and we will leave at daybreak. You will be of no use to me if you exhaust all your strength." In any case, our horses needed a night's rest.

We had planned to set out at first light, but we were further delayed by the disappearance of my escort, Don Ascanio. I was concerned, for Don Ascanio had a reputation for carousing and brawling. Directly I realized he was missing, I set out to search the public houses of Naples. Thanks to my association with my Master, I was well familiar with the most sordid places where Don Ascanio might be loitering. The public houses were all closed by this time, but I soon found him, fast asleep in an alley behind the Gatto Nero. I was unable to awaken him from his drunken stupor, and he was a great lump of a man that I couldn't hope to haul onto my horse alone. But a kindly passerby agreed to help me, and together we hoisted him afront the saddle, and I lugged him back to the doctor's, where we tossed him unceremoniously into the back of the cart.. So it was midmorning by the time we finally got under way, the doctor and Don Salamone in their cart with Don Ascanio snoring in the back, crowded in with medicines and with the doctor's violin, I on horse. For the doctor, travel was extremely difficult. At home, he knew every corner, every obstacle, and could move about the house and the garden as competently as if he had sight. Away from home, however, he had to be led everywhere by the hand. Strong as his constitution and his will were, it was very trying and tiring for him. Moreover, the cart was cumbersome and rocky, an uncomfortable ride even for a sighted man. We traveled slowly, and stopped for the night at Avellino. By the time we finally arrived in Gesualdo, two days and a night had passed. We ascended directly to my Master's chamber, where we found him, considerably recovered, sitting up in his bed. At his side were his wife Donna Maria, Don Fabrizio, and Don Pietro. The Prince was reading a document, that I could see was an accounts sheet. He called Pietro over, pointed out some details from the sheet, and instructed him to deal with the matter. He then turned to me. "Ah, Ludovico, you have returned. And you brought the doctor. Excellent."

"I see you are much recovered," said the doctor.

"I feel much better, though I am still quite weak."

"Ludovico told me about your seizure."

"Happily, I have no recollection of it. None whatsoever. I only remember awakening in the morning, feeling completely exhausted, and clean. Clean, yes. The maids had apparently washed me and changed all the linens. I understand I made quite a mess!" He chuckled.

I was glad to see this complete reversal in my Master's condition, but my pleasure was tempered by the towering question that hovered over the castle. But I didn't have to ask, for my Master read my thoughts.

"She has not returned. Perhaps she shall not return. In the meantime, the curse seems to be lifted and life has returned to normal." With that, he turned to his wife, and took her hand.

By the following morning, the Prince had completely recovered. He spent the morning in the great hall, sitting in judgment on disputes from within his realms. He reviewed the accounts, and determined that the following day he would tour the village with the doctor, to check reports of an outbreak of rinderpest among the cattle. The following day he planned to go hunting with Don

Fabrizio. That evening, for the first time since the witch had arrived in the castle, the *capella* sang madrigals, and the *camerata* performed a *symphonia*. It was a huge relief to the musicians, whose forced idleness was a frightening onus.

These days passed as planned. My Master spent the night, and the following night, in the chamber of my Mistress. The cattle disease, the doctor determined, was not rinderpest at all, but a digestive disorder, apparently caused by distemper. Bleeding the animals of a pint of blood seemed to remedy the problem. The following morning, with sunrise, I set out with my Master and Don Fabrizio, heading into the forest below the castle in search of a hart or wild boar to slaughter. We rode for several hours, finding nothing. We spotted a deer grazing in a meadow, and we followed it as stealthily as we could as it browsed its way across the field. At one point it lifted its ears, and turned anxiously in our direction, sniffing the air. My Master immediately shouldered his cross-bow and fired an arrow, but it narrowly missed the animal, who turned and bolted before anyone could get off another shot. We followed in the direction it fled, not actually expecting to find it, but for having no better course of action. We halted for a noon meal, and then remounted. We had ridden about another hour, when we heard a sound from deep in the forest. It sounded decidedly like whimpering. The hairs on the back of my neck stood. "Let us flee this place," I said. But the sound had entranced my Master. He dismounted and pushed through the brush toward the sound. Don Fabrizio and myself followed with great trepidation. We pushed our way through to a small meadow. There, at the edge of the meadow, sat the witch. She was filthy. Her hair was caked with mud, her dress torn and stained with dark brown splotches. She knelt in a state of exhaustion. She heard our arrival, but did not lift her head.

"Why did ye come?" she said.

My Master, overwrought with emotion, rushed to her to hold her. "Bring wine," he commanded.

"Why did ye come?" she repeated. "I could ha' died here."

Don Fabrizio approached with a skin of wine. My Master took it and held it up to her lips. She sipped at it, and then collapsed in a spasm of coughing.

I spoke with as much decision in my voice as I could muster. "My Lord, let us leave her here. You heard her, she herself said, she wishes to die."

"I cannot let her die," replied my Master, his voice shaking, his eyes filling with tears. "Do you not see? I must not let her die."

The witch looked at him with dead eyes and an expressionless face. "Well, if I must live, let's fuck." And she lifted her skirt, exposing her swollen pubes and the hairs of her legs stiff with clotted blood.

Without hesitating, and with his own eyes clouding over as if in a trance, my Master there stripped off his pantaloons, and lay on the witch, penetrating her with his long, slim priapic member. There in the grass, they coupled, an exhausted, vacuous and painful coupling. It lasted for only a minute or two, as Don Fabrizio and I stood by and watched. In the end, my Master gave a weak cry, not of sexual ecstasy, but of pain. He rolled over on his back, eyes glazed, body limp. There he lay for a minute or two, then rose heavily, and mounted his horse. "Lift her up to me," he commanded.

"I shall not, my Lord," I replied. But Don Fabrizio lifted the witch gently, and set her on the horse in front of the Prince. My Master turned his horse, and led the way through the forest back to the castle. During the course of the ride, they twice more copulated. I shall not describe the technical difficulties posed by copulating while riding; in any case, the act gave them no pleasure, but only left the both of them in a state of enervated lassitude.

Upon our return to the castle, I went directly to the doctor. He was packing his things, in the belief that his services were no longer needed. But, apprised of the return of the witch to the premises, he accompanied me to my Master's chamber, where my Master lay on his back, the witch over him humping listlessly. The doctor could not, of course see them, but he immediately understood what was taking place. When they finished, the witch fell back on the bed beside the Prince.

I was curious how the doctor would proceed. What he did was completely unexpected to me. He spoke to them in a steely voice of command: "Sit up, the both of you, and face me!"

This speech was such an extreme breech of protocol, that I was unsure how the Prince would respond; for, to address thus the Prince of Venosa, one of the most titled noblemen of the land, would be grounds for imprisonment. Moreover, the witch, from however lowly a station she may come, was not a person to be trifled with. Her powers were proven, and who knows what additional powers she had acquired during her initiation into the coven. Yet the two of them rose like two obedient children, and sat on the edge of the bed, awaiting their instructions.

"I am a medical doctor, I treat diseases of the body. I am therefore unable to assist you in ridding yourselves of the evil that has possessed your souls. For that, I urge you or your associates to call an exorcist, or a representative of the Inquisition, to deal with the witchcraft here. I am prescribing an admixture of rue, saltpeter and chasteberry. This should relieve your Priapism, and," addressing the witch, "your compulsion for incessant coition.

"I emphasize again, this treatment is not a cure, but only a palliative that will relieve the most egregious symptoms of your curse. Do not expect your lives to return to normal in any respect."

"Then," said the witch, "I shan't be dyin'?"

"No, madam, you shall not die. This treatment will prevent you from succumbing to an excess of sexual congress."

I could see tears welling up in the witch's green eyes. The doctor turned to his assistant. "Don Salamone, prepare the potion please. To the witch's dose, add a measure of opium and half a measure of hemlock. One glass in the morning and one in the evening." He turned to me. "I have enough medicine here for a week. Send a messenger to my home, and I shall provide you with sufficient quantity for a month." With that, the doctor turned and left the room, Don Salamone leading him by the hand.

The doctor remained with us another day, to evaluate the efficacy of his treatment. The potion had the expected effect: my Master's nightly priapism was relieved, and the witch limited her demands on the Prince to once a night, in the early morning, when the medicine's effects were diminished prior to the morning dose. My Master was thus able to recover some of his vitality, and resumed his administrative duties, albeit in a less intense manner than before. In the evening, the doctor played his violin, and my Master was truly delighted to listen. Indeed, the entire *camerata* gathered to hear this remarkable new instrument that they had never heard before. My Master again expressed his desire to own one. "Perhaps you should go to Cremona and bring me back a case of them," he suggested to me. The doctor, however, on his departure, took me aside and urged me strongly against such a journey. "Your Master may seem somewhat recovered, but he is in a very fragile state. Moreover, there are those in his court who seek to do him ill. I am very concerned about your Mistress's dream. I urge you to stay near to him. He trusts you, relies on you, and you are one of the few members of his household who I believe can protect him."

The doctor's concern was well founded, for, though his medicine mitigated the most virulent manifestations of the curse, the other effects of the curse remained: he was unable to engage in intercourse with his wife or with his friend and lover Don Fabrizio, no matter how much he might have desired it. He would still occasionally invite Don Fabrizio to his room, and they would caress, though anything else was impossible. His wife he eschewed altogether. "I cannot go to her," he told me. "It is too shameful that I cannot be a man to her." His emotional state was extremely fragile. He woke frequently, at least once a night, from the red dream. It was I who entered his chamber and comforted him, for the witch, drugged by the opium and hemlock, usually was asleep. His periodic depressions were more frequent than usual. The doctor left several lumps of hashish resin, which I prepared for him and which mitigated the depressions. He was unable to write music, though he would occasionally agree to listen to us play or sing for him.

Donna Maria was well-nigh distraught by his abandonment of her bed. "Does he no longer love me?"

"I believe, My Lady, that he does still love you. But he is so deeply ashamed that the curse has rendered him impotent in your presence, that he is embarrassed to approach you. I know this for he has told me so himself."

"But he need not be ashamed. I love him still, even in his impotence. I only wish to be with him."

I conveyed this message to my Master, but he was firm in his refusal. "How can I approach her? She is so passionate that she has actually loved her former husbands to their deaths. And I cannot even..."

I interrupted him. "My Lord, expunge that thought from your mind. It is a gross falsehood, invented by the coward Don Giulio. Both her husbands died of natural causes, I know this to be a fact. Repulse this lie."

"Of course, of course," agreed my Master. But it was clear to me that this slander had firmly planted its poisonous roots in my Master's soul.

Nor was this the end of the slanderous tales that Don Giulio invented. A month had passed since the witch's return – a month in which we succeeded in reestablishing a semblance of routine to the curse-inflicted castle – when my Master called me for a private and urgent conference.

"Ludovico, I have reason to believe... I have reason to doubt..."

I waited while my Master composed his thought.

"Ludovico, I do not trust my wife."

"In what way do you not trust her, my Lord?"

"I believe she might be unfaithful to me."

"And who has implanted this absurd notion in your mind? Don't tell me. It was Don Giulio." Sarcasm was dripping from my voice. But it was completely lost on my Master.

"Don Giulio says that Donna Maria has been dropping hints to him. Making little gestures..."

"Don Giulio suggested that my Mistress was propositioning him? That slimy puddle of fat? You surely cannot believe that, my Lord."

"No, of course, it is incredible, isn't it?" he replied. "He says she gave him unmistakable signs."

"And what might those be?"

"He says she invited him to her room. He says that, at supper a few nights ago, she looked at him boldly, and pulled at her blouse, exposing the pink of her breast."

I took a deep breath. "My Lord, you have been married to Donna Maria for almost three years now. For three years you have loved her. I believe you still love her, even if you are incapable of showing it. For that time, I too have come to know her and to love her. My Lord, knowing her as you do, knowing how devoted she is to you, how completely she is concerned for your welfare, how could you possibly entertain such an absurd notion. And coming from that repugnant slanderer – it is too ridiculous to take this seriously."

"Well, Don Giulio claims he has appointed an assignation."

"And when is that to be?"

"This evening after supper in her chambers."

"And, I suppose, you are invited to observe."

My Master looked surprised at this remark. "How did you know that? Yes, he has suggested that there is a room across the courtyard, where I can look into her chamber. I cannot hear what is said, but I can see well enough."

"Then I shall join you," I said. At this, too, my Master seemed surprised, but he readily assented. And so, after supper, we made our way to the small chamber.

It was a tedious wait. My Master took a chair, the only one in the room, so I stood. Donna Maria was a long time in coming. By the time she arrived an hour had passed, and my legs were aching. She entered with her maid, who assisted her in dressing for bed. She was wearing her nightgown when she and the maid looked toward the door. Don Giulio pushed the door open and entered. Donna Maria looked angry, and seemed to speak harsh words. Don Giulio did not respond directly, but looked faint, and lay down on the bed. He spoke, pressing his hand to his forehead. Donna Maria looked irritated, but turned and spoke to her maid. The maid turned to leave, but Don Giulio lifted his head from the bed, and called her back. He then seemed to dismiss her, and she stepped out of the room. Left thus alone, Don Giulio rose from the bed and faced Donna Maria. There was a brief conversation. Donna Maria appeared violently upset. She slapped Don Giulio hard in the face, and gestured for him to leave. Don Giulio rubbed his cheek, and turned to leave. As he was leaving, the maid returned with a wet towel. Don Giulio seized the towel and left the room.

"What do you make of that?" asked my Master. "I am not sure what exactly we witnessed."

"It seemed pretty clear to me, my Lord. Giulio entered the room, and found some pretext to dismiss the maid. He then made an indecent proposal to your wife, who took gross offense, slapped him, and sent him on his way."

"I suppose that is right," said my Master. We were about to leave, when Don Giulio entered the room, apparently highly agitated.

"Did you see that? Did you see it? The hussy!" he cried.

"She did not appear to be a hussy at all to me," replied my Master, somewhat coldly. "You propositioned her and she rejected you. To me, she seemed to have behaved entirely properly."

"No, no, you have completely misunderstood!" exclaimed Don Giulio. "I came to her to tell her that I was rejecting her indecent proposal to me. She sent the maid away, and she approached me with a most seductive, even lewd, gesture. I reiterated my determination to reject her, at which she grew angry and slapped my face."

"I did not see a lewd gesture," said my Master, looking puzzled.

"Did you not see how she pulled at the neckline of her nightgown and exposed her breasts to me? Of course, perhaps she had her back to the window."

"My Master did not see the gesture, because there was no gesture," I interjected angrily. "There was no lewd gesture and there was no indecent proposal. We saw the entire interaction. You have invented this incredible story to undermine my Master's faith in his wife. Do you think we are idiots?"

"I believe Don Ludovico is right," said my Master. "It indeed appeared to me that she was rejecting you."

"And this red mark on my cheek, do you think that, too, is my invention? She slapped me, because I rejected her. With her breasts hanging out like a common whore! Surely you saw that!"

"Perhaps I missed it," said my Master, confusion in his voice. "Ludovico, did you see that?"

"Of course I didn't see it, because it never happened. My Lord, this man is pouring poison in your ears. Reject it, reject it utterly. Disdain these insidious and nonsensical insinuations."

My Master turned to Don Giulio, and said in a voice filled with ambivalence, "Yes, Don Giulio, I believe Don Ludovico is right. I believe I did not see any lewd gestures. At least I don't remember seeing such a thing. Surely I would remember something like that, don't you think, Ludovico?"

I looked on my Master with exasperation. "You certainly would have remembered, my Lord."

"Good. So, for the time being, we will set aside any suspicions of my wife's fidelity. Thank you for your concern, Don Giulio."

"I only wish to serve, my Lord." Don Giulio bowed, and, like green slime sliding on the face of a pond, oozed out of the room.

The following three months were a bloodless war for my Master's mind. Whenever I was not physically present at my Master's side, the witch and the pseudo prelate worked to erode his sanity. Whether they were working in consort I knew not, but they were certainly working toward a common end. The witch enervated the Prince with the power of her curse and her daily sexual demands. She rendered any physical love between my Master and my Mistress impossible; by sapping his seed daily, she left him in a state of flaccid pusillanimity, so that he could barely carry out his duties of administration, and had abandoned his musical composition completely. He no longer hunted, he no longer philandered, and, though the *camerata* and the *capella* performed nightly, he listened listlessly and often stole off in mid-performance to take to his bed.

In parallel, Don Giulio was insidiously filling my Master's ear with the most vile and ludicrous insinuations of his wife's infidelity. The Prince would usually come to me directly with these slanders, and I would, sometimes patiently, sometimes angrily, refute them. By far the most ridiculous of these slanders was that Don Fabrizio was conducting an affair with Donna Maria. "He goes to her room, where he keeps his wardrobe," my Master told me. "Under pretense of dressing, he has seduced my wife. That is what Don Giulio has told me."

"My Lord, you know Don Fabrizio. You know him well. You know that in the last few years, he has lost all interest in the female sex. You know that his visits to Donna Maria's chambers are something that you yourself initiated. You know that he keeps his female wardrobe there, You know how devoted he and your wife are to your well-being. All this you know. So how could you possibly entertain such an absurd notion?"

"Oh, Ludovico, you are right, I know in my mind you are right. But in my heart, there is doubt."

"It is this unctuous pretender who has planted these doubts in your heart. Banish him from your presence, my Lord. Rid yourself of this vile vermin."

In the end, my Master would always agree with me, and would decide to send Don Giulio away. But he never did. On the contrary, despite my efforts, the evil duo gained more and more control over my Master's will. I resolved to be in attendance at my Master's side as constantly as possible. I stopped attending rehearsals of the *camerata* and the *capella*, and dogged my Master's footsteps throughout the day.

As the months passed, my Master's life became characterized by violent swings of mood. One day he would be filled with choler, would rail against his wife, and swear to murder her and his friend Don Fabrizio. During these rages he would beat himself with his fists, tear at his hair, and, on occasion, grab his sword and slash violently at the empty air. I would chastise him, and sometimes grasp him (at great risk to myself) to restrain him from harming himself or others. My chastisement led to a complete flip in mood, from choler to melancholy. The Prince would weep, pray, kneel before the cross and beat himself with his belt, beg me to beat him. He would sometimes refuse all food and drink for days at a time, closing himself in his chamber and refusing to admit anyone but the witch, and her but once a day for her daily fuck. These days of depression would end in a rise of phlegm; the Prince would lose all interest; he would ignore matters of state, he would refuse to speak with friends, he would lie the entire day on his bed or on the lounge in the great room, and stare dully at the ceiling. During this time I would linger in his presence, to prevent Don Giulio from approaching. With the passage of days, the phlegm would subside, and my Master would enjoy a few days of normality. He would attend affairs of state, he would listen to music and compose, he would occasionally take to the hunt. But, invariably, at some point, the schemer would find a way into my Master's presence, they would speak, and the cycle of choler – melancholy – phlegm would begin again.

This recurring pattern suggested to me that the witch's curse was effected by a cyclical imbalance of the humors in my Master's body, and that this imbalance could be mitigated by administration of herbs and other treatments to stabilize the balance of humors. To this end, I wrote to my mentor, the Dottore Moise Amani, without whose advice I would certainly not proceed. I suggested a potion of black hellebore to counteract the black bile that gave rise to his choleric episodes. The doctor replied directly:

My dear Ludovico,

You have learned your lessons well. I sometimes regret you have become a musician; you would have made a fine doctor.

Your suggestion of black hellebore is excellent. The effect of this purgative is most strong: it induces vomiting and diarrhea, and an excess can, as you know, cause severe illness and even death. It is, however, the most effective antidote for a rise in black bile. So you must administer it judiciously. Begin with a small dose, and increase it over time to achieve the best effect.

I recommend that, before you begin your course of treatment, you track your Master's cycle of choler-melancholy-phlegm-health over a time. If you find the cycle to be regular, I would suggest that you administer the hellebore not upon the onset of the choler, but a day or two before. I also advise you to mix the hellebore with a portion of bishopwort, which is known to be effective against spells and witchery.

I also urge you not to ignore the iatric value of music. He should hear music at least an hour a day, this will most certainly have a salubrious effect on him. Let me remind you that music in the Dorian mode encourages stability and temperance. Certainly avoid music in the Phrygian mode, which inflames the passions and would most likely exacerbate his fits of anger and violence. Were I able to come, I would play for him the music of the Saracens – I have found melodies in particular Maqamat (the Islamic forms of musical modes) to be very effective therapeutically.

My dear Ludovico, how I wish I could be at your side in this difficult time. Alas, as you know, it is well nigh impossible for me to make the journey in my disabled state, even with the assistance of my devoted assistant Don Salamone. Nonetheless, I have complete faith in your abilities to best attend to your Master in this difficult time.

Your devoted mentor,

Moise Amani

How he wished he could be here now? Oh, how *I* wished he could be here now! For there was no greater force on the course of my life, save my father, than Dottore Moise! At his side, I learned all that I know beyond music: Science, art, philosophy, history. From him I learned to love Plutarch, I was introduced to the wonders of Pythagoras and Aristotle and St. Augustine. A man of tremendous erudition, he had – while still he had eyes – read

Avicenna in the original Arabic and Maimonides in the original Hebrew.

I discovered Don Moise – or, perhaps, was discovered by him – when I was 12 years old. I was wandering about the city with my buddies, when I heard the strains of his violin. I was drawn to the sound like a fly to flame, and immediately became enamored of this remarkable man. Whenever we were in Naples (that is, when we were not in Gesualdo, where we sojourned several months each year), I spent two or three afternoons a week at his feet, watching him treat his patients, listening to him as he explained the beauties of our world. My father agreed wholeheartedly to my spending this time with the Dottore. For my father, too, was a learned man, and wished for his son to be the same.

But not only the disciplines of the sciences and the arts did I learn from Don Moise; I also learned the moral life. It must seem strange to you that I, a believer in the one true savior, our Lord Jesus Christ, should learn the Christian virtues of mercy, love, charity and humility from a Jew. Yet there you have it: I have known no man of such moral rectitude, so merciful, so forgiving, yet so modest, as my mentor. I remember especially one conversation I had with him when I was 15, a few short months before I entered the service of my Master the Prince. By then, I had been with Don Moise for more than three years, and an intimacy had grown between us that emboldened me to ask him about his blindness. He told me the story of his trial before the archbishop Carlo Borromeo, my Master's uncle.

"You must hate him very much," I said.

"Hate, my son," he said, "is an emotion unbecoming of the human soul, and revenge is an act unbecoming human society. No, I do not hate him. In fact, I once treated him for an ailment."

I was duly astonished. "He came to you for treatment?"

"He did indeed. He had a furuncle on his glans, and he feared to go to a Christian doctor, who might suspect the French disease. That would mean he violated his vow of chastity."

"And was it the French disease?"

"Oh no. I believe the Archbishop lived by his vows to this day. In that sense, he was, perhaps, a truly saintly man. No, the furuncle was unlike anything I had ever seen. I lanced it, and a great volume of pus flowed from it, with a distinctive odor, like that of a billy goat. In any case, I have no doubt that it was not transmitted to him through sexual concourse.

"In any case, Ludovico, it is difficult to judge men. While he dealt me with, I believe, excessive cruelty, he was true to the ideals of his own church. In many ways, his life was exemplary. No, it is not my place to hate him, no matter how vilely he has treated me."

While Don Moise never directly taught me music, I believe his impress upon me has made me a better musician. I lament that many musicians have no general education beyond their specific technical skills. Music is a demanding profession. Many of my fellow musicians spent their entire youths mastering the technical challenges of musicianship and of their instruments. For these players, music is a skill and little more. They have no understanding that music is far more than a skill, more even than an art: music is a science. The ancient philosophers tell us that music is a branch of astronomy; that the laws that govern the harmonic movement of the bodies of the heavens are the selfsame laws that govern the harmony of a motet. These musicians do not know that music is the living heart of this glorious edifice we call our universe. This boorishness characterizes many musicians of my generation, and many more of the generation of musicians who came after me. I believe this boorishness is a cause of this new fashion in music, the opera. Don Monteverdi, the leader of the new operatic trend, so popular today, is himself a man with great musical talent but of indifferent learning. This I know first-hand because I count Don Monteverdi among my friends: I made his acquaintance during my sojourn in Cremona, of which I will write later. I believe that the rise of this – I might say, pathetically simple-minded – style is the result of lack of general education among the new generation of musicians. These musicians do not appreciate the beauty of polyphony, nor do they understand the centrality of music to the workings of our world. I can only hope that this new fashion will be as ephemeral as it is vapid and insipid, and that the glories of polyphony will once again reign supreme.

But the events of which I write here occurred long before Monteverdi came forth with his new style of opera. In the days of which I write, polyphony was still king; and, though the ancient forms of modal music passed on from the Greeks – the Dorian, the Lydian, the Phrygian – had fallen out of style, there were still to be found madrigals and motets written in these archaic modes. I therefore conferred with Maestro Bartolomeo Roi, the *capo* of the *capella*. Maestro Roi, a deeply conservative man who delighted in the ancient forms, agreed immediately to prepare a program of motets in the Dorian mode. He knew a good number of them, and, since we had no part books for them, agreed to copy out the parts from his remarkable memory. Within a few days of intense rehearsal, we were thus able to implement this element of my Master's treatment, and I believe I saw some modicum of improvement in his condition.

The second aspect of his treatment, the medicinal, took an additional couple of months, For, following my mentor's advice, I tracked the course of my Master's accursed malady of anger-depression-lassitude over three full cycles. The cycle, I found, was indeed quite regular: choler for two or three days, a week of remorse, a week of phlegmatic inactivity, and a period of six or seven days of normality. So, on the sixth day of the end of the third cycle, I administered a small dose of the black hellebore, mixed with bishopwort. My Master felt nauseous and suffered from cramps the next day, but this dose had no perceptible effect on the course of the curse. I therefore increased the dose the following cycle. This time, my Master vomited violently, and suffered intense diarrhea. He was much weakened by the treatment, and the choler which followed was indeed greatly mitigated. I couldn't know if the hellebore had actually reduced the rise in black bile, or that the purgation had simply weakened him so much that he was too exhausted to be angry. In any case, I considered the treatment a success. I decided, however, to administer the bishopwort separately, for I feared that, given concurrently with the hellebore, it would simply be vomited up and not have the desired effect. At the end of the third cycle, my Master strongly resisted the administration of the hellebore. Indeed, I quite understood him, for the treatment was most unpleasant. However, I prevailed upon him to take the dose, and thus, for the next couple of months, I succeeded in mediating the violence of his emotions.

In the battle for his mind, however, I was losing steadily. The poisonous insinuations of the vermin Giulio, and my Master's sexual enslavement by the witch, combined to breed the green-eyed monster in my Master's heart. His former love for his wife turned to a venomous jealousy, that grew into hatred, that grew into indifference. All my efforts to convince him of the absurdity of his suspicions were, if not entirely in vain, at best merely temporal.

"In my mind, I know you are right," said my Master during a period of normality. "But my heart, Ludovico. My heart is filled with doubt."

"You must follow your mind, my Lord," I said. "In this case, your mind is true, your heart is a prisoner of dark forces. Let me take you to your wife now, right now. Speak to her. You will see for yourself that she still loves you and is as true as the wafer is God's flesh."

"I cannot, Ludovico, I cannot." And my Master buried his face in his hands, torn between what he knew to be true and what his troubled soul feared to be false.

What I spoke of his wife I knew first-hand to be the truth, for I visited her frequently. I can vouch that throughout this terrible time, the only man with whom she had physical contact was myself. For it happened that often during my visits, she would fall upon me weeping, dreading the loss of the husband she loved. It was, alas, cold comfort that I could offer, faced with the abandonment of her Lord and Master.

My visits to Donna Maria were necessarily abbreviated, for I had resolved to spend every possible moment in attendance to my Master, in order to ensure the exile of the vermin Giulio from his presence. In the main, I succeeded in this; when Giulio approached, I would immediately find some pretext to send him away – that the Master was resting, or working, or in his bath. On occasion, I would even resort to the threat of violence, taking him firmly by the arm and directing him out. The vermin was quite docile, and retreated always, if not always willingly. It was, however, impossible for me to be in attendance without interruption, and invariably when I was forced to leave my Master even for a moment, the vermin seized the opportunity to visit my Master and vent his poison.

It was late one evening, after I had put my Master to bed, that I retired to my room, and sat contemplating this unfolding tragedy. I was trying hard to apply my mentor's lesson to hate no one, but finding it increasingly difficult not to hate the vermin Giulio. I was thus engaged in thought when there was a knock on the door, and, without waiting for a reply, the door opened and in walked the vermin himself. I rose to my full height, intending to expel him at once. But he spoke before I could utter a word.

"I must have a word with you, Don Ludovico."

"I have nothing to say to you. Please leave at once."

Giulio did not leave, but rather took the chair and sat. "My Master wishes for you to leave Gesualdo," he said.

I looked at him with incredulity. "I know not who your Master might be. But I know who my Master is, and he does not wish for me to leave. But I wish for you to leave. So please leave now."

Giulio smiled wryly, and for a moment did not reply. Then he spoke. "Yes, my Master..."

I interrupted him. "Yes, your Master. You live in this castle, you eat my Master's food, you sleep in a bed provided by my Master. You are a leech affixed to my Master's flesh, But you do not serve my Master. You *dis*-serve my Master. So I have no further desire of words with you. For the third time I ask you, nay, I instruct you to go."

Giulio made no move to leave. He gazed at me with a look of melancholy and self-pity. "You don't like me very much, do you?" he said.

"I do not like you at all. On the contrary, I despise you. If you were not so destructive, you would be unworthy even of my disdain."

"But you are everyone's friend," he said in his whining voice.

"I am not your friend," I replied coldly.

"You are even the witch's friend."

"Whatever gave you that absurd idea?"

"She told me. She said you were her only friend."

"Well, she is lying or she is deceived. I am not her friend. In fact, I despise her as I despise you. You can tell her that. But then, why would she listen to anything you say?"

"Because I have something she needs."

"And what might that be?"

Giulio looked at me slyly, and did not reply.

"Well, it matters nothing to me," I said angrily. "I want only one thing from you, and that is for you to leave my room."

Giulio rose slowly. "I came to ask your friendship."

"You came to tell me to leave Gesualdo."

"I came to beg your friendship. And you spurned me. I shall remember that."

I looked at him angrily. "If you want my friendship, there is one thing you can do. Leave Gesualdo. Leave now. Never return. That is the only gesture of friendship you can make towards me."

Giulio's features distorted, his brow wrinkled, and he looked as though he was about to burst out in tears. "I cannot. I cannot leave Gesualdo."

"There is nothing at all to keep you here. What, do you need a horse? I shall go with you directly to the stable and arrange one for you."

"No. I cannot leave. I am not a free man."

"No, you and the witch. You are not free men," I said sarcastically. "I have no more patience for you. Leave now, or I shall kick you out." I made for him with menace. This urged him on his way, and he shuffled gracelessly to the door. On the threshold he paused and turned to me.

"You don't know. You don't know how alone and frightened I am."

"You are not alone," I said, with as much disdain in my voice as I could muster. "You have your witch." And I slammed the door in his face.

I returned to my chair, and sat, my whole body shaking uncontrollably from this encounter. I did not for a moment abide his pathetic appeal for pity, and considered it merely another slimy subterfuge, to ease his access to my Master. Had I known then what I know now, I would perhaps have related to the episode differently. I might, perhaps, have asked myself, who is this vermin's master? What is it that the vermin has that the witch needs? Who is it that demands my departure from Gesualdo? But even if I had asked those questions – and, in my agitated state, I did not – I don't believe this would have informed a different course of action. For, within a week, a dramatic development took place.

We were in the great hall, myself and my Master, alone. We were, as we often were, discussing his wife. For a change, I felt I was making real progress. My Master had been free of humoral imbalance for a week, and was most reasonable. I argued that the current situation was intolerable: while they lived in the same household, they rarely met. She rarely left her chambers, took her meals in her room, and ventured into the court only when she knew her husband would not be there. He, on the other hand, had allowed his suspicions to blossom without ever confronting her. After lengthy argument, he agreed to visit his wife. But at that moment, an attendant entered the hall and said that my Mistress had urgently requested my presence. I therefore took my leave of my Master, and hastened to my Mistress's chambers. I found her there reading a book. She was delighted to see me, but told me she had not sent for me. I immediately understood that there was some dirty business afoot, and dashed back to the great hall. There, sitting with my

Master were the witch and the vermin. My Master turned his gaze to me, with eyes glazed as though in a trance.

"Ah, Ludovico, come, we were just talking about you." His words were welcoming, but his voice was flat and expressionless. He sat on the edge of his chair, his back straight and stiff, as still as a statue – except for his hands, which fidgeted on his lap incessantly. To his left, the vermin sat, the hint of a smug smile on his lips; to his right, the witch, whose face was contorted into a mask of suffering, as though she was about to break into tears.

I bowed deeply. "I am at your service, my Lord."

My Master spoke as through from a prewritten script, without shifting his eyes. "We were talking about the violin. As you know, I have wanted one since I first heard it at your doctor's."

"Yes, my Lord."

"I have decided to send you to Cremona, to order the construction of a chest of violins, and to bring them back."

I went pale. "That is quite impossible, my Lord. You are not well, and I have taken upon myself to treat you, according to the doctor's instructions. It would be extremely dangerous to your own person were I to abandon your treatment now."

My Master said nothing for a few moments. He turned his head stiffly towards the vermin, this without bending his back or ceasing the constant fidget of his hands. The vermin looked him sternly in the eye. He turned his head back to me, still without changing the frozen, expressionless gaze of his eyes.

"My attendant Don Pietro will continue the treatment. You will instruct him in the preparation of the potions. And you will instruct Maestro Bartolomeo to continue his musical therapy."

"My Lord," I replied, "I see you are not in a free state of mind right now. I shall wait and discuss this with you tomorrow, when you are feeling better."

Again, my Master turned to the vermin, who again stared and nodded at him sternly. He returned his sightless gaze to me.

"My mind is made up. You shall leave tonight."

I looked desperately for excuses. "My Lord, this is a very difficult and dangerous journey. I cannot undertake it alone. I will discuss this with your chancellor and head of the guard, and will see what arrangements can be made. It would be impossible to depart before a few days have elapsed."

Like an automaton, my Master again turned to the vermin to receive instructions. "All has been arranged. The captain of the guard, Ascanio Lama, will accompany you."

In a flash I understood. Ascanio Lama, a solid block of a man, a man of no mercy and no morals, who had murdered dozens in the service of the Prince, was, I had no doubt, given the mandate to murder me as soon as we left the castle. This was, you may recall, the same Ascanio Lama I had retrieved sleeping in a Neapolitan alley a year prior. I had to buy time until I could speak to my Master when he had emerged from his trance.

"I shall speak with Don Pietro Bardotti, and explain the treatments. But these are not simple potions, it will take me at least a few days to teach him the proper preparation."

The vermin rose from his chair. "You have been given a direct order from your Master," he said. He was trying to make his wheedling voice sound commanding and authoritative, but in his reedy tenor he sounded only ridiculous.

"I shall serve my Master as I see fit," I replied, with venom in my voice.

"You shall do as you are commanded," said the vermin. "How dare you defy your Master's will?"

I turned to my Master. "My Lord, your mind is not free. I will wait and speak to you when you are more in command of yourself."

My Master replied as though the vermin were implanting the words in his mouth. "Don Giulio is correct. It is not for you to judge the state of my mind. It is insubordinate, treasonous." These words, so loaded, were yet spoken in a flat, toneless voice that belied the total subjugation of my Master's will to the vermin and the witch.

135

"I command you to go, and to leave tonight. I bid you farewell." And now, his lip quivered and I saw a tear in his eye. "Farewell, Ludovico, my friend."

I bowed and walked out of the hall. There was nothing to be done. My Master had indeed given a direct command, and, though every cell in my body rebelled. I had no choice but to obey. And to obey, I believed, meant going to my death; and leaving my Master to a fate unknown, but a fate worse than death.

LIB

m'inuolate hor chi redete il core

On one count, at least, I was wrong: I was not sent to my death. Don Ascanio, murderous and violent as he was, was given no mandate to murder me. On the contrary, the trip was as great a surprise to him as it was to me. My Master had called him to the great hall immediately after me, and instructed him to accompany me. Don Ascanio, unlike myself, was delighted; new lands meant new drunken rivals to do battle with, strange wines to quaff, exotic women to debauch.

I really never had grounds to fear. For Don Ascanio was as devoted to me as a mutt collected from the street is devoted to its master. Ever since I had recovered his insensate body from that alley in Naples, he felt he owed me a debt of gratitude that bound him to me forever. Don Ascanio was of Sicilian ancestry, which would explain the extremes of his affections. It would also explain his physical strength. He was entirely square: square head atop a torso as thick and square as a brick, legs straight and square as brick chimneys. His hands were larger than most men's feet, his fingers short and fat, with narrow fingernails outlined by a narrow black line of grime. He had, apparently, no sensation of pain. I saw him pummeled mercilessly in a bar fight by five men, on his face, his eyes, his nose, his genitals, without a flicker of his eyelid, before he hammered the lot of them to the floor. This fight I witnessed in Bari. We arrived in Bari from Gesualdo, and from there sailed to Venice, on our way to Cremona. As luck would have it, we sailed at dawn the day after the fight. Lucky, because the local constabulary was looking to arrest the victor, because one of the vanquished, suffering from a smashed eye socket, was a minor baron with connections in the police.

Incidentally, as tough as Don Ascanio was, he had no stomach for the sea, and spent the entire four days sail from Bari to Venice leaning over the rail and spewing the contents of his mostly empty stomach into the dark green water.

m'inuolate hor mi redete il core

The ninth day of February, Year of Our Lord 1590

Venice

To His Excellency Carlo Prince of Gesualdo, Count of Conza, Marquis of Laino Rotondo, Duke of Caggiano, Prince of Venosa:

May God grant my fervent prayers for your well-being and prosperity! I write to inform you that your devoted servant and his bodyguard have arrived in Venice. However, an unfortunate circumstance has caused a serious disruption in our travels. Don Ascanio became regrettably involved in a brawl, and killed a man. The man was, unfortunately, a cousin to a member of the Great Council, and the constabulary is demanding 800 ducats for his release. As I do not have this sum readily available, I beg you to advise me how to proceed.

I will not burden your Excellency with details of how Don Ascanio got involved in the melee that led to his arrest, nor shall I regale you with tales of Venice. Suffice it to say that Venice is a remarkable place in every respect, and that the music here is of exceptional interest. And I hope and pray that when the Good Lord sees fit to restore you to full health, you will visit here and see for yourself.

I await your instructions.

Your humble servant

Ludovico Forcella

m'inuolate hor mi redete il core

This 19th day of February, Year of Our Lord 1590

Gesualdo

Don Ludovico Forcella

My friend Ludovico,

Our Master has asked me to write this reply to your letter. I must tell you that your letter brought tears to his eyes. "Why did I send him away?" he lamented. When I suggested that you recall him to Gesualdo, he heaved a heavy sigh, but was unwilling or unable to give the command for your return. Alas, the influence of the witch is still bearing heavily on his soul.

However, I must give you this good news: I have expelled the faux priest Giulio from Gesualdo. Two days after your departure, and without consulting our Master, I went to the blackguard's room before dawn, grabbed him by the collar of his nightshirt, and marched him to the stable, set him upon a horse, and, accompanied by two of the Prince's guards, sent him off to Naples, with orders never to return.

The removal of this vermin, as you call him, had an immediate and salubrious effect on our Master. Some of his vitality returned, his descents into depression – already mitigated by the treatments prescribed by the doctor and by yourself – have become yet milder. For sure, the influence of the witch is still bearing heavily upon him and, indeed, on the entire court. But there is unquestionably an overall improvement in our Master's mood and function. And most important, he has ceased to obsess over the absurd slanders of his wife's infidelity. True, he still has not visited her, but I would not be surprised if such a visit were to occur in the next few days or weeks.

I should also note that, surprisingly, our Master has not remarked the absence of the faux priest, despite the fact that prior to his exile, he was a frequent and dominant presence in the court.

Our Master beseeches you to abandon your reticence and send him detailed descriptions of every moment of your journey. For, while, on the one hand, your letter caused him much regret and longing for your company, he yearns to hear from you. So, my friend, write! Fear not the prolix!

As for the problem of Don Ascanio, our Master asks that you show the attached letter to the Jew Abraham Ben Shaul, who will provide you with the 800 ducats required for Don Ascanio's release.

Finally, while I have written this response, I suggest that you continue to address your letters directly to our Master. If he does not respond in his own hand, it is because he is still too preoccupied or conflicted to do so.

Your friend and servant,
Pietro Bardotti

m'inuolate hor mi tédete il core

This second day of March, Year of Our Lord 1590

Venice

To His Excellency Carlo Prince of Gesualdo, Count of Conza, Marquis of Laino Rotondo, Duke of Caggiano, Prince of Venosa:

May God grant my fervent prayers for your well-being and prosperity! I send you the good news that your servant Don Ascanio has been freed from prison. Our journey, alas, has been further delayed, for while in prison, he contracted an ague, and has been unable to travel. I believe the disease will pass in a week or two, and we shall continue our way to Cremona. I ordered a doctor to examine him, and he prescribed a vile-smelling concoction that he called teriaca, but I have little faith in its curative powers. Indeed, the doctors here seem all to be the basest quacks. This doctor, for example, detected blood in Don Ascanio's urine, and concluded he was suffering from an inflammation of the kidney. He put forth the absurd notion that the function of the kidney is not, as we all know, to produce black bile and modulate melancholy, but to purify the blood and produce urine! How can you put faith in someone who believes something so ridiculous? Nonetheless, I am optimistic that Don Ascanio shall recover, through his own bodily curative powers if not through the ministrations of this mountebank.

The story of Don Ascanio's arrest is this: Venice, as you may know, is a city of canals and bridges. Some of the largest bridges are commandeered by gangs of thugs, who charge a toll to cross. These gangs bear an intense animosity to each other, and often do battle for control of the bridges. Upon our arrival in Venice, Don

Ascanio set off for the nearest public house to consume prodigious quantities of wine such as only Sicilians can consume without collapsing. It was there he befriended members of one of these gangs, who were plotting the overthrow of a rival gang to control one of these bridges. Don Ascanio, with the option of a brawl at hand, naturally readily volunteered his services, and the thugs set off to do battle. The objective of these battles is to toss your rivals into the canal. Should you fall into the canal, you should pray to drown quickly; for, should you be drawn from the water alive, you shall die anyway within three to five days, in the most exquisite pain, with blood and vomit pouring from your mouth and nose and ears. This disease, canal pestilence the locals call it, fells almost everyone who is immersed in these noxious waters; and, if you survive, you will be blind and feeble-minded, and will have to be set out with a cup to beg.

Venice is the most beautiful of cities, built on the most pestilent of swamps. The Venetians have built palaces and piazzas of the most magnificent and graceful design, the most artful construction, and executed by the artisans the finest of all Christendom. The waters they have channeled into canals, that serve as their streets. Boatmen – mostly Moors – paddle long, graceful craft with a single oar. It is a site of beauty and grace to see.

On the other hand, the waters of these canals are so fetid that the entire city is enveloped in a vile stench. In the back canals, where the water is completely stagnant and filled with sewerage, the stink is so bad that it is impossible to move about without covering your mouth and nose with a kerchief. In the broader canals, there is, apparently, a mild current so that the filth is less. Nonetheless, the stench is pervasive, though the Venetians themselves are so inured to it that they seem not to notice. But, then, these Venetians are strange in many ways. For example, they speak a type of Italian so barbarous that it surprises me how they can understand each other.

Indeed, after Don Ascanio's arrest, I applied for an audience with Leonardo da Ponte, the victim's cousin who had ordered the incarceration. He had set the blood ransom at 600 ducats. The interview took a long time, for I had great difficulty understanding him and making myself understood. But I finally succeeded in making him understand that the culprit was in the service of your Excellency. He was familiar with the Gesualdo name (though, of course, he had no inkling of your musical genius), and promptly raised the blood payment to 800 ducats. I was affronted by this – did he have no respect for the Gesualdo family? "Respect yes. But respect is not an issue here," he said. "Gesualdo is so rich, 600 ducats is a piss in the pot for him." So, while little of value was achieved by this interview, at least I now know how to say "piss in the pot" in the Venetian dialect.

I mentioned your musical genius, yet I have so far told you nothing about the music of this city. Well, the music here is not merely good, it is astonishing. I went to hear a mass in their Cathedral, San Marco. They have choir bays with consorts and wind bands scattered strategically throughout the cathedral. The groups sing in antiphony – that is, one group sings, then passes the music to the next group. As the cathedral has a strong and long resonance, the concluding tones of the one group are still ringing through the hall as the next group begins, creating an ethereal sense of floating in an ocean of sound. Moreover, the wind bands accompany the singers – something unheard of in the south. Our vocal ensembles are always a capella, never accompanied. Indeed, it is a violation of church canon to allow instrumental accompaniment in holy music, as it makes the words unintelligible. And, as a matter of fact, the words of this incredible music are impossible to make out (not only because of the barbarous pronunciation). But these Venetians care not a whit for the laws of the church, they are in fact a Godless and rebellious lot, who often speak freely against the church. Be that as it may, I have never felt so uplifted by sacred music. My spine tingled for its entire length, my hair bristled, and my limbs felt as though they were being lifted by angels.

My Lord, I do hope and pray that the day will come when you are well enough to journey here, to hear this incredible music.

Don Pietro tells me that your state is much improved. Allow me to exhort you to take your medicines, unpleasant though they may be. Of course, my greatest wish would be for you to expel the witch who has enslaved your mind and body, if necessary with the aid of an exorcist. I fear this wish is bootless, knowing how thoroughly she has insinuated herself into the very fiber of your being. Barring her expulsion, I beseech you to return to composing. Your music, My Lord, is, I believe, the most powerful palliative that can weaken her hold on you, and, eventually, free you.

If you send me a manuscript of some new work, I can show it to people here. For, as I have said, the Gesualdo name is known here, but people have no inkling of your musical creations.

My Lord, you asked for details, and I hope you will excuse my poor powers of description in my attempts to fulfill your wish.

I pray daily for your well-being and for a full reconciliation between you and your beloved wife, to whom I ask that you deliver my heartfelt regard.

Your servant,

Ludovico Forcella

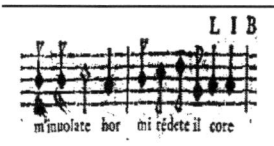

LIB

m'inuolate hor mi tedete il core

This 10*th* day of March, Year of Our Lord 1590

Gesualdo

To my devoted servant and friend, Ludovico Forcella

My Dear Ludovico,

Your letter gave me great joy, and brought tears to my eyes by reminding me of my sorry state. How right you are that I am a slave to this witch, and unable to free myself from her clutches.

I find myself too weak and too overwrought to write you a long letter. There is so much I wish to tell you, indeed, to recall you to Gesualdo. But even this I cannot do.

However, I have taken your suggestion, and have resumed composition. I find it now takes me much longer to write a simple tune, but with perseverance I have succeeded. I send you a copy of this, as you have suggested, as a sample of my work to show to others. But, more than that, I am hoping for your advice and encouragement. Friends I have few – Don Pietro, Don Fabrizio, yourself – but in matters musical I trust no one but you.

Your Master and Friend,

Don Carlo Prince of Gesualdo

m'inuolate hor mi redete il core

Enclosed with this letter was a manuscript. With hands shaking in anticipation, I took the pages and read through the music. It was so complex and unconventional that I had trouble reconstructing the sound of it in my mind, and had to read it through several times before my inner ear could hear it. At first, I thought it was like nothing I had ever heard, by far the most bizarre piece my Master had ever written. Gradually I came to understand it. My mouth went dry, there was a lump in my throat. My hands grew clammy, a cold sweat broke on my brow. This music was terrifying. I recognized its source – it was the music of the witches, the music we heard that fateful night in the forest. Not identical, mind – no, it was a new creation by my Master's bewitched mind, in the strange, frightening style of the witches. Music with no modal or tonal center, music that defied all the laws of composition; music that challenged our very notion of what music is. Visceral, terrifying, captivating. The music, strange, depressing, was ideally suited to the words:

Moro, lasso, al mio duolo,
e chi può darmi vita,
ahi, che m'ancide e non vuol darmi aita!
O dolorosa sorte,
chi dar vita mi può,
ahi, mi dà morte!

I die, alas, in my suffering,
And she who could give me life,
Alas, kills me and will not help me.
O sorrowful fate,
She who could give me life,
Alas, gives me death.

My tears flowed freely as I came to understand this strange and beautiful new music. Listening to it, I understood the prison in which my Master lived, the prison that cramped his soul; and the inner musical voice that, should he succeed in freeing it, could change forever the way we hear music.

This 11th day of March, Year of Our Lord 1590

Gesualdo

To my servant and friend Ludovico Forcella

My dear Ludovico,

I am distraught. I heard the camerata rehearsing a new madrigal. With great joy in my heart, I understood that my husband had returned to his composition. I went down to the great hall, where they were singing. I listened intently.

This music was nothing like the beautiful madrigals my husband wrote when he was courting me. It was strange, frightening. I tried to make sense of the harmonies, to no avail. But I cannot say I was unmoved – on the contrary, I felt a knot in my stomach and a dryness in my mouth.

I then listened carefully to the words. They were hard to make out because the different voices moved about so unpredictably. But as I came to understand, it added immeasurably to my terror. "She who could give me life, alas kills me and will not help me." Dear God, is he writing about me? Am I killing him? Does he wish to be free of me?

O, Ludovico, I am in the depths of despair. If this is what he wishes – to be free of me – I will leave tomorrow. For I love him so, I would gladly die if it would make him whole again.

Your Friend,

Maria of Gesualdo

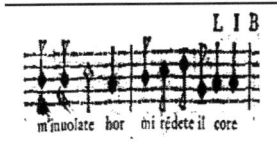

This 22nd day of March, Year of Our Lord 1590

Brescia

To my Mistress Donna Maria Princess of Gesualdo

My Dear Mistress,

I do not know if what I have to tell you will please or disappoint – a little of both, I suppose.

The subject of this composition is not yourself, but the witch. It is she that my Master wishes would leave or die. It is she that is stealing his life, it is she that causes his suffering, it is she who gives him death.

Rest assured that his estrangement from you is the result of a diseased mind, a mind vanquished by an evil curse. I assure you that his greatest wish – a wish that he, alas, cannot express – is to be free of this curse and return to your bosom. And let me encourage you that our friend Don Pietro has opened a small window of hope; for he has written me that, with the expulsion of the faux priest Giulio Gesualdo, our Master's mind is somewhat eased. Witness to this is that he has returned to his composing table.

Your reaction to this madrigal – fear – was, indeed, the same as mine. I, like you, felt an intense physical reaction to this music, as though a snake was winding across the floor toward me. I thought of your terrifying dream of being enveloped in vermin. You are right that this is unlike any music that went before. It is born of the cursed disease of his mind, and, while it is terrifying and perverted, I believe it is also momentous. For I have never been so moved. God alone knows where this will lead.

Your friend and servant,

Ludovico

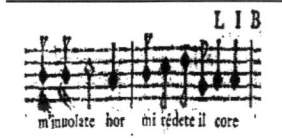

After I arranged Don Ascanio's release from the Venetian dungeon, and nursed him to health so we could continue our travels, he became – if that were possible – even more devoted to me than before. He took to calling me "Master", even though, in the formal hierarchy of the court he outranked me. His devotion to me was so total, that it bordered on the ridiculous.

Before we set out for Cremona from Venice, I called him for a stern talk. "My dear Ascanio, from now on not a drop of liquor shall pass your lips."

"Yes, Master," he replied, standing at attention, but with his head hanging like a reprimanded cur.

"And you shall strike no man except I give you explicit instruction."

"Yes, Master."

"I shan't be bailing you out of prison again, do you understand? Next time, you are in for good."

"Yes, Master."

"Now go and prepare the horses."

And so we set off for Cremona, Don Ascanio much chastised. But, resolved as he was, his violent nature ran deep, and I knew there would be no restraining him forever. The following incident will demonstrate this.

The road led through Padua, Vicenza, Brescia. The road was quite well maintained for most of the route, for the King of Spain had recently made a visit and the roads were repaired for his passage. However, it was a most annoying passage, for, at every bridge and every crossroads there was an armed *cavalliere* who extracted a toll for the local Lord. Our guide, whom we did not completely trust in this matter, made a small show of negotiating with the soldier, and then assured us that he had bargained him down to the lowest possible rate. Helpless to dispute, we paid and went our way. This proved to be time consuming and expensive, and immensely aggravating. When we reached the bridge over the river Oglio, the soldier, mounted on his horse, and armed with sword and mace, demanded a full ducat to cross. At this, Don Ascanio lost his temper, rose, and went to strike. I let out a cry, "Don Ascanio, you shall not touch that man. Did you not promise to strike no person without my explicit direction?"

Don Ascanio paused in his march, a mix of emotions contorting his features. On the one hand, his fury at these, truly unreasonable, demands, and on the other hand, his dogged obedience to me. Finally, he approached the soldier, pulled back his arm, and threw a tremendous blow just below the horse's eye socket. There was a sickening crunch, the horse staggered backwards several steps, weaving left and right, and then her knees buckled and she tumbled to the floor in a heap, with the soldier ignominiously cast into the mud. There he sat speechless, and we proceeded to cross the bridge unimpeded. I must admit, this was an imaginative resolution of Don Ascanio's quandary – for he struck no man, yet gave violent release to his anger and frustration, and ensured our safe passage.

Alas, it was clear that such imaginative solutions would not abide us forever, and the day was not distant when Don Ascanio would again lead us to trouble. And, indeed, not two months of our sojourn in Cremona had passed, when Don Ascanio's resolve to do my bidding was overwhelmed by his own stubborn nature, he stole out of our apartments to the public house, filled himself with wine as only a Sicilian can, and, weaving his way home, encountered the *cavallieri* of the *gonfaloniere*. This was not far from our residence, and I heard the fracas from my window. By the time I descended, four of the soldiers were sprawled insensate on the ground. "Halt, Don Ascanio. Desist immediately!" At the sound of my voice, Don Ascanio froze like a statue, as did the remaining two soldiers, who were standing warily, a safe distance from the savage, their swords drawn.

Had I not intervened, heavens knows what the outcome might have been – possibly the two of us could be expelled from Cremona, thus putting an awkward end to my mission. However, at this point Don Ascanio meekly cast his eyes down, and the two soldiers – still keeping a safe distance behind him – directed him to the prison.

For the next three years, I dutifully visited my bodyguard in his cell once a week. The authorities were in something of a quandary as to what to do with him – on the one hand, he was a violent criminal who had attacked the constabulary; on the other hand, he was a senior official of one of the richest and most powerful families of the peninsula (albeit from the South). So the *gonfaloniere* took the most prudent course. He did nothing: did not bring Don Ascanio to trial, and did not release him. This was fine with me, for I had no sentiments about his imprisonment. After three years had passed, I negotiated his release, and traveled with him to Ferrara, where my Master was now residing.

Indeed, in the four months since I departed Gesualdo, I had undergone a momentous change. For the first time in my adult life, I was not in the orbit of my Master. I had lived – indeed all of us in the court had lived – like moths circling a flame. But that flame was not a flickering candle, it was a fiery ball of violent, sulphuric eruption, that colored our every moment and sucked us inexorably into its vortex. Every violent mood, every perversion, every inspired moment of musical creation, found its reflection in the soul of each of his retainers. And the witch's curse had not infected the mind of my Master only; it had cast a pall on the entire court, and on the entire principality of Gesualdo.

And now I was free of this. It was a new and exhilarating – and, indeed, confusing – period. For, though I reveled in this newfound freedom, my soul was tied to that of my Master by bonds stronger than service. I was not only his servant, I was his friend, his consort in music, his closest confidante, his confessor. It was, perhaps, our tie of music that was the strongest – for we both felt the same visceral thrill when we heard music we loved, and, foremost, the music that my Master created.

Be that as it may, it was clear that I was embarking on a new phase of my life. I quickly established myself in Cremona, making new friends, and finding valuable ways to fill my time while I awaited the manufacture of my Master's instruments. I had planned to apply to the brothers Amati, Antonio and Girolamo, who carried on the luthier business established by their father. I arrived at Antonio's shop, believing it to be that of the brothers. I was greeted with frost by a crusty and unpleasant old man – not so old in years as in character – who dismissed me out of hand. "I have two years of back orders," he said curtly. "Come to me in another year, perhaps then we can talk." He refused to say what had happened to his brother, but an inquiry at the public house revealed the truth: the brothers had quarreled two years ago, and Don Antonio had left and set up his own atelier across town. I went to visit the original studio, now used exclusively by the younger brother, and found a man of entirely different character. Jovial, receptive, Don Girolamo greeted me with a warm handshake, and within minutes we were more friends than client and artisan.

"I am instructed by my Master to remain in Cremona until I have six violins to bring him," I said.

"I fear you will have a long wait," replied Don Girolamo. "Everyone wants violins today, and there are only three or four *liutai* who know the secret of their construction. I myself have orders from the King of France (who has already received 30 instruments), from the King of Spain, from the Queen of England, not to mention my near neighbors the D'Estes in Ferrara, the Medicis in Florence, the Gonzagas of Mantua, the Doge in Venice. It will take me a year to supply your order.

"But do not despair. Since you are here for a while, join us at the *accademia* this evening. The Duke will be delighted to meet you."

The *Accademmia dei Animosi* met in the town hall of Cremona. The Duke, His Grace Asdrubale Anguissola, was a tall, aristocratic looking gentleman, with high forehead and aquiline nose. He was dressed in the Spanish style, with a jet-black over-jacket and a massive ruff of pure white linen, starched so it stood like a board and forced him to hold his head in an artificially erect position. He greeted us in Latin. Girolamo replied readily, and I dredged up my indifferent Latin to make an appropriate reply. Luckily, the rest of the evening was in Italian; I don't know how I would have fared if I had been expected to chitchat in Latin.

Among the guests was the young Claudio Monteverdi. Monteverdi was quite the prodigy: at 23, he had already published two books of madrigals and a number of part books for three and four voices. He would go on to be the innovator of opera, a style that, as I have mentioned before, I execrated. But at that time he was still a musician and composer of marked conservative bent, and his madrigals – which I later read and performed in consort with him – had none of the imagination and daring of my Master's.

Girolamo had brought a violin for my use. The musical part of the *accademia* consisted of myself and Girolamo on violin, Monteverdi on theorbo, and His Grace on cembalo. We played some *canzonetti* by Salamone Rossi, a new composer from Mantua, which we found delightful. His Grace was a more than passable cembalist. We then had a spirited discussion of polyphony and its place in sacred music. Monteverdi argued vociferously that the more advanced forms of polyphony had no place in the Church.

"The Council has determined that polyphony obfuscates the words," he argued. "The words are paramount. The music is only to serve the message."

"Then why not merely recite?" I said. "Why have music at all?" And I answered my own question: "The music does not serve the message; the music is what conveys the message. When a king enters the hall in his nightshirt, he is still the king; but when he enters in his regal robes, with scepter and orb and crown, he is not merely king, he is regal."

In fact, Monteverdi in his music assiduously adhered to the Church's edict, just as my own Master assiduously ignored it. And I would take my Master's music over Monteverdi's any day.

But Monteverdi's opinion in this matter was not merely a matter of ideology; it was a matter of character. For, in all things, the young composer was dogmatic to the point of obsessive, dour and complaining. He was lanky, with a long, narrow face and eyebrows arched in a look of perpetual disapproval. He was especially critical of Cremona, which he considered a provincial backwater lacking in culture, an impediment to his considerable talent. He had been trying anxiously to find a position in Mantua or Brescia, so far without success.

"It has been more than a month since I wrote to the Duke of Mantua, and have heard no reply," he complained testily at dinner.

"My dear Claudio," said His Grace, "Have some patience! Surely you know the Duke is preoccupied with the war against the Turks. He may soon have to take the field himself, and Lord knows how he will fare."

"Well, he might have the courtesy to reply," said Monteverdi, picking at his food. "That would be the proper thing to do."

This preoccupation with dogma and propriety struck me as odd, as his father, who was also at table with us, was quite the opposite. Jovial, optimistic and open-minded, Baldassare Monteverdi was a doctor, who, it seemed to me, was quite open to the latest ideas. He mentioned the theory that the role of the kidneys was the purification of the blood and the production of urine, the theory that I had previously scoffed at.

"But we have known for a thousand years the kidneys are the receptacle of black bile," I said. This I had learned from my mentor and friend, *Il Dottore* Moise Amani.

"Yes, that is what Galen wrote," replied Don Baldassare. "But the northerner Vesalius has dissected the human body and discovered the actual tubes that bear the urine from the kidneys to the bladder."

His son looked at him with extreme distaste. I understood him – for even I was jolted, if not offended, by this gross trespass of canon law prohibiting dissection. Don Baldassare smiled.

"These Northerners are a Godless band. Protestants. They have no respect for the laws of the true church. But never mind – in their sin, they have made great advances in our understanding of the human body. Quite revolutionary, really."

In one matter, however, the younger Monteverdi was right: Cremona was, indeed, a backwater provincial town. For a place that was known world-wide as the center of musical instrument manufactory, there were surprisingly few musicians. There was the *capella* of the cathedral, with its 10 singers (Claudio Monteverdi was one of them). The local aristocracy kept no *camerata*. The *piffari* – the town musicians – were five mediocre wind players who were drunk most of the time, and played horribly out of tune. This was one of the reasons that my appearance in the town was welcomed so felicitously. I immediately became a permanent guest at the *accademia*, and His Grace compensated me respectably (if not lavishly) for my performances there. Don Girolamo also brought me new instruments to try out. He himself played only indifferently, and he was eager to hear how his violins sounded in the hands of a competent player. He was constantly innovating in his design, varying the thickness of the top, the position of the bass bar and the *anima* (the soundpost wedged between the belly and the back of the instrument), adjusting the shape of the F-holes and the dimensions of the body. With each experiment, he gave me the new instrument, and we discussed the resulting tone. For this, he paid me a commission.

What was much more momentous for the future course of my life was my introduction by Girolamo to Frederico d'Abruzzo, a local maker of instrument strings. He, too, was constantly experimenting to find the best combination of weight, twist, density and material to produce the finest tones. With each batch of new catgut, he would give me a set of strings. I would set up one of Don Girolamo's violins, and we would together analyze the effects.

It was, however, not because of his strings that my meeting with him was momentous. It was because of his daughter, Beatrice. The moment I set eyes upon her, I was smitten, and knew I wanted to marry her. She was a true Southern beauty, with olive skin that glowed like the lacquer on one of Girolamo's violins, black hair as smooth as silk, sparkling brown eyes, and a shy, engaging smile. She was working aside her father in the yard behind their home when I first saw her, scraping the sheep guts to extract the fine *filo* fibers that ran the length of the intestines, and that made up the raw material for catgut strings. It was hard and unpleasant work; the intestines stank, and they were soaking in a foul solution made from the dregs of wine barrels, which burned the eyes and hands. But Beatrice worked hard, and smiled brightly at me when she saw me. We had little opportunity to chat, but I felt instinctively, from that very first encounter, that she felt about me as I did about her. Being an orphan, I applied to His Grace to act as a go-between, and he quickly negotiated an agreement to wed.

Dear reader, I fear I have carried on a bit about my reception to Cremona. This memoir is about Don Carlo Gesualdo, and not about me. But I feel you must understand how I became so rapidly acclimated and accepted in my new home, in order to understand the following letter that I sent to my Master on the 15th of May, Year of our Lord 1590:

To your most Serene Lord, Your Excellency the Prince of Gesualdo, Prince of Venosa, Count of Conza, Marquis of Laino Rotondo, Duke of Caggiano:

May God grant my most fervent prayers for the health and prosperity of you and your Beloved Wife.

My Lord, it is with the most powerful feelings of trepidation and joy that I lay my most humble plea at your illustrious feet. Trepidation, for I fear that my suit might, God Forbid, place a pall on the deep obligation of servitude I feel toward you, indeed, the deep bond of friendship and of music that binds us inexorably together. Joy because what I come to ask is the consequence of a great and uplifting change that has stirred me to the very quick in the last few months.

I shall come directly to the point: I love. I have met the woman whom I wish to marry and with whom I dream of cojoining 'til the day of our death. And, to my boundless joy, she has agreed to my suit, and consented to marry me. I therefore beg you, with all humility and respect, to allow your devoted servant to marry this woman.

My Lord, this suit is the motive force of my being since my arrival in Cremona. But this love has engendered other changes which have affected me so deeply that I know not how to express them in this letter. For in Cremona, in its people, in the scent of its air, in the beauty of the instruments that it produces, I have found a new home. My bride to be is bound to this town by ties of family. I myself have found, in the brief span of two months, a people so receptive, so serene, that I feel as though I have come home.

My Lord, nothing on earth can mitigate the love I feel for you, can weaken the ties of music and love that bind us. But since my arrival in Cremona, I feel I have come home.

I therefore humbly beg of your Excellency to release me from your service, and allow me to reestablish my life in the town of my bride and mistress.

Know that I would never ask this of you, had I not had assurances from my friend and your servant Don Pietro Bardotti that your condition is steadily improving, that you have returned to composition, and have, to my great delight and relief, resumed concourse with your wife, may God grant her years of happiness in the glow of your Excellency's aura. For your welfare is far more valuable to me than my own insignificant happiness. But, knowing that you are on the road to recovery from the awful curse of the witch, I have gathered the courage, and, indeed, the audacity, to place this suit by your humble servant at your glorious feet.

Be assured, that, should you agree to my release from service, though I will no longer be your servant, I shall always be your friend. And I shall continue to visit, to write, and to offer you the same support, in friendship and in music, that it has been my good fortune to provide you until now.

Your servant and devoted friend,

Ludovico Forcella

It was with considerable trepidation that I submitted this plea. For one thing, I had no doubt that his condition had not improved, despite my friend Don Pietro's assurances to the contrary. So long as the witch cast her appalling spell upon my Master, any show of improvement was bound to be superficial. True, the vermin Giulio was out of the picture, and that removed any immediate danger to his person and that of his wife. But the situation was fundamentally unstable, and, in light of the profound warnings my mentor Doctor Moise had given me, I had no reason to believe my Master was on the road to recovery.

My comment that he had resumed concourse with his wife was also a distortion. I had received three accounts of his encounter with Donna Maria: from her, from Don Pietro, and from my Master himself. The facts are these: My Master met his wife in the great hall, quite by accident. She had descended from her chambers to hear the *capella* rehearse. My Master saw her, and was too overcome with emotion to speak. He went to her, and embraced her wordlessly. He then rushed to his own chambers, closed the door, and, by his own testimony to me, shook uncontrollably in his whole body for several minutes. He then stripped off his chemise, knelt by the cross, took his rope and beat himself on the back until the blood came. "The pain was so great," he wrote, "I grew faint. I turned and saw the witch standing by the door. Her lips were turned up in a strange forced smile. Tears were streaming from her eyes. Her hands were shaking."

This, I aver, is not a resumption of concourse with his wife.

Moreover, I knew the depth of my Master's dependence on my support. True, I was now forcibly expelled from his physical presence. But our correspondence (which I have not reproduced here) was at least twice weekly – me writing long descriptive letters of life here, and he mostly baring his soul in his misery and subjugation. He had sent me a few more of his compositions, as well, and eagerly sought my opinion. So, while I specifically wrote that our correspondence and our friendship would continue, I suspected that he would feel bereft and abandoned were I to leave his service.

In any case, his reply did not tarry.

The 21st day of May, Year of Our Lord 1590

Gesualdo

To my servant and friend, Ludovico Forcella

My Dear Ludovico,

I know not where to begin this letter. For your letter to me filled me – as, you say, it did you – with dread and joy in equal measures. Here, let me begin with the easiest part: of course I grant you my permission to wed, and, such as may be a blessing from a man living under the curse of the Damned, my blessing.

As for your second request: I believe I have answered that, as well. For I am a man living under the curse of the Damned. Your conjecture that my condition is improving is wrong. I am as oppressed as from the day I drank the lady's menstrual blood from her lips. I am awakened by the red dream at least twice a night. Don Pietro does not hear my cries, because the witch stifles them by sitting on my face until the foul stench of her fica overwhelms the terror of drowning in red velvet. While I am no longer under the deceptions woven by my cousin Giulio, I am still unable to address my wife.

O, Ludovico, sending you away was the most terrible punishment that the witch could inflict on me. How I wish I could have you at my side again. How can I bring myself to give you the order to return? How can I impose my own will on that of the damned creature that rules me?

And now you yourself no longer wish to return. Few friends had I: you, Don Fabrizio, my wife. Now I cannot speak to my wife, you are gone, and Don Fabrizio spends his days in Naples while I waste away here. Don Pietro? He is so dependable, so efficient, so wise, so dedicated; but a friend? I could not call him that.

No, I am alone. I and my witch. I and the rope I use to beat myself.

And so, no, I cannot release you from my service. I cannot make you want to return to me. But I can make you return.

But I shan't. Remain in Cremona. Continue to be my servant. I shall continue to send your letter of exchange monthly. Make your life there.

But the day will come when I shall need you at my side. When that day comes, if it is in my power to command, I will call for you. And, as my servant, you shall come.

I am sorry. I cannot do your bidding. This is the best I can do.

Carlo Gesualdo

My Master – yes, he would continue to be my Master – enclosed two new madrigals, which, like *Moro, Lasso*, were strange and terrifying and mesmerizing. If anything could awaken in me the ties that bound me to him, it was these manuscripts. I felt a tinge of conscience that I had even presumed to ask for my release; yet, pulling in the opposite direction were the new feelings of freedom and love that drew me to this new place.

On reflection, my Master's letter promised me the best of all worlds. I would continue to live my life here, with my new wife and my new friends. I would be free to work and develop as I saw fit; yet my ties to the Master who had become part of me would not be severed. Moreover, financially this was a great boon: I would continue to draw my handsome salary and expenses. I would supplement this with the modest but sufficient income I earned from commissions and from my appearances at the *accademia*. I would continue to receive my rents from my father's house in Naples. I had become a man of means.

Beatrice and I married. We wasted no time. At the end of June – the 30th of June – we took the vows of holy matrimony.

m'inuolate hor mi redete il core

October 1st, Year of Our Lord 1590

Naples

To my friend Ludovico Forcella

My Dear Ludovico,

I beseech you to return to Naples immediately. A terrible turn of events has put us on the brink of disaster, and the Master needs you by his side.

His Eminence, our Master's uncle, visited Gesualdo. He brought with him the vermin Giulio. They ordered our Master to move immediately to Naples. His Eminence instructed our Master to instate Giulio as his confessor. Our Master called me, and in a voice entranced, as was his voice when he ordered your exile, instructed me to move the court to San Severo.

We have been in Naples two weeks. Giulio has reinfected our Master's mind with his ludicrous slanders against our Lady. Our Master's soul is as one obsessed, now ranting, now weeping, now retiring to his chamber and self-flagellating. He does not sleep – I hear his cries through the night, only periodically stifled, I presume by the witch. During the day he frequently calls your name in distraction.

Come, my friend. Come now. Do not tarry. It may already be too late.

Pietro Barlotti

My wife had missed her time for two months now, and showed all the symptoms of being with our child. I had been invited to attend an *accademia* in Mantua, together with Monteverdi. We were to perform with a young singer, Claudia Cattaneo, who would, in a few more years, become Monteverdi's wife. The appearance was at the invitation of His Grace the Duke of Mantua, Vicenzo Gonzaga; the meeting was of utmost importance to my friend Monteverdi, as his appointment as court violinist, and perhaps *Maestro di Capella*, depended on it.

There was nothing to be done. I made my apologies to Monteverdi, and departed the following morning. I made my way directly to Genoa, there I boarded a boat to Naples. I arrived on October 19th and went directly to the *palazzo* in San Severo.

The house appeared deserted. The door was ajar. No one responded to my cries. I went up the marble staircase, and walked the hall with the pink walls and the space where the hunting scene by Giovanni Antonio di Amato the Younger had hung before it was removed to Gesualdo. On the white marble floor of the corridor were pale brown stains. I opened the door to my Master's chamber. The room was in disarray, bedclothes ripped off the bed, clothing and personal items scattered about the floor. Among the shambles were a few valuable pieces of jewelry strewn about. Why had no one been in and looted them, I wondered. I left the room, and followed the trail of brown stain to the room of my Mistress. With shaking hand, I pushed open the door.

In the center of the room, an overturned chair. And, hanging from the chandelier by a rope, the bloated black body of Giulio Gesualdo.

L I B

m'inuolate hor mi redete il core

I leaned my head against the wall, fighting back the nausea. I had exited and shut the door to stifle the stench, but the smell of death was everywhere. I pressed my kerchief to my nose, and, breathing shallowly so as not to inhale the noxious fumes, opened the door again and pushed in.

The corpse had, apparently, been hanging there for a while, several days at least. The eyes bulged from the sockets, the black tongue hung stiffly from the open mouth, which appeared to be fixed in a hideous grin. I saw that his hand was wrapped tightly about what appeared to be a package, the paper stained with blood and with the fluids escaping through the pores in death. Gingerly, I reached out to take the package. The fingers were stiff with *rigor mortis*, and refused to give it up. Removing the kerchief from my nose and mouth, I used both hands to pry open the fist, and retrieve the small bundle. I took it out of the room, and again closed the door against the stench.

The blood and bile that coated the outside of the parcel had dried, and the paper was stiff. I spread it open carefully on the floor. Inside was a ring, oversized to fit over a gloved finger, wrought in gold with elegantly chased shoulders, the table set in a large, square emerald, deep and green, faceted, its face engraved with a seal of a cross. The ring of an Archbishop.

On the paper there was writing. I lifted it carefully. The stains obscured the text, but it was still legible. I read:

Ludovico,

I wanted to be your friend. Why does everyone hate me so?

Tell Don Carlo I beg his forgiveness. I thought I did not want to do it. I thought the ring made me do it. I know better now.

I would have liked to pray first. It has been so long since I could pray. No, God will not forgive me. I do not even ask.

Dying will be the easiest part.

How did he know I would find the letter, I wondered. I again turned my attention to the ring. It was strangely warm to the touch. I gazed into the emerald. It appeared to have infinite depth; entranced, I felt myself being pulled into the vast interior of the stone. I saw a swirl of red, like smoke, curling out of its depths. The red cloud grew and grew, gathered substance, and became a mass of red velvet that enveloped me entirely. I felt myself suffocating in the soft cloth, and felt a sharp pain in my side. I felt myself falling, falling into the red cloud. Suddenly I heard a cry. It was the voice of my Mistress, calling out of the depths. I could not make out the words, it sounded like pleading. I heard a second cry, a man's voice – Fabrizio! I felt myself spiraling down, down, into the red void. I heard the sounds of weeping. One man, then a second. I heard laughter – not mirth, but satanic laughter. One voice, then another. Angry shouts. I was losing consciousness. I felt a burning in my hand that became more and more intense, until I shook my hand in pain. The ring fell to the floor. The moment the ring left my hand the hallucination stopped. I looked at the ring. It lay on the marble, glowing bright red, and casting supernatural waves of heat toward me. I looked at my hand. The top layer of skin had peeled away, and a large blister swelled there. It was intensely painful.

I sat on the floor, pressed my kerchief to my hand, and waited for the initial pain to subside. As I waited I saw the ring lose its red glow, as it cooled. With the pain slightly relieved, I rose, gingerly lifted the ring, and dropped it into my pouch. The letter I left on the floor. I returned the kerchief to my nose, and reentered the room. On the bed, laid out neatly, were a gentleman's shirt with frilled, starched cuffs, green breeches, a doublet of fine yellow linen, green silk hose, white cotton pantaloons. On the floor, torn and bloodstained, was a lady's nightshirt, but greatly oversized. It was frilly, with silk lace straps and a diaphanous body. There were numerous tears in the fabric, and a large hole in the stomach with black char marks about it. I recognized it as one of the absurdly sexy garments that Don Fabrizio kept in my Mistress's closet, for his encounters with my Master. Alongside it was a second nightdress, cotton and quite unalluring, the size of my Mistress. It too was stained deep brown and black, and, besides numerous tear marks all over the bodice, there was a large hole ripped in it in the area of the stomach.

I left the room undisturbed and proceeded slowly down the corridor. Most doors were ajar; doors that were closed I opened and peered in. It was late afternoon, and the sunlight streamed in through the western windows, lighting up the western rooms with a dazzling light that highlighted every cast-off item in the chaos. Clearly, the household had left in great haste. Where was the skeleton staff that should have been left behind to keep the mansion clean and ready?

I heard a soft sound of whimpering. I opened the room of Silvia Albana, Donna Maria's personal maid. Silvia was crouched in the corner of the room, arms wrapped tightly around folded legs, rocking and weeping quietly. I went to her, knelt beside her, and wrapped my arms around her. Her skin was dry as leather. Though she was sobbing, no tears came. I had a wineskin, I offered her a sip. Her hand shook as she reached up to bring the wine to her lips. She took a few drops in her mouth and swallowed; then she retched violently, though expelled nothing. I held her for a few more minutes.

"Silvia, will you come with me?"

She shook her head.

"Silvia, you must come with me." I tried to lift her, but she pulled away.

"Silvia, if you remain here, you will surely die."

Silvia pulled her arms away and wrapped them again around her legs. Without turning her sunken eyes toward me, she replied, "I must stay and serve my Mistress."

"Silvia, your Mistress is not here. Do you know where she is?"

"O, Sir, they have killed her! They have killed her! Dead! She is dead!"

"Who killed her? Who Silvia?" I wanted to grab her and shake her; but I could not bring myself to hurt the poor creature.

163

Silvia's eyes widened in a look of terror, but she made no reply.

With heart heavy with trepidation and pity, I rose and left the poor child rocking on the floor.

Further inspection of the premises revealed no other living creature. The rooms were all deserted, clearly in haste, everywhere clothing and possessions scattered, as though the residents had packed up whatever they could take and rushed off. I could see no profit in remaining there; moreover, a pall hung over the entire building, more than mere abandonment; there was an aura of terror about the place, a feeling that it was cursed. I recalled the terrified feelings of the clearing where the witches were gathered. As the darkness gathered, I resolved to repair at once to Gesualdo, there, I suspected, the court had retired after whatever catastrophe had befallen the household. In the twilight, I made my way to the stable, there I found three mares in their stalls. Clearly no one had tended the horses in several days. They were agitated, stomping and kicking at the walls of their stalls. When they saw me approach, they laid back their ears and bared their teeth, and whinnied mightily, stomping their hooves and making a racket.

I pitched hay into their stalls, and with a bucket filled their trough. They munched the straw eagerly. I could see that one of the mares had capped her hocks, and would be unsuitable for riding. A second was so agitated that I dared not approach her. The third ate avidly, and seemed to calm after eating and drinking. When I reached out to pet her snout, she bridled, but, after a third attempt, she agreed to be touched. For the next quarter of an hour, as the stable plunged into darkness, I kept up my petting, and hummed quietly, until I felt confident I could saddle her and ride to Gesualdo. I took her from her stall, cinched a saddle and bridle on her, and set off. Outside, there was still enough light to find my way out of Naples, so I rode to the home of the Dottore Moise. I needed a place to spend the night, and was also eager to apprise him of the situation, as I did not doubt I would need to call on his services in the next days and weeks. He accommodated me gladly; I slept until first light, and then set out again for Gesualdo.

I rode hard, and arrived in Gesualdo in mid-afternoon. A strange sight greeted me: the thick forest that had grown up to the walls of the castle had been cut down, the hewed timbers lying scattered where they had been felled. About 100 *canna* of woods had been thus cleared. At the edge of the forest still standing a team of about 20 peasant men were vigorously chopping with axes at the stand of trees. Every few moments there was a crash as another tree fell to the axe.

In the center of these peasants, stripped of his shirt, was my Master. He was chopping like a fiend, his body shiny with sweat, and sweat dripping off his nose and into his eyes. His eyes were wide and wild. His bare back was crisscrossed with angry red welts. The muscles of his long, thin arms rippled under his skin. He chopped as one amok. He was not a man of strength or stamina, yet he chopped furiously, not seeming to tire.

I dismounted and approached him. "My Lord," I said.

He paid no attention, but continued his chopping.

"My Lord," I said louder.

"Take an axe, and get to work. Kill these trees," he said, without pausing or taking his eyes from the wounded tree.

"My Lord, it is I, Ludovico."

The sound of my name apparently gave him pause. He lowered his axe and stared straight ahead into space with a puzzled look. He then resumed his chopping.

"You are not Ludovico."

"My Lord, I am, I am your servant Ludovico. Look at me and you will see."

"Ludovico is in Cremona. You are not Ludovico. Go away."

"My Lord, I am come from Cremona, to be at your side in this hour of trial."

My Master made no response, but continued to chop.

"My Lord, why are you chopping down the forest?"

"Kill the trees. We must kill the trees. Nothing can live where I live. I must be surrounded by death."

"My Lord, this is most unwise. I beg you to desist. Call off your men. Let us go up to the castle for a rest. Then we can discuss this more reasonably."

My Master turned to me, axe held in both hands at the ready. He stared at me with his hollow, unblinking eyes. His features were twisted with emotion; but which emotion it was impossible to tell: Anger? Sadness? Confusion? After a long moment, he spoke.

"Who are you?"

"My Lord, I am Ludovico, your servant and your friend, who has come from Cremona to be with you now."

"You are not Ludovico. Ludovico is dead."

"My Lord, I assure you, I am not dead."

My Master raised his axe. "Begone!" he shouted. "You imposter! Ludovico is dead, dead!" He slid his hand along the shaft of the axe, preparatory to a swing that would cleave my head in two. But I stood and did not wince.

"My Lord, stay your hand!" With the axe suspended in midair, he froze, and his lips turned in a visage of perplexity. "My Lord, you are not well. You shall come with me to the castle. Lay down your axe now!"

To speak thus to my Lord and Master was tantamount to sedition, and he would have been justified in killing me right there. Instead, he slowly lowered the axe, never taking his eyes from me. His lower lip began trembling, his hands shaking. He looked at his trembling hands, and gripped the handle of his axe with all the strength he could muster. His knuckles turned white. Then he raised his eyes to me again. "Go to the castle and await me there," he said.

"Very well, my Lord." I turned to go. I felt there was no longer any immediate profit in this exchange, and decided to seek the aid and advice of my friend Don Pietro. I had gone only a few steps, however, when I heard loud sobbing. I turned and saw my Master fallen to his knees, the axe dropped at his side, his hands on the ground, and his whole body wracked with sobs.

"O, Ludovico, do not leave me, do not leave me!" I went to him and pressed his kneeling body to me. Thus we remained, my Master's arms about my waist, blubbering, me patting him on the back in comfort.

"Why did you abandon me, why, Ludovico?"

"I did not abandon you, my Lord. You sent me away."

He suddenly lifted his head, and looked about in a panic. "They are coming! We must hide! Stop! If you beat me they will stop. Beat me, Ludovico, beat me!"

While the details of this catastrophe were still unknown to me (and, indeed, would remain so until the days before my Master's death), this much was clear: my Mistress and my Master's best friend were dead, most likely by my Master's own hand, in a crime that was as dastardly as it was incomprehensible. For this reason, my Master's invitation to me to beat him I did not reject out of hand. For, at that moment, I felt a fathomless fury and, yes, loathing, for the Master who had once been my closest friend and mentor. Yet the bonds of love that had grown up of years of constant companionship and the ties of music that bound us prevailed. I helped him to his feet, and we made our way up the hill to the castle. As we walked, my Master kept casting panicked glances behind, as though some invisible furies were pursuing him. As we left, I called back to the woodsmen to lay down their axes and desist from this sylvan massacre.

Once in the castle, he shut the door and threw the bolt, then scrutinized the great hall, as though searching for one of these furies that had somehow penetrated the castle. After a few moments of his eyes darting about like a hunted hart, he sat on the stone floor and leaned back against the wall, exhausted. Waiting in the hall was Don Pietro, who stood silently aside until our Master sat. He then approached with a skin of wine, and offered it. Our Master took it and drank greedily. He then fell back again against the wall, in an exhausted stupor.

There was nothing to be done but to wait while our Master regained his strength. We stood by respectfully, without speaking. I was eager to talk to Don Pietro, to hear from his lips what tragedy had unfolded in Naples. I also hoped to speak to him about the ring. This cursed ring, I believed, could well contain the secret to the curse that hung over Gesualdo and its Lord, and so could, perhaps, be our deliverance. When Giulio visited me that night to say that he had something the witch needed, it was, I surmised, this selfsame ring. And the magical powers with which it was endowed – the supernatural way it heated to furnace red – tied it in my mind to my Master's uncle, his Eminence Alfonso Gesualdo – the same who, it seemed, had made it a purpose in his life to embitter every living moment of my Master.

However, all discussion of this would necessarily be postponed, as protocol demanded our silent attendance while our Master rested. But his rest was not to be long. For not ten minutes had passed, when he suddenly snapped out of his stupor and looked to the great stairway with a panicked cry: "Stop it, stop it! The red cloud! Ludovico, stop it!" He rose and rushed about the hall, as though dodging some invisible monster. He grabbed a vase off a table and hurled it toward the stairs. It shattered with a sickening crash. He then grabbed the table itself, a heavy side table, of thick maple top and legs elegantly carved, and with almost superhuman strength lifted it and threw it as well in the direction of the imagined cloud. He then retreated into a corner of the hall, cowering and covering his head with his arms, shouting all the time, "Stop it! Stop it!" He rolled over and grabbed his side as though he had been stabbed, and let out a blood-curdling scream. This whole episode took only a few seconds. By the time we could move to his assistance, he was huddled in the corner. Both Don Pietro and myself reached out to restrain our Master from doing himself harm, but he beat us back, howling in imagined pain.

And then, down the steps came the witch. She was wearing a plain gray shift, her hair was disheveled and she walked as though somnambulating. Her steps were hesitant as she descended, her hand gripping the bannister to keep from falling. She went to my Master, lifted her shift, and kneeled down, pressing her sex against his face. His cries ceased immediately and he lapped lackadaisically at her crotch. "My baby ha' a bad dream?" she cooed, as she rubbed herself against her exhausted victim.

"Let's fuck," she said. She rose, and with a single motion pulled off his tights, exposing his priapic member. And so, without a drop of shame, before all the servants and subjects passing through the great hall, she lowered herself onto him, and, with a face contorted with pain, humped him, fucking like two dogs, until he jerked weakly. She rose, pulled down her shift, and started to walk away, leaving our Master lying prostrate and exhausted, his now flaccid penis exposed for all to see.

Don Pietro went quickly to our Master, and pulled up his tights, covering his private parts. I turned to the witch. "I believe we must speak," I said to her.

"Don Ludovico, ye wish t' speak wi' me? What an honor." I could not tell if this remark was sarcastic or genuine; but then, nothing the witch did was unambiguous. I turned to the door, unbolted it, and walked out across the moat bridge, with her at my heels. I strode a few paces down the road, then stepped off the pavement and turned to her.

Wordlessly, I withdrew the ring from my pouch. I had tied it to a leather thong, as a precaution should it incandesce again. I dangled it on the thong before her eyes. She stared at it blankly for a moment. Then she slowly began to understand what it was, and her eyes became wild. She leapt forward to snatch it from me, but I yanked it up out of her reach.

"Give it me, give it me!" she shouted. "It belongs t' me!"

With one hand I held the string high, while with the other I fended her off, pushing her on the chest. She struggled frenziedly in an attempt to grab it.

"It may be yours, but I have it now," I said. "If you wish to have it you will obey me."

"I'll do what ye want! Ye want t' fuck? Here, ye kin fuck me." With that, she grabbed the neckline of her shift, and ripped with all her might, so the fabric tore down the middle, exposing her fallen, sere breasts. I took a step back with a look of disgust on my face.

"No I do not wish to fuck you, madam. First, I want to know whose ring this is."

"Give it me now. I tell ye what ye want t' know, just gi' me the ring!"

"You will tell me now," I commanded. "Whose ring?"

"It's his, the cardinal's. Now gi' it me!"

"Madam, if you want this ring, you will leave Gesualdo forever. You will leave now. I will send an escort who will take you far to the north. There, when I have established your intent never to return, I shall instruct the escort to commend the ring to your possession."

The witch stopped her struggling, stood back, and looked at me with a nasty, appraising look. "O, yer a sly one, ain't ye? I know yer type. Ye mean t' keep it, an' send me packin'.

"Well, I'll do it. I'll go where ye say. An' if'n ye d'not gi' me me ring, I'll come back an' I'll kill ye. Yes I will. I'll kill ye all."

But as she spoke, I felt the heat emanating from the ring. I looked and saw it turn a pale pink, and slowly glow fiery red. The thong by which it was suspended started to smoke, and then gave way. The red hot ring fell to the ground. The witch leapt forward to grab it, but I stepped quickly to hold her back.

"Do not touch it, madam. It is extremely dangerous."

And then, the ring slowly sank into the ground, as though the solid earth were a viscous pit of tar. I looked on astonished, as the witch pitched forward, scrabbling furiously at the dirt. "Ye fool, ye lost it! It's gone. 'Twer me only hope. Now we all be doomed!" She fell weeping on the ground.

Indeed, I, too, despaired at the loss of this ring. For, as I have said, I believed that the ring carried the key to exorcising the curse. And now the earth had swallowed it up; and so long as the ring remained buried beneath this village, the inhabitants would live in a cloud of misery.

It was thus with heavy heart that I turned, left the witch groveling in the dirt, and returned to the castle. Don Pietro and my Master were no longer there, but I heard my Master's cries from the direction of his bedchamber. I followed the sound, and found my

Master sitting on his bed. On either side, standing at attention, were four of the palace guard, waiting for Don Pietro's instructions.

My Master had his hands clamped firmly on his ears. "Stop the singing! Stop it! It is killing me!"

"There is no singing, my Lord," I said.

"Do you not hear it? Do you not hear the witches? Their singing! It is killing me!"

"Perhaps if I played for you, my Lord, it would drive out the song of the witches."

My Master dropped his hands from his ears, and gesticulated wildly. "No, no music! No! I must have silence!" He then started clawing at his face with his fingernails. Don Pietro nodded to the guards. Two guards grabbed his arms and pressed them to his sides, so he could no longer injure himself. Don Pietro turned to me. "I fear we shall have to restrain him. Otherwise he will do himself serious damage."

I nodded. Clearly our Master had taken leave of his senses. With the ring gone, I had only one hope for our Master's recovery: to call upon the ministrations of Dottore Moise. "I shall call for the Doctor," I said. I went to the guard room, and ordered a messenger dispatched at once. By the time I returned, my Master's limbs were tied to the posts of the bed, the cords loose enough so he could move about, but could not reach his face. He lay motionless on his back, eyes closed, snoring erratically.

I turned to Don Pietro. With the crisis now in hand, I was eager to speak with him, and to hear what had transpired in Naples. He, too, wished conversation: our eyes met, and we retired to another chamber, where we could speak in privacy. I now looked at him for the first time. There were dark circles below his eyes, his hair was disheveled, he looked as though he had not slept for a week. Normally his dress was immaculate and meticulous. But now, his doublet was soiled, his cuffs, usually starched, were limp, his blouse crumpled and stained. He saw a chair in the corner of the room, and fell into it exhausted. I stood by patiently, waiting for my friend to regain some strength. After a few moments, Don Pietro turned to speak.

"I have spoken with our Master's father. He will resume the duties of governance, until our Master has sufficiently recovered."

"May God grant him a rapid and full recovery."

"Amen. I have stopped his medication for the time being. It seems hardly relevant to his current state."

"I agree. I hope the doctor shall arrive in another two days, and will have a course of treatment that can restore our Master's sanity."

We fell silent. I felt the tension in my shoulders, my hands were clenched in anxiety. My heart was consumed by a battle between my desire, nay, my need, to know what had transpired, and my dread at hearing what I had already surmised. But there was no need to ask, for Don Pietro, without being asked, spoke:

"Our Master discovered that his friend Fabrizio Carafa had cuckolded him. He resolved to take his revenge. He announced he was going hunting; but late at night, he descended to his wife's chamber, there he discovered her and her lover in lecherous concourse. He slayed the adulteress and her lover, and departed immediately for Gesualdo."

I was astonished. "Don Pietro, you know this story is preposterous. You know that Donna Maria was faithful to her husband, and you know that Don Fabrizio was no – well, what can I say? It is absurd."

Don Pietro's voice was flat, as though reciting a prewritten script. "There was an official inquest the day after the murder. There were two witnesses to the events – myself, and Donna Maria's maid, Silvia Albana. Our stories both corroborate what I have told you. There is no more to be said of this."

"I spoke with Silvia. She was in the palace in San Severo. She was deranged, and refused to leave. I was unable to give her any succor. There was no one else about. I assume she is dead by now."

Don Pietro gave a heavy sigh. "It is as I feared. I knew she would rather die than live with the truth buried in her heart."

"Then you know this story is false."

Don Pietro looked at me sharply. "This is the story to which we swore in the inquest. It is the only story. There is no other truth."

I understood what he was saying, but it was not something I could live with. Surely, as his friend, he could trust me. Surely he could tell me the reason for this implausible lie, and tell me what had truly transpired.

"Perhaps, one day, my friend, I will be free to tell you – more details. But for now, this is all that can be said. Now I believe His Excellency would like to speak with you."

It was a dismissal. There would be no more questions. I didn't know whether to be angry with my friend, or piteous; for it was clear that he was bearing a heavy burden, a burden of a truth he would not or could not tell. So, without further ado, I thanked him, and went to seek my Master's father – now, once again, the ruler of the realm.

I knew he was not in the great hall, so I went to seek him in the solar. There he was sitting in his special chair, a chair fitted with wheels so he could be rolled about. Though he was infirm and weakened by age, His Excellency's mind was still as sharp as ever. I approached and bowed deeply.

"Ludovico, our most precious servant. I am so glad to see you have returned to us."

"Thank you my Lord. I am deeply honored to be welcomed so, though it is a shame that it is in such tragic circumstances."

"I understand you have called for the assistance of your Jewish doctor. Let us pray that he will find a way to restore my son's mind."

May it be God's will."

"Ludovico, I understand you asked my son to be freed from your service with us. Is that so?"

"It is, Your Excellency."

"You are not happy in your service?"

"Your Excellency, since my Master sent me to Cremona, much has changed in my life. I have married, and my wife is with child."

"Well, I am happy for you. However, the question is moot, for my son has not freed you, is that so?"

"That is so, Your Excellency."

"Well, I am not like my son. Were you my servant, I would have let you go. Know that, should my son not recover, I shall free you from your service. However, I do wish for you to stay with my son until his senses are restored."

"Thank you, Your Excellency, I will certainly remain as long as I can be of assistance."

"Or," he continued, with a sound of dread in his voice, "until it is clear that they shall never be restored."

"God Forbid, Your Excellency."

The Prince sighed. "The events of the last week weigh heavily on my son's soul. Don Pietro told you what happened?"

I hesitated. Should I tell the Prince that this story that my friend Pietro told was fabulous? But before I could speak, the Prince continued.

"My son caught his dear wife fornicating with another man. It was an offense that justified both their deaths."

"Your Excellency, I ..."

The Prince raised his hand to stop me in mid-sentence. "I know you find this story incredible. But you must understand, Ludovico – adultery makes this slaying justifiable. Any other explanation would make this murder, and would expose my son – indeed, all of us – to the wrath of the d'Avalos and Carafa families. There would be war in all Avellino. So there can be no questioning of this version of the events."

"I understand, Your Excellency."

"I have wondered if, had you not been sent away, had you been at your Master's side, you could, perhaps, have averted this tragedy. But I suppose not. There are powerful forces here, far beyond the human ken, beyond what you already know and imagine. In a way, though, it is a blessing that you were away. For we have all had our souls tainted by the dark forces that have twisted our fates. You are the only one who can see us through eyes unsubverted by witchery.

"But I have said too much already. Go, minister to your Master. God grant you the powers to make him well again."

There was no more to be said. "Thank you, Your Excellency." I bowed and exited.

During the next two days, as we awaited the arrival of the doctor, there was little to be done. Don Pietro and myself took shifts by our Master's bedside. Our Master spent his waking hours either weeping, or screaming at some creature of his imagination that tormented him, or attempting to beat himself – something his restraints prevented him from doing. We had to feed him like a baby; for, if we released his hand to allow him to eat, he would immediately tear at his face and ears. He was unable to scratch himself, as we had trimmed his fingernails almost to the nub. The only thing that gave him solace was the witch, who came twice a day for her rut. As horrified we were at this, we were oddly impotent to stop it. Rather, we stood helplessly by in a sort of trance and watched with disgust as the witch and the Prince coupled without the least shame. It was clear that the ordeal was not pleasurable for either of them; on the contrary, the witch grimaced with pain throughout the whole act. The Prince barely moved, and fell back exhausted when he had spent.

With nothing to do but babysit the Prince, I had the opportunity to have several conversations with my Master's son, Emmanuelle. The young Master at age four was as precocious and as repugnant as he had been when he was two. He conversed like one twice his age, he littered his language with the few words of filth that he knew, and the thoughts he expressed were vile. As I write this, after raising two children of my own and living in the house with my own grandchildren, I marvel that I could call a child of four repugnant. Are not all children adorable, do we not overlook their foibles without actually being aware of it? Yet, when I remember little Emmanuelle, I can think of him as nothing but repulsive.

This in spite of the fact that he rather seemed to enjoy my company, and during the next few days and weeks sought me out. I was, perhaps, the only person who would converse with him. His nurse he despised, the other children his age in the castle shunned him, and other adults he ignored as though they were invisible.

"Ludovico, I am glad to see you," he said when he first saw me that day. It was in the great hall, and I was on my way to take some air after my shift with the Master.

"Hello, young Master. May God bless you."

"Papa murdered Mama," he said.

As you can imagine, I hardly knew what response would be appropriate to such a bold assertion. After a hesitation, I replied, "Alas, it is true that your Mother is dead."

"Murdered," he insisted. "I'm glad."

"Glad, My Lord?"

"Yes, glad, I hated her."

I drew myself up. "My Lord, if I may speak freely, gladness is an inappropriate sentiment to express at a time like this."

"Inappropriate?"

"Improper, my Lord."

"Well, fuck proper. I hated her. I'm glad she's dead. Murdered, that is."

I said nothing to this.

"You should have been there, Ludovico. It was real exciting."

"You... witnessed it, my Lord?"

"Well, I could hear some of it, Enough to know what was happening. I wanted to go watch, but they wouldn't let me out of my room."

"What, exactly, did you hear, my Lord?"

"Well, they came up the stairs, made an awful racket. Nurse peeped out of the room, then shut the door and locked it. She told me to hide under the bed, but I told her to go fuck herself. I went to the door to listen, but she had the key so I couldn't get out.

"I heard them open the door to my Mama's room. There was some arguing, I couldn't tell what they were saying. Someone shouted, "Take the weapon!"" Then two huge bangs – that would be the arquebuses. I guess. There was more talking. I heard Papa crying, No, she's not dead, she's not dead! Then I heard another voice, But she is dead, Your Eminence! "Do it now!" shouted someone. Then some laughter and more crying. Then they all went downstairs again."

"Could you tell who was with your father?"

"I couldn't make it out. But I don't care. Papa murdered Mama. And now Papa's crazy."

"We hope and pray to God that his condition is temporary."

"I don't."

"You don't what, my Lord?"

"Hope and pray. Fuck him. He deserves to be crazy. I like him better this way."

You can see why I considered the child repulsive. His language was filthy as a street gutter, as were the sentiments he expressed. His hatred of his parents knew no bounds. Indeed, I suspect that his own death, three weeks before his father's, he planned purely out of spite; for he knew that nothing would pain his father more than the loss of his sole heir and the end of the house of Gesualdo.

Be that as it may, during those two days, I had a number of conversations with the young Prince, as well as afterward. For I remained in Gesualdo for two months, attending my Master as he recovered – in a fashion – a fragile sanity that allowed him to resume his life, such as it was. During those two months, I was myself deeply conflicted over my feelings toward my Master. The murder of my Mistress was a crime that I was unable to deal with. That it was my Master's hand that felled her I found myself unable to forgive. Yet I did not doubt that this was not an act of volition, but that dark forces beyond his control were what moved him to this dastardly deed. Did this make him less culpable? Could I forgive him for doing what his will did not command? The answer was no: in my heart I despised him for killing the single soul that brought light to this cursed house.

Yet the bonds of love could not be severed. I continued – perhaps in quite another chamber of my heart – to adore my Master, to love him, to care about his foibles, to guide him out of the quagmires he created for himself, to save him again and again from his own hand. This bond was nurtured by the music we shared. Especially now, with the astounding madrigal he had sent me, I was captivated by his genius.

Fortunately for me, I did not have to resolve this conflict. For I was bound to my Master by law of servitude, and so long as I was in his service I would respect and obey, and work tirelessly for his welfare. The protocol of service freed me from having to deal with my conflicting feelings toward him. And so I was able to toil for his recovery.

That recovery began with the arrival of il Dottore Moise. The doctor went from his carriage, accompanied by his assistant Don Salamone, directly to the patient's bedroom for an initial examination. My Master was at that moment screaming that someone should cover his ears, to block out the witch music. "How is he restrained?' he asked. I explained that his limbs were tied to the posts of the bed, such that he could thrash but could not reach his head or body to inflict injury on himself. The doctor nodded approval. "I will retire and rest, and I will then make a detailed diagnosis. Please collect his stool and his urine for me to examine." I led him and Don Salamone to their chambers.

A couple of hours passed, and the doctor and Don Salamone returned to my Master's bedside. My Master's eyes were glazed, he was sobbing and coughing. A chair was brought for Don Moise, who sat, and took my Master's hand in his hand. My Master turned his head toward Don Moise, and stared in his direction without actually seeing him.

"Why are you weeping, my Lord?" asked the doctor in a quiet voice.

"The witches. They are singing. They are always singing. The pain."

"What pain, my Lord?"

"In the side."

Don Moise, reached across my Master's body, and felt his side.

"Would you like for me to play some other music, my Lord? I know a tune that might soothe your pain."

My Master's eyes filled with sudden panic. "No, no music! No music!" He pulled his hand away, and started struggling against his restraints. "The red! The red is coming!"

Don Moise gestured to Don Salamone, who approached my Master, and pressed a sponge to his nose and mouth. My Master struggled furiously, shouting and twisting. But Don Salamone held the sponge firmly against his face. The sponge gave out a sweet, pungent odor. Gradually my Master's struggles became less, and he finally fell back on the bed in exhaustion.

Don Moise rose, and gestured for us to follow. Don Salamone took his hand and Don Pietro and myself followed them into the solar, there we sat about a table. We waited for my Master's father to join us. Don Moise spoke.

"The Prince's derangement is deeply rooted in visions that have savaged him since his childhood. Clearly it has been brought to a head by the witch's curse and by the tragic events of the last weeks. The condition is profound, and only extreme measures have any chance of effecting a cure. And those measures in themselves are dangerous, and can lead to his death.

"Nonetheless, I am of the opinion that we should proceed. He cannot, I believe, continue much longer in his present state; without treatment, his visions will no doubt intensify, and he will soon die.

"The treatment I recommend is threefold: first, I shall administer a course of valerian and opium to achieve an immediate sedation. Second, I shall perform a trepanation. The derangement, I believe, has the form of a stone within the Prince's skull. By penetrating the skull with a trepan, without tearing the meninx, we will aerate the stone and cause it to dissipate. I should tell you that I have performed a trepanation six times in my career. Three of those times the patient died, but the other three times the procedure brought a meaningful recovery.

"The third aspect of the treatment will be music. Music is to be played at his bedside throughout the hours of daylight. The music is to be in the Dorian mode, which is known to have a calming effect and to restore the humour balance in the body. The performance can be repetitive. The music is to be performed, without regard to the Prince's protests. He will likely protest loudly at first, but the music is to continue, now matter how loudly he screams.

"Since this course of treatment is not without risk, I ask for your approval before I proceed."

We all looked at His Excellency. It was his decision. He returned our gaze with decision. "Proceed," he said.

m'involate hor mi redete il core

The following week saw a remarkable change in my Master's condition. The threefold treatment recommended by Don Moise effected a gradual recession of hallucinations. My Master ceased his screaming, his attempts at self-injury, his episodes of panic and tears. There was, to be sure, a curious flatness to his personality: his speech became less animated, almost monotonic; he showed no particular interest in anything; he did not initiate speech, but would reply when spoken to; and the only topic on which he was prepared to hold an ongoing conversation was music. Since Don Pietro's knowledge of music was limited, ongoing attendance to my Master fell primarily on my shoulders. However, it was no longer necessary to restrain him or to sit with him throughout the night.

The most interesting part of the treatment was the trepanation. I had never seen this operation, and to see it performed by a blind physician was fascinating and thrilling. Don Moise proceeded entirely through feeling, smelling, and listening; the acumen of his other senses more than compensated for his lack of sight.

The patient was strapped to a chair, and, in particular, his head was strapped to the backrest to render it immobile. To his head was fitted a kind of frame, with a drill shaft attached to its center, a crank to turn the drill, and another handle on the top to adjust the pressure of the drill head against the bone. The drill head itself was a cup about two finger-breadths in diameter, with a finely serrated edge, the teeth razor sharp. I have included a sketch of the device – please forgive my slim skills at portraiture.

Once the trepan was strapped securely to his head, the patient was sedated by inhaling a mixture of valerian and opium, until his eyes drooped and his muscles relaxed. Having seen head wounds before – usually caused by sword blows – I expected there would be a great deal of blood and pain. In fact, the operation was almost painless, and there was only minor bleeding. Don Moise ran his fingers over my Master's pate, feeling the shape of the skull below the skin. With a sharp razor, he shaved an area of the head where the drill would enter. He then made a crisscross incision precisely below the head of the drill, and peeled back the skin from the scalp. Don Salamone dabbed at the wound with a cloth soaked in cimolian and wine, which stanched the bleeding almost entirely. Don Moise cranked the drill head down so it was just touching the exposed bone, verifying the location of contact with his fingers. He then turned the drill head, which spun rapidly, gradually cutting into the skull. Don Moise paused frequently, touching the drill head with his finger. If the drill began to heat, he removed it and dipped it in cold water, reattached it, and resumed drilling. He constantly adjusted the pressure to control the depth of the cut.

Don Moise drilled until the bit had nearly penetrated the skull. He then took a spatulated tool with a sharp edge, and carefully pried out the round disk of bone that he had cut. He took great care not to cut or puncture the gray fibrous sheet below the bone. The skull thus opened, we waited about ten minutes while the brain aerated, and the stone of my Master's insanity evaporated. Don Moise frequently sniffed at the wound, attempting to identify any vapors that might issue from the hole. When he was satisfied the stone was gone, he placed a small round silver disk over the hole. Don Salamone scraped away the cimolian, and pulled the flesh tightly over the skull and the disk. He applied a paste of honey and vinegar over the wound. The trepan was removed, and the patient, still in a stupor, was released from his bonds and carried to his bed. Don Salamone tied a bandanna over the wound and under the chin, to prevent the patient from scratching the wound.

My Master slept for twelve hours following the trepanation, and awoke much refreshed, and in an entirely new frame of mind. The hallucinations were gone. He continued to be troubled by the witch music, which he asserted he heard clearly from the adjacent room. When the *capella* came to begin the music therapy, he complained bitterly and insisted they stop. When, in accordance with the doctor's instructions, they continued to sing, he rose from his bed in a fury, with intent to strike them. He was, however, too weak and dizzy to do this, and fell back on his bed quite out of breath. I approached him and took his hand. "My Lord, you must suffer this music for a while, it is an essential part of your treatment." My Master clamped his hands over his ears to shut out the sound, but, after a short time, his hands dropped to his sides. He appeared to be intensely unhappy with the music, but did nothing to stop it. And, as the days passed, he grew more and more relaxed, and occasionally paid attention to what was being performed.

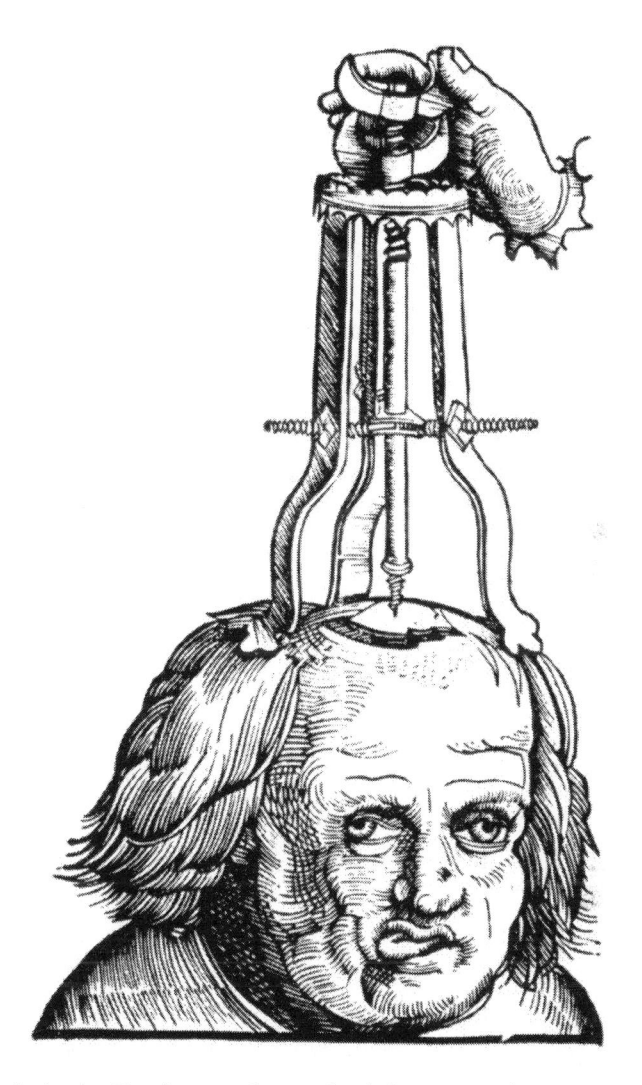

For music in the Dorian mode, we had the songs that our *Maestro di Capella* Don Bartolomeo had transcribed from the previous time we applied this treatment. In addition, my friend the *oltramontane* Giovanni de Macque wrote a lovely instrumental suite in the Greek style, that we must have played a dozen times over the next weeks..

It was a pleasure to once again make music with my friends in the consort. Playing with my friend Don Scipione was a particular pleasure. When he played continuo, he would introduce such surprising and amusing embellishments that the whole consort would sometimes break down in laughter; well, except for Maestro Bartolomeo, who would shake his long white beard in disapproval. Before my move to Cremona, we would often retire after a rehearsal or performance for a boot of *Fiano* wine, Don Giovanni would tell jokes, and the *castrata* Battista di Pavola would brag about his sexual exploits. Don Battista had since left His Excellency's service, so, while the choir lost a good deal of its shimmering, glorious sound, the company was much improved. For Don Battista was a tasteless boor, even if he had a magnificent voice.

When I was not performing, I spent a good deal of time with my Master, either listening to the other musicians or attempting to engage him in conversation. He had lost interest in almost everything. He had no wish to hunt, and certainly not to whore, and completely neglected administration. Though no longer plagued with hallucinations, he would often, sometimes in mid-sentence, break down in a tumult of weeping. He rarely explained these seizures. On one occasion, he did address me in his tears: "O, Ludovico, it was a terrible, terrible thing that I did. There will be no atonement, none, none." Any attempt to draw him out on this ended in silence. I once said to him, "My Lord, you must repent and recover. Think of your uncle Carlo – live up to his expectations." My Master gave me such a bizarre look – a look that defied interpretation – that I never again attempted to advise him on the matter. In any case, these seizures of weeping ended as suddenly as they began.

Of course, the witch continued to demand her twice daily fornication. As I have said, we were powerless to resist this, for the moment she entered the room we were rendered pusillanimous. As our Master was continually attended by someone, their coupling was always a public affair. Neither she nor my Master showed the slightest shame or modesty about the matter, and the whole thing was executed as though they were buying fruit at the market. The witch always grimaced in pain as she unceremoniously stuffed his penis into her, nor did he show any sign of pleasure.

His nights were surprisingly peaceful. Since the trepanation, the red dream ceased to plague my Master's rest. I found this curious, for the dream was deeply rooted, and long anteceded the onset of his madness. In any case, the black hellebore treatment was no longer necessary, and this was a blessing, since this medicine had a seriously debilitating effect on him.

Throughout this time, my mixed feelings toward my Master continued to disturb me. As his friend for years, I truly desired to see his full recovery. Yet the vileness of his deed was never far from my thoughts. On a number of occasions, during his bouts of weeping, he would beg me to beat him. Though I have always been a most peaceful man, I was sorely tempted to accede to his requests. I sometimes imagined to myself what it would be like to apply the switch to his bare back: would it expiate my anger toward him? I even considered writing to Don Moise about this. Perhaps, I thought, a good beating would be therapeutic for both him and me. In the end, I did not write, but I did not put the thought out of my mind.

We did have a number of interesting conversations about music. I had brought with me a number of madrigals, written out in score, by the Ferrarese composer Luzzasco Luzzaschi, whose chromatic style bore a striking similarity to my Master's better works. This is the same composer whom my Master had studied, admired and criticized on a previous occasion, a composer who, in the not distant future, would become an associate and a rival of my Master when he moved to Ferrara. My Master was greatly interested in these new scores, as I knew he would be, and discussed them with me at a length that eventually became tedious. This was especially so because of the flat, monotonic inflection that his voice had taken, probably a result of the valerian and opium medication that he continued to receive.

The doctor left Gesualdo after a few days, and returned at the end of a month and a half. He examined the patient, and called us together for a second consultation.

"I find the patient greatly recovered," he told me, Don Pietro, and his Excellency, my Master's father. "He is, in some respects, better off than he was before his madness. He is, for example, no longer troubled by his red dream. This development suggests to me that he has somehow resolved the conflict that gave rise to the dream. Perhaps the trauma of the murder dredged up an episode from his distant past, which relieved the tension giving rise to the dream. That he has not shared this memory with any of us suggests that it will remain a secret until the day of his death.

"Despite the recovery of his faculties, he is still deeply troubled, as his seizures of weeping suggest. I would recommend a complete change of environment, for an extended period."

"He has spoken of his desire to visit Luzzasco Luzzaschi in Ferrara," I said. "He has mentioned it several times, and I know the D'Este family would consider a union with him. This was, I understand, prior to his illness, but I suspect it would still hold now that he is recovered."

"Ferrara would be excellent," said the Doctor.

"I will attend to it," said Don Pietro.

It would be, however, another year before a move could be arranged, for His Excellency's health had taken a turn for the worse. My Master's father had begun to cough blood, and had grown increasingly weak. Within six months, he died. It took another six months to order the affairs of the estate, something that fell entirely on the shoulders of Don Pietro, and only after that was it possible to move the court to Ferrara.

In any case, all this took place in my absence. For two weeks after the Doctor's departure, I asked my Master for permission to return to Cremona and rejoin my wife. On hearing my request, my Master reacted with real emotion: tears came to his eyes, not the tears of his bouts of weeping, but honest sadness at the departure of a friend he truly loved. He nonetheless granted my request, and I happily set off for home.

L I B

m'inuolate hor mi redete il core

How like a spider's web is a lie. The hapless fly is caught in its strands, and its struggles only serve to tighten the fibers that bind it. Then the spider wraps its prey in layer after layer of filament, wrapping, wrapping, until the fly disappears in a small silvery ball, suspended by the gossamer web. The spider injects its poison, and sucks the juices out of the encrusted insect, until there is no fly left, only the dissolving shell in the heart of the ball. The web itself spreads across the ceiling, from eave to eave, fibrillating with every puff of air, with every beat of a victim's wings trapped in its grip.

So it was with the story of my mistress's murder: a web of prevarication, so carefully spun, so deftly wrapped layer by layer over the truth, that the truth, like the fly, dissolved into a poisonous residue completely hidden from human ken. And the entire web hummed while the truth died in its silken prison.

For the story of the murder of Donna Maria d'Avalos and Don Fabrizio Carafa spread through Italy like an enormous spider's web. The story soon grew to mythic proportions: poets sang of it, chroniclers reported it, and with each retelling, the fabrication grew more and more fantastic. Don Fabrizio and Donna Maria were as renowned and star-crossed lovers as Dante and Beatrice, Boccaccio and Fiammetta, Petrarch and Laura. The story, as it developed through endless tellings and retellings, had all the earmarks of high tragedy and romance: a pathetic and beautiful woman, spurned by her husband, falls into the arms of a dashing cavalier; their love blossoms as a mighty tree. As our friend, the poet Torqueto Tasso wrote:

O Weep, ye Graces, lovers, weep and fear!
For lovers true whose death was their reward,
A green-eyed envy put them to the sword,
Their lovers' bed turned gruesome funeral bier.

My Master himself is portrayed as the horned husband, a jealous and intolerant villain, but with the law – if not justice – on his side. Consider this poem, published shortly after the murder, by Fra Filippo Carafa, a distant relative of Don Fabrizio:

Your sin so great it stinks to Heaven's gate,
To strike with halberd, dirk, and arquebus
A man defenseless, woman without blame,
How could you think spilt blood would purge
your shame
While you wallowed in gross sin licentious
And cared not keep your couch inviolate?

Accounts of the murder grew embellishments with each repetition. The most popular account, *Successi tragici et amorosi de Silvio et Ascanio Corona*, widely distributed in manuscript throughout Southern Italy, knew to tell intimate conversations between the two lovers, to which they alone could have been privy. Donna Maria is portrayed as a strumpet unable to rein in her lusts, her "bosom filled with impure desires and a libidinous and unbridled appetite for illicit love"; while Don Fabrizio is a pusillanimous wimp who accedes to her every desire, no matter how dangerous and absurd. The Prince is a vengeful, scheming blackguard. He broke all the locks of the house, and gave out that he was going hunting. He then broke into his wife's chamber, where the lovers were in the throes of embrace, and slaughtered them.

How absurd! These characters were not the people I knew and loved. The Prince would never go hunting if not accompanied by Don Fabrizio; I could not bring myself to breathe the name of Donna Maria and "lustful" in the same sentence.

But the story of Ascanio and Silvio Corona was a work of fiction. Far more disturbing was the report of the inquest, conducted by the Chief Justice of the Grand Court of Vicaria, Dominico Vicene. His

Honor Don Dominico entered the premises while the bodies of the victims were still sprawled in puddles of blood. He examined the bodies, the wounds, the pile of bloodied weapons left behind in the Prince's chamber, and then ordered all members of the household to remain in place until he could interview them. Don Pietro, however (so I understood from the subsequent testimony) sent everyone in great haste to Gesualdo, leaving behind only himself and Donna Maria's Lady in Waiting, Donna Silvia. Why, I wondered, did he do that? It could only be because he didn't want other members of the household – who were present during the murder and could possibly contradict the story he had fabricated – to speak with the interrogators. And, indeed, when the interrogators arrived two days later, they found only Donna Silvia and Don Pietro.

Don Pietro begins his testimony with the words – well, let me quote his testimony in its entirety, so you can judge for yourselves:

> On being asked why Don Carlo left that night, and with whom he had gone, Don Pietro replied "My Lords, I shall tell you the truth. On the Tuesday evening, which was the 26th day of the present month, the said Lord Don Carlo dined at three hours of the night in his apartments on the middle floor, undressed himself, and retired to bed as he was wont to do every evening, and those who served him at supper were witness, Pietro de Vicario, a man servant, Alessandro Abruzzese, and a young priest who was a musician. And when he had finished dinner the aforesaid Pietro de Vicario and the others departed while witness remained behind to lock the door After he had secured the door the Lord Don Carlo composed himself to slumber, and witness covered him up and, after undressing, went to bed. Being thus asleep, it would be about six hours of the night when he heard the Lord Don Carlo calling for him that he should bring him a glass of water. Witness went to the well to draw water, and when he had descended to the courtyard he noticed that the postern gate, opening on to the street, was open at that late hour. And on taking up the water he beheld Don Carlo up and dressed in doublet and hose And he told witness to give him also his long cloak to put on. When witness asked him whither he was going at such a late hour of the night, he replied that he was going a-hunting, and on witness observing that it was not the time for going to the chase, the said Lord Don Carlo replied to him "You shall see what

hunting I am going to do." So saying he finished dressing, and told witness to light two torches, which done, the said Lord Don Carlo drew from beneath the bed a curved sword which he gave to witness to carry under his arm, also a dagger and a poignard together with an arquebus

Taking with him all these weapons, he went to the staircase which led up to the apartment of the Lady Donna Maria d'Avalos, and while mounting by it the said Lord Don Carlo spoke to the witness, saying

"'I am going to massacre the Duke of Andria and that strumpet Donna Maria." And while mounting the stairs, witness saw three men each of whom was carrying a halberd and an arquebus, which men, witness attested, threw open the door at the head of the stairs which led to the apartments of Donna Maria. And when the three men had entered into the said apartment of Donna Maria. the Lord Don Carlo said to them "Slay that scoundrel together with that strumpet! Shall a Gesualdo be made a cuckold?" Then witness heard the sound of firearms, but heard no voices, because he had remained outside the room After that he had remained a short while thus, the three men came out, and he recognised one of them to be Pietro de Vicario, man-servant, another to be Ascanio Lama, and the third to be a confidential servant called Francesco and they departed by the same staircase by which they had come up armed Then Don Carlo himself came out, his hands covered with blood, but he turned back and re-entered the chamber of Donna Maria, saying

"I do not believe they are dead." Then the said witness entered with a torch and perceived a dead body near the door. The said Don Carlo went up to the bed of the dead Donna Maria and dealt her still more wounds, saying "I do not believe she is dead." He then commanded witness not to let the women scream, and the said Lord Don Carlo Gesualdo descended the staircase by which he had come, and witness heard a great noise of horses below, and in the morning saw neither the Lord Don Carlo, nor his confidential servant, nor any of the members of the Court or of the household of the Lord Don Carlo.

And this is that which the witness knew

Signum crucis

Two things struck me about this testimony: first, Don Pietro begins with the words "My Lords, I shall tell you the truth." Why would he make such a statement? Was he suggesting that, under some other circumstances, he would not tell the truth? Or, perhaps, he was worried that the magistrates would not believe him. For, while his detailed account has the ring of veracity, it is, in fact, a total fabrication, as I – and certainly he – knew. Don Fabrizio, once philanderer and courtesan *par excellence*, now totally eschewed any sexual concourse with women, and preferred to dress in women's clothes. His Excellency the Prince, was a shriveled, pewling shell of a man, dominated by a witch, indecisive, helpless, certainly not capable of such assertive action and speech as Don Pietro had portrayed. So, I concluded, the opening words of Don Pietro's testimony were an attempt to ensure the magistrates' acceptance of his testimony, without further investigation.

The second puzzling element of his testimony was his assertion that the Prince was accompanied by Don Ascanio Lama. He knew, and I knew, that Don Ascanio was at the time of the murder languishing in a prison cell in Cremona. Few others in the court knew where Don Ascanio was, for we had left, you will recall, in haste and without announcement. So this lie would be obvious only to me. Surely, Don Pietro was trying to send a message to me – a message that this testimony should in its entirety be rejected as fantasy. But that I, and I alone, should recognize its fantastic nature.

There were other small details that troubled me about the whole affair. There was a claim that, following the murder, The Prince and his cohorts dragged the bodies into the hallway, there an unnamed priest fornicated with Donna Maria's stiffening corpse. This detail kept cropping up in various accounts, and, while it had the ring of fiction, it was oddly disturbing. Wherefrom would such a bizarre and vicious rumor arise?

And then there was the matter of the ring. Whose ring was it? What was its strange power? Why was it in the possession of Giulio – who lived in the thrall of His Eminence DonAlfonso – and why did the witch desire it so? In any case, it appeared to be gone now forever, swallowed up by the earth. Yet, if its power was to enslave the witch and my Master, its disappearance did not end their travails; on the contrary, the witch seemed to think it could set them free, and that its removal killed all hope of ever being free of the curse.

These matters greatly occupied my mind over the next years. I assiduously collected every scrap of information, rumor, and fabrication related to the murder. Don Pietro kindly copied out and sent me the complete text of the inquest, with a note that said: "Here is copy of the outcome of the official investigation into the sorrowful events of October 16. This, Ludovico, is now the only truth. Let all other theories of what happened that day remain locked in your heart until the day of our Master's death."

And so matters remained for the next eight years. I did not see my Master after departing Gesualdo for Cremona for another year. We maintained a desultory correspondence, the Prince inquiring into the progress on his case of instruments, me advising him on that progress. By the time he moved to Ferrara, the work of my friend Don Girolamo was completed, and I personally delivered the instruments to my Master – accompanied by Don Ascanio, whose release I had finally arranged. Thereafter, at his command, I visited Ferrara once or twice a month, and spent a few days in his service and companionship before returning to my life in Cremona.

My Master was much changed. Gone were the bouts of tears, the recriminations and self-flagellation, and, on the other hand, the fits of ecstasy, the manic activity. He spoke rarely, and then in a monotone, his upper lip trembling slightly as though holding back a sea of emotion. The only topic on which he would speak at any length was music, and once on that subject, he could hold forth for hours, not really conversing but lecturing. He was greatly interested in the music of his colleague Luzzasco Luzzaschi, whose compositions shared, to some extent, the harmonic daring of my Master's. He would spend hours discussing his analysis of Don Luzzasco's works, applying the modal theories of Zarlino and others with whose theoretical works on music I was familiar. My grounding in musical theory, sound as it may have been, was slim indeed, compared to that of my Master; nonetheless, any lack of understanding on my part did not for a moment give my Master pause, and he would carry on, apparently pleased just to have another person in the room as he spoke.

Though my theoretical knowledge was inferior to his own, this never impinged on his complete faith in my musical judgment. Every time I visited him, he presented me with a new batch of his compositions. He worked at these for most of his waking day, and his production was prodigious. In the space of his four year sojourn in Ferrara, he composed hundreds of works, edited most of his past works, and published six volumes of madrigals. These publications were, to my taste, a landmark in the development of music. They were so shockingly original, so intense, that they instilled in me a visceral reaction. Even with my limited theoretical knowledge, I could tell that these works – especially the sixth volume – challenged the very foundations of musical theory. Moreover, I could hear in these works the voice of the witches of the forest – their influence on his musical *oeuvre* was palpable and frightening. I had never before thought that a piece of music could be frightening; but hearing these madrigals chilled the marrow of my bones, sent shudders up my spine, and dried my mouth as though filled with cotton.

One reason that my Master could be so productive in Ferrara was that the witch he had left behind in Gesualdo. I found this remarkable: how did he free himself from the power of her spell? But when I asked him about this, his answer was most unsatisfying.

"My Lord, tell me how it is that you have left the witch in Gesualdo?"

"I told her not to come."

"How tell her not to come? Were you not under her spell? What strength of will did you have to tell her not to come?"

"Perhaps."

"Perhaps what?"

"Perhaps I was under her spell."

"And when you told her not to come, what did she say?"

"She said, alright."

How odd. How frighteningly odd! He was "perhaps under her spell?" And perhaps not? The menstrual blood, the soup with the mixing of their seed? His sexual enslavement? The murder, the madness? It was all "perhaps" a spell? I could make no sense of this reply. I thought again of the ring. Perhaps with the ring gone, the power of the witch's magic had waned. And what had it left? A man without display of emotion, or interest, or curiosity. A shell of a man. Yet a man with an inner voice of astounding creativity.

Be that as it may, he was no longer a slave to the witch's lubricious demands. In her absence, his natural venerous tendencies revived, and he resumed the promiscuous ways of his youth. He limited himself, however, to the company of the *cortigiani di lume,* common street whores. He had no sense of propriety whatsoever, and would often have these women about his house when entertaining guests. In the midst of supper, he might rise, without excusing himself, and accompany one of these women – who would actually join him at table – to the boudoir. He also had a reputation for treating these whores violently, striking them, twisting their arms and breasts until they cried out in pain. He thus earned a reputation as a client to be avoided. This reticence on the part of the whores was overcome by my Master's generous payments to those who served him; there was no lack of women who would submit themselves to his violent tendencies for the right sum. However, the inevitable result of this behavior was that he was shunned by almost everyone in Ferrara.

Which explains why Leonore d'Este, the granddaughter of His Grace Alfonso II, Duke of Ferrara, reacted so violently when the Duke proposed she marry my Master. I was not present, so I cannot verify any of the accounts. According to one version, she screamed her refusal so vehemently that she had to be physically removed from the room. According to another version, she rushed out and vomited. Regardless of the details, what was certain was that she had no stomach for such a coupling. His Grace was, however, adamant. For he had no heir, and, without a successor, Ferrara would be incorporated into the Papal states on his death. A union with the nephew of the most powerful cardinal in the College would certainly be a step toward rescuing his realm from the greedy hands of the Church, especially if the successor was the son of that nephew.

(I should note here that my Master's other cardinal uncle, His Eminence Don Carlo Borromeo, had died a year before. His death coincided with the onset of my Master's madness, following the murder. I had intended to tell my Master of the sad event, but, following his strange reaction to my suggestion that he should live up to the expectations of his Uncle Carlo, I decided against it.)

Donna Leonora's revulsion at the match notwithstanding, the couple were wed on the 21st day of February, in the Year of Our Lord 1594. I had the opportunity to make acquaintance with the bride only after the wedding. She was a dour, unattractive woman, with slightly bulging eyes, receding chin, and chest flat as a board. I know not how she was before her marriage, but after she had every reason to be sullen and nasty. For my Master kept her locked in her chambers for most of the day. She joined him for supper; between her and her husband sat one of my Master's many whores, who would – always at my Master's urging – try to engage Donna Leonora in conversation. Aside from this daily humiliation, my Master paid her no attention whatsoever. He did, however, have intercourse with her once, apparently on the night of their betrothal; for nine months after the wedding, she bore him a son, who died while still an infant. There were no more offspring.

A few months after child was born, my Master determined to return to Gesualdo. He announced his decision at supper. The Duke, his wife, and his son, Donna Leonora's father, were in attendance.

"I have decided to return to Gesualdo," my Master announced.

The guests looked at each other in stunned silence. Then the Duke spoke.

"This comes as a surprise. I thought you were quite satisfied with your life here."

"My life here is fine. But the time comes when one must return to his ancestral home."

"I see. When are you planning to make the move?"

"I will be leaving within the month."

"You will move your entire court the entire length of the Italian peninsula, in a month's time?" The Duke was incredulous.

"Whatever cannot be moved within a month shall be moved later."

Throughout this exchange, Donna Leonora sat with a face of stone. I assumed that this was the first she, like the others, had heard of these plans. But now she spoke.

"Well, I shall not be ready to move within a month, so I shall remain here."

My Master looked at her sharply. "No, wife, you shall accompany me to Gesualdo."

There was steel in her voice as she replied. "No, husband, I shall remain here until I am quite ready and able to move." She looked my Master directly in the eye, unflinching.

In that moment, I thought of the witch. A woman of iron will, who had the personal powers, not only the mystical powers, to dominate my Master. And my Master submitted to her totally. Just the opposite of his first wife, modest, pliant, obedient, devoted. That obedience he could not abide, and finally murdered her. And now he was confronted once again with a woman of iron will. But today he was a changed man. The vicissitudes, the moods, the subservience, all were gone. How would he react now? This was, perhaps a long and complex thought; but I had the time to think it, for Donna Leonora's insubordination had struck everyone dumb. In the pause that followed, one could have performed a complete villanella of seven verses. Finally, my Master spoke.

"Very well." He took up his shank of lamb, and ate.

That was the end of the conversation. Within a month, the entire court was packed and ready to move. It was a masterful work of planning by Don Pietro. Half the household left for Genova, to sail to Naples, while half set off southward via the overland route. The move had momentous implications for me. Soon after his announcement, he called me to his chamber.

"I wish for you to continue your service with me when I have returned to Gesualdo," he said. "In the same manner that you serve me now – a sojourn of several days every few weeks."

The current arrangement served my needs exceedingly well. I was drawing a salary of 500 *scudi* a year, plus all my expenses. In addition, I was earning 20 to 100 *scudi* a month from my performances at the *accademia* and in commissions for helping my father-in-law and my friend Don Girolamo. I was taking in rent of 6 ducats monthly from my father's house in Naples, which was sent to me by letter of credit. I had saved enough in the first two years of my service in Cremona to buy a house of comfortable size. I kept a horse for my trips to Ferrara, a cow and two goats, which we kept in a barn on the ground floor of the house. We had two servants. Last year, Beatrice's father died, and his business had passed to her brother. Beatrice received a stipend of 400 *scudi*. So we were well off.

My Master's request would entail our leaving Cremona and moving south. I certainly did not want to return to Gesualdo. The thought of living again in the shadow of the witch, in the castle that bore the curse, caused my skin to crawl. On the other hand, I missed my friends, and I missed the music. Though Cremona was a town that lived by music, the reality was that there was very little performance of merit there; that is why Monteverdi was so eager to get out. The arrangement that my Master proposed – two or three days of service every few weeks – would allow my family to live in comfort in Naples. We could occupy my father's house, and I could supplement my income there, as I did in Cremona, by performing at *accademia* and events. My services, I knew, would be in great demand; for the violin was becoming the rage in Naples, as it was throughout Italy, and there were very few musicians there who could play it competently.

And so it was that, concurrent with the move of my Master's court to Gesualdo, I packed up my household in three wagons, and we set off, myself, my wife, my son of four years, and my daughter of two years, on the week-long trek to Naples.

m'involate hor mi tèdete il core

After waxing prolix about the first eight years of my life with His Excellency Don Carlo Gesualdo, Prince of Venosa, I have compressed the next nine years into a single *ottavo*. In truth, there is very little to be said of this period. My life continued, mostly apart from my Master. His new persona – reclusive, incommunicative, all emotion suppressed – demanded no intervention on my part; no longer was I my Master's companion, nor was I his babysitter, as I had been. During my visits, he would spend a good deal of time with me. This time was spent almost in its entirety in discussions of music. In order to better serve my Master, I had begun studying in greater depth the theoretical bases of the music which I knew in practice – most particularly, the writings of Zarlino on modal structure. I must admit that, the more I understood these theories, the more dissatisfying they became; for, I felt, they did not adequately capture the real underlying structure of music as we played it. My feelings on this matter, shared by my Master, were reinforced by the development of a new compositional technique, the figured bass technique, which was becoming current in the North. I won't go into the technicalities of this matter; suffice it to say that my discussions with my Master, while sometimes discursive to the point of tedium, were, for the most part, interesting to both him and me.

The witch, of course, was in the castle awaiting my Master's return. He came home, and they took up where they had left off five years previous: twice a day they would copulate, often in public places, she grimacing in pain and he with a look of exquisite boredom. Their life together more and more looked like a jaded marriage: what had begun as a vengeful curse had devolved into a conjugal routine of a bored couple in middle age. As before, the witch's sexual demands sapped my Master's energy, so he had no urge to philander. They became, the ultimate irony, faithful to each other.

Living with them was Emmanuelle. The obnoxious child had grown to be an obnoxious youth. At nine he had taken up riding, and rode like a maniac, dashing through the streets of Gesualdo at full gallop, scattering the villagers, often falling, exhausting his steeds. He refused to study. He avoided his father as much as possible. If he encountered him by chance, he would spit and fart, and then turn his back on him without speaking. When I was in Gesualdo, he would frequently seek out my company, and tell me how much he despised his father, and how he spent hours thinking of ways to cause him pain.

Thus passed four years. And then, something happened.

m'inuolate hor chi tédette il core

As I approached the castle in the spring of 1599, I heard shouting. As I grew nearer, I could make out the words: "Why didn't you tell me, you stupid bitch? You have wasted nine years of my life!" "I'm sorry, m'Lord, How'd I aknow you was interested?" "Interested? This would have made me Pope! Now it may be too late!" I heard the sound of a slap echo through the hall.

I entered to see the witch sitting on the floor, rubbing her cheek, and weeping softly. Standing with his back to me was His Eminence, Don Alfonso. He turned and gave me a scowl. "You! What are you doing here?"

Here was a question to give pause. "I am still in the service of His Excellency, Your Eminence."

I could well have asked what he was doing here. For, though he bore the Gesualdo name, he had not visited his nephew for ten years at least. I wondered the reason for this unexpected visit. But my curiosity was not to be satisfied just then, as he turned without saying another word and left the hall.

I continued in his footsteps, intending to greet my Master. But His Eminence entered my Master's chambers ahead of me, and shut the door with decision. I understood, and waited outside while they conferred. Half an hour passed, and Don Alfonso swept out of the room. "Go in now, he is waiting for you." With that, he turned and left. I did not see him at Gesualdo again.

"Ludovico, my dear friend, I am so glad to see you." My Master attempted to inject a note of levity into his monotone; but his features displayed no emotion whatever.

"I am at your service, My Lord," I replied with a bow. "I met His Eminence your uncle in the hall, What an unexpected honor."

"Yes, quite so," replied my Master. There was a pause.

"Ludovico, I have a task for you."

"Command and I shall perform."

"You know my uncle Carlo is to be canonized?"

This caught me by surprise. The last time his maternal uncle was mentioned he had reacted so strangely that I never mentioned his name again. "Yes, My Lord. I am glad you have noted that. I thought perhaps you would wish to attend the ceremony."

"No, no, I am not able to make the trip. But I wish you to go."

"It will be my honor, My Lord."

"And bring back some bones."

"You wish to make a reliquary, My Lord?"

"Yes, a reliquary. That's it. Go now."

"Now, My Lord? Right now?"

"Yes, Ludovico. There is no time to waste. Go."

"Very well, My Lord." I turned to leave.

"Bring me some bones."

"Yes, My Lord."

"And, another thing. If you get the bones before the ceremony, you needn't wait. Bring the bones right back."

"I understand, My Lord."

The truth was that I did not understand. Why this strange haste in making a reliquary? Did a reliquary have any value before a man was sainted? Why this sudden interest in his uncle's earthly remains? For years, I thought, my Master had avoided any mention of Carlo Borromeo, and now, suddenly, he was seized with a desire to commemorate his memory with a reliquary.

No purpose in idle speculation. I immediately made ready, and set off by horseback to Rome. There I purchased a fine silver case in the shape of a cross, studded with ruby and emerald, elegantly decorated with repoussé and inscribed with the Saint's name. At the Vatican, I obtained an audience with the Prefect of the Sacred Congregation for Rites. The Prefect acted as though he had been expecting me, and proffered three fragments of bone, without the usual demands of fees and without the usual dickering. The canonization was due to take place in another week, but, in accordance with my Master's wishes, I did not wait, but returned immediately to Gesualdo.

I arrived in the afternoon, a week before Holy Week. I was filthy and tired from the road, and eager to wash and rest. But, knowing my Master's anxiety to receive the reliquary, I went immediately to his chamber. There he was hard at work, finishing his setting of the *Tenebrae.* When he saw me, he directly laid off his work, and rose from his seat. "You have the bones?"

I did not even have a moment to greet him properly. "They are here, My Lord," and I handed him the reliquary.

He turned the reliquary over in his hand, laid it face down on the table, and opened the back. He took out a small leather bag, removed the bones from their silver house, and dropped them into the bag, drawing the strings of the bag tight. "Come with me. We haven't a moment to lose." He swept out of the room, me at his heels.

He led to the stables, where two horses were saddled and ready. We mounted and headed south into the forest. The sun was low in the sky; in a few hours it would be dark, and there was no way we would find our way. "My Lord, this is no hour to go riding into the forest. Let us postpone this until the morning."

My Master made no reply but kept up a quick trot along the narrowing path. The sun set and a full moon rose in the east, a huge blood-orange disk peeping through the trees. As the moon rose in the sky, it cast fantastic shadows on the forest floor. The path disappeared, and we wove our way between the holm oaks, beech and towering cypress trees. Although in a pathless forest, my Master rode on as if guided by an inner compass. We rode thus for more than four hours. By this time, the moon was almost directly overhead, and I had no idea where we were or in which direction we were headed.

Then I heard it. In the distance, strange singing. I recognized the music at once. It was the music of the witches that I had heard 12 years ago. Terror seized me as we approached. This time there was no stealth, no attempt to hide our presence. My Master rode up to the edge of the clearing, and we dismounted. There, as before, was the muddy pond, the coven of witches in black standing around it, the wooden platform with the inverted cross. But there was no goat tethered on the dais. Instead, on the platform stood His Eminence, Don Alfonso Gesualdo.

My Master stepped to the edge of the pond, and kneeled on both knees in the mud. The witches fell silent. The cardinal spoke.

"You brought the bones?"

My Master lifted the leather bag and held it up for the cardinal to see.

"Bring it here."

My Master rose and started to wade across the pond. But the stentorian voice of the witch queen, who stood at the foot of the podium, stopped him.

"Halt! Strip off your clothes first, *stronzo!*"

My Master waded back to where I awaited him. Slowly, he removed his shirt, his doublet, his breeches, his hose, and laid them neatly on the ground. Then he turned to face the witches, and, stark naked, with the leather bag in his hand, waded across the pond. On the other bank, facing the podium, he fell again on his knees. The cardinal stepped off the platform, stood before him, and held out his hand. My Master gave him the leather bag.

The cardinal loosened the string, and peered into the leather pouch. He was dressed in full choir dress: ankle-length cassock, with an embroidered *fascia* about his waist, surplice, *muzzetta*, and a broad-brimmed *galero* on his head. In the pale white moonlight, all colors faded to gray; but, when the cardinal moved, a moonbeam would sometimes catch the moiré silk of the *muzzetta* and give a flash of scarlet. He probed the pouch with his fingers, and drew out the fragments of bone. He held them up to the moonlight, turning them and examining them. Satisfied, he dropped the bones back into the pouch, and tightened the lace. He held the bag over the ground. As if on cue, the witches again took up their strange, seductive chant. The cardinal shut his eyes, and intoned:

> *"Fiat Lux, smaragde annulum,*
> *"Fiat lux smaragde annulum,*
> *"Quod ego sequi,*
> *"Fiat lux, smaragde annulum,*
> *"Inveni annulum!*
> *"Venit ad ossa Domini tui*
> *"Venit ad ossa Domini tui."*

The ground began to shake. Then, as though floating up from the depths of a viscous sea, the ring rose out of the ground, and lay upon the mud.

The cardinal lifted the skirt of his cassock, so as not to sully the hem in the mud, bent down and lifted the ring. He held it high, admired the dark gleam of the emerald flashing in the moonlight. Then he gestured to the witches, who fell silent. He turned to my Master. "I have waited too long for this, because of your stupidity."

My Master made no reply, but stared stonily at His Eminence's feet.

"Hold out your hands. Palms up."

My Master lifted up his hands. In the palm of his right hand one could still clearly see the scar where the red-hot ring had burnt him on the day of his wedding.

"Grasp his wrist." The witch queen grasped my Master's left wrist in an iron grip.

The cardinal held up the ring to the moonlight. It started to glow, at first a dull yellow, growing slowly to a fiery red. Standing across the pond, I imagined I could feel the waves of heat emanating from the infernal ring; but the cardinal's fingers were unscathed as he held it lightly. When the fire reached its peak, the cardinal took the ring and pressed it down hard on my Master's upturned palm. My Master screamed with pain, and squirmed in the grip of the witch. The cardinal held the ring on the hand for several seconds, then lifted it. The witch queen released my Master's wrist. He fell writhing and screaming to the ground. Thus we stood, frozen, for several minutes. My Master's screams faded to exhausted whimpers. The cardinal gestured to the witch queen. Two witches lifted my Master by the armpits, and held him before the cardinal.

"You should be glad, nephew. Now you have stigmata on both hands, like a true martyr.

"What say you, shall we go a round? For old times' sake?"

The cardinal mounted the podium, followed by the witch queen, and the two witches bearing my Master. They stretched his naked body face down across the table, the same table where, twelve years before, we saw the novice witch raped by the goat. They held his wrists firmly so he could not move. The queen took up a long, thin switch cut from a fresh branch of silver spruce, stripped of its bark and gleaming white in the moonlight. The cardinal lifted his cassock, stroked himself a few times, then thrust his erection deep into my Master's buttocks. While he pumped slowly, the queen laid stripe after stripe on my Master's back. Ugly black welts crisscrossed his back.

This torture lasted for less than a minute. For the cardinal's tumescent member quickly reached climax. He pumped vigorously for a few seconds, and then, spent, withdrew his penis and straightened his cassock. "Finally it is my turn," he said. "I always had to do the whipping." He nodded to the witches holding my Master down. They released him, and gave him a shove. He tumbled off the podium and fell into the mud, lying curled in a ball.

The cardinal and the witches descended from the podium. The cardinal led the way into the forest, the coven following in single file, singing softly. I waited until their song had completely faded away. Then I rushed through the pond to my Master. I wrapped him in my traveling cloak, and held him tightly. He was only half conscious, shivering and moaning. We lay together in the mud, closely embraced. And thus I fell asleep.

m'involate hor mi cedete il core

When I awoke, the sun was already filtering through the trees. The podium was gone. The pond had disappeared, in its place was a grassy meadow. Across the meadow I could see my Master's clothes laid out neatly where he had arranged them, and beyond, the horses tethered to a tree.

My arms were still wrapped about my Master's torso. I slowly released him and looked at him. He remained unmoving, but his eyes were wide open. He was still shivering and weeping silently.

"My Lord?

"Can you speak?"

My Master turned to me, and nodded. His shivering stopped, the weeping stopped.

"Yes, Ludovico, I can speak."

"It was your uncle, wasn't it? Your uncle Carlo?"

My Master nodded.

"The red dream – that was Carlo."

Another nod.

"Your uncle Carlo raped you. It was his hand you bit."

There was a long pause. "It was both of them," said my Master. "Uncle Carlo would rape me while uncle Alfonso beat me. But Uncle Carlo was the boss. Alfonso was only a lackey."

We sat in silence, gazing across the meadow.

"And the murder?" I asked.

"Carlo, Alfonso, and the slave Giulio. They led me up the stairs. They gave me the arquebus. They said, 'shoot.' I shot. First Fabrizio. Then my wife."

"They did not resist?" I asked.

"Fabrizio looked at me. He said, 'My Lord. I love you. If you wish to kill me, I die happily.' And then I shot him." My Master began again to weep.

"And Donna Maria as well?"

"The same."

"And then?"

"They gave me a knife, and told me to stab her. I did it. They gave me a sword, and told me to stab Fabrizio. I did that, too.

"I knelt beside the bed. And Carlo said, "You have killed your best and only friend, and your faithful wife. She was faithful. You knew that, didn't you?' I nodded. 'You killed them, but you were no cuckold. You did it because you wanted to, didn't you?' and I nodded again. 'And now they are dead.'

"'Maybe she is not dead' I said.'Maybe she still lives. Let her live!' And Carlo said, 'If she lives, stab her some more.' and he gave me the dagger. I said, ' No, maybe she lives, maybe she lives!' and as I said it, I stabbed her again and again.

"And then, Carlo said, 'Well, if she was faithful to you in life, let her cuckold you in death. Giulio, fuck the bride.' Giulio looked on us with horror in his eyes. 'But she is dead, Your Eminence,' he said. 'Just do it,' shouted Carlo, and slapped him. And Giulio lifted up his cassock, and lay upon my wife, his body wracked with tears, and he fucked my wife's body while it was still warm. Then he, too, fell to the floor. He grasped my hand. 'Forgive me my Lord. It was not me, it was the ring. The ring made me do it.'

"And then Carlo slapped him again, and said, 'The ring? The ring does not make you do anything. You do not understand the power of the ring. The ring does not enslave you and make you do its will. The ring frees you, it frees you to fulfill your own will. It releases your own most secret desires, the desires you yourselves are afraid to acknowledge. You Giulio, raped a dead woman because you wanted to. You, nephew, you murdered your wife and friend, because in your heart, you cannot abide love. You murdered them because you wanted to.'"

My Master could not go on. His body shook with sobs. I again embraced him, and we sat thus on the edge of the meadow until the sun was high in the sky. Then I rose, brought him his clothes, helped him dress, helped him mount, and rode with him out of the forest. The ride in took more than four hours, but we headed north and reached Gesualdo in little more than an hour. I helped my Master dismount, half carried him up the stairs, and laid him in his bed.

My 20, 1600

I am sitting in the veranda of my home in Naples with my friend Don Scipione. In my hand is the manuscript containing my Master's transcription of the witches' music. Don Scipione, my Master, and myself are the only ones who will have seen this music. For, in a moment, I will burn it.

On that fateful day, as my Master slept, I mulled over the things that had happened. The truth of what I heard – the power of the ring to free a man's darkest desires – made me shudder. I realized the truth of this – that my Master had, indeed, murdered the Mistress I had loved and served, the friend who was faithful to his last breath – murdered them in cold blood, because he could not abide their love. This realization filled me at once with a violent fury and hatred, and love and pity that frightened me to the bone. It was in this state that I was in, when my Master awakened, and begged me to beat him. And – perhaps this too was the power of the ring – I acquiesced.

For the next three weeks, I beat my Master daily. I laid the lash on with vigor, expiating the fury in my heart. But no amount of flagellation could cleanse the sin. This torment was but a foretaste of what awaited him in the next life.

Nor was the physical torture the greatest he had to bear. For, on the same night of our encounter with the witches, his son Emmanuelle was pitched from his horse. Emmanuelle's neck was broken, and he died instantly. And thus, the obnoxious youth found the ultimate weapon to torment the father he despised.

Within three weeks, whether from the suppurating wounds on his back, or the infection from his scorched hand, or from a heart broken by a thankless son, my Master died. And thus came to an end the life of the Master I had served and left and returned to, who brought to my heart light and dark, thrill and torment, through the music he created and through the power of his presence.

I walk with my friend Don Scipione to the kitchen, where my daughter-in-law is cooking a fish stew. I take the pages of the witches' music, and drop them into the flames of the cook fire. The fire flares up briefly as the pages char and curl. It is the end of cursed music. But the curse of Gesualdo, I am certain, will hover over the castle of Gesualdo for hundreds of years to come.